The Business Af...lius Caesar

The Business Affairs of Mr Julius Caesar

Bertolt Brecht

Translated by Charles Osborne

Edited by Anthony Phelan and Tom Kuhn
with assistance from Charlotte Ryland

Bloomsbury Methuen Drama
An imprint of Bloomsbury Publishing Plc

B L O O M S B U R Y
LONDON · OXFORD · NEW YORK · NEW DELHI · SYDNEY

Bloomsbury Methuen Drama

An imprint of Bloomsbury Publishing Plc

Imprint previously known as Methuen Drama

50 Bedford Square	1385 Broadway
London	New York
WC1B 3DP	NY 10018
UK	USA

www.bloomsbury.com

BLOOMSBURY, METHUEN DRAMA and the Diana logo are trademarks of Bloomsbury Publishing Plc

Original work entitled *Die Geschäfte des Herrn Julius Caesar*, published in the *Bertolt Brecht Grosse kommentierte Berliner und Frankfurter Ausgabe* (vol. 17), Suhrkamp Verlag, Frankfurt am Main 1988-2000

Copyright © Bertolt-Brecht-Erben / Suhrkamp Verlag

Introduction copyright © 2016 Anthony Phelan

English language translation © Charles Osborne, 2016

Anthony Phelan and Tom Kuhn have asserted their moral rights to be identified as the editors of this edition. Charles Osborne has asserted his moral right to be identified as the translator of this edition.

British Library Cataloguing-in-Publication Data
A catalogue record for this book is available from the British Library.

ISBN: HB: 978-1-4725-8273-7
PB: 978-1-4725-8272-0
ePDF: 978-1-4725-8275-1
ePub: 978-1-4725-8274-4

Library of Congress Cataloging-in-Publication Data
A catalog record for this book is available from the Library of Congress.

Typeset by Fakenham Prepress Solutions, Fakenham, Norfolk NR21 8NN
Printed and bound in India

Contents

Introduction

Bertolt Brecht and Julius Caesar

Brecht's sustained interest in the figure of Julius Caesar, particularly in this unfinished novel, might at first sight seem frankly eccentric. Plans for *The Business Affairs of Mr Julius Caesar* only became clear towards the very end of 1937. In November that year Brecht was still writing to friends sketching out a play dealing with Caesar's rise to power, which he hoped to put on in Paris. Perhaps plans for that production fell through, or the dramatization of a significant chunk of Roman history, from Brecht's political point of view, presented insuperable problems. Whatever it was that led him to rethink the project as a prose narrative, Brecht set about his novel with a will, using material he had been collecting over a number of years, and it became one of the works he was specially committed to during his exile from Nazi Germany.

Brecht's interest in the life of Julius Caesar went back much further, however. He learnt Latin at school and had read parts of Caesar's commentaries on the *Gallic War* and *Civil Wars*; later he studied Plutarch's life of Caesar, and seems to have been particularly interested in the story of Caesar and the pirates that is one of the first legends about him to be debunked in Book One of the novel. But Brecht's historical research on Caesar took him far beyond Plutarch. He made notes on Suetonius and Sallust as sources for the political psychology of his central character; as well as pursuing these Roman authors, with the help of Margarete Steffin Brecht he gathered critical material for his fictionalized life and read many of the most well known modern and contemporary Roman historians. Brecht's exile in Denmark made his study of such material difficult, and he pressed his friend, the Berlin lawyer

Martin Domke, who was based in Paris, to provide summaries of works he couldn't access himself; in one case Domke sent a volume that Brecht needed to the family's new home near Svendborg. Chief among the sources he consulted is Theodor Mommsen's *History of Rome*, but he also made use of more recent and sometimes controversial authors such as Jérôme Carcopino (*César*) and Eduard Meyer (*Caesar's Monarchy and Pompey's Principate. An Interior History of Rome 66–44 BC*).

Brecht's own copies of some of these books, kept in his library at the Bertolt Brecht Archive, Berlin, allow us a glimpse of things that had caught his attention because they are highlighted by a pencil mark or marginal comment. It is clear from many of these remarks that Brecht's use of the ancient historians he read is partisan, heavily influenced by his own perspective on Caesar and his contemporaries. One passage that attracted Brecht's pencil, for instance, is a good example of how Mommsen attempts to reimagine Rome as a modern city:

> If we try to conceive to ourselves a London with the slave-population of New Orleans, with the police of Constantinople, with the non-industrial character of the modern Rome, and agitated by politics after the fashion of the Paris in 1848, we shall acquire an approximate idea of the republican glory, the departure of which Cicero and his associates in their sulky letters deplore. Caesar did not deplore, but he sought to help so far as help was possible.[1]

The passage that Brecht noticed echoes Mommsen's earlier description of Rome as 'this city – which in every respect might be compared to the Paris of the nineteenth century'. Mommsen is perfectly willing to rethink the ancient world and the political conditions of the Late Republic in contemporary terms: Paris and London, New Orleans and even Istanbul can be drawn into the comparison. In this respect Brecht's novel follows a line already established in such traditional historiography. The effect

---

[1] Theodor Mommsen, *Römische Geschichte*, 4 vols (Berlin: Weidmann, 1856–85), 493.

of modernizing Roman history in this way matches Brecht's own instincts, however – so that when he reads in Carcopino that Cicero 'didn't have the guts' to deal with the Catilinarian conspiracy, he jots in the margin: 'Perfect! That is Herr Cicero's weakness'. His obvious pleasure as he turns up material that confirms his own view is patent: this research remains opportunistic as he hunts both for material and for a *style* that can be used for his presentation of the Late Republic in contemporary economic and political terms.

In the years after 1933, the historical novel provided a genre that many German writers living in exile from Nazi Germany were able to adopt, to provide an alternative view of political dilemmas in relation to humane values in their own times; or to offer some personal account of recent history and the emergence of the Third Reich. Heinrich Mann's trilogy of novels on the French renaissance king, *Henri IV*, is perhaps the most distinguished of these works, and in some respects, like Brecht's *The Business Affairs of Mr Julius Caesar*, it allows the reader to understand the contemporary world at the time of its writing through the prism of an historical narrative.

Brecht's reimagining of the first century BC seems more focused, and from an early stage in the development of the material he is clear that the emphasis has to be economic – to present a Caesar driven by venal financial motives as well as political ambition. This clear-eyed and contemporary analysis of the figure could only be managed by simultaneously undermining the image of Caesar as one of the great men who according to the German historian Treitschke famously 'make history'. In one sense, the *Caesar* novel asks the same questions of history as those that appear in the exile poem 'Questions of a worker who reads'

> [...] The great city of Rome
> Is full of triumphal arches. Who set them up? Over whom
> Did the Caesars triumph? Did Byzantium, so much praised in
>   song
> Have only palaces for its inhabitants? Even in fabled Atlantis
> That night when the ocean engulfed it, the drowning
> Roared out for their slaves.

Young Alexander conquered India.
Was he alone?
Caesar defeated the Gauls.
Did he not have so much as a cook with him?
[...]

Between 1932, when he discussed the possibility of reworking Shakespeare's *Julius Caesar*, and 1945 Brecht repeatedly takes up classical material, here in the poem questioning the clichés of history as it is taught, or in other texts challenging legendary figures ('Empedocles' shoe'), or suggesting by reference to or imitation of classical metres, specifically the dactylic rhythms associated with the hexameter, that the 'heroic' qualities of antiquity might be identified in the modern world in the opening of the Metro in Moscow ('The Moscow workers take possession of the great Metro'). This enthusiasm for classical models, and particularly for Latin precedents, in poems written in his Danish exile, is taken up at the end of the war in Brecht's partially realized plan to produce a contemporary didactic poem in the spirit of Lucretius, which would attempt to rewrite *The Communist Manifesto* as a long poem that redid the Roman poet. There is an early mention of this plan in Walter Benjamin's diary of his visit to Brecht in Denmark in September 1934. However, his most sustained interest lay with the politics of the Late Republic: he produced a radio play about Pompey's old rival, famous in retirement for his indulgent lifestyle, *The Trial of Lucullus*, which Paul Dessau later used as the basis for his opera *The Judgement of Lucullus*; Brecht's novel draws out this sense that the political and economic environment in which Caesar comes to power as dictator, seen through the prism of the late 1930s, can be *instructive* as well as entertaining to contemporary readers.

Telling stories
Brecht's interrogation of history is pursued in *The Business Affairs of Mr Julius Caesar*. In a letter to his friend and mentor Karl Korsch, written from Denmark in November 1937, Brecht sketches the difficulties he faces in what is still conceived as a theatre project:

And now I'm setting about a – Caesar play: 'The Business Affairs of Mr Julius Caesar' for Paris, where there is a chance of performance. It's difficult and you are seriously missed. I don't want to do a *pièce à clef*, conditions are so different in antiquity. Nevertheless, Caesar is the great model, and I can throw light on at least two things: 1) the way the dictator swings between the classes and in doing so conducts the business of one single class (in this case the equites) and 2) that wars (in this case the Gallic War) are undertaken to exploit one's own people, not just the ones under attack. For France the whole thing has a note of piquancy (Roman Caesar with his new imperium and Gallic War). The difficulty: Caesar nevertheless signifies some progress, and the inverted commas round 'progress' are hugely difficult to dramatise.

Some of these difficulties remained. Book 5 of the novel, which would have dealt with the Gallic War, was left as notes and fragments when Brecht abandoned the book, but the question of which party Caesar adheres to in the Late Republic keeps returning. Brecht identifies the period of Caesar's life he is dealing with as the moment when a largely patrician Senate increasingly comes into conflict with the *equites* or Equestrians, the Romans whose ownership of property was sufficient to oblige them to provide the legionary cavalry; in earlier periods the Senate included not just members of distinguished families and those who had held high religious office, but also members drawn from those who met the Equestrian property qualification.[2] By the middle of the first century BC the Equestrian class had gained an independent identity, which Brecht associates with the financial interests he brackets together as 'the City', imagined as bankers, financiers and merchants. The difficulty he envisaged lies in the fact that, for all his corruption and shady dealings, Caesar in serving these financial interests is also a socially and economically *progressive* force because he engineers a movement from the dominance of land-owning patricians to a more highly evolved social form in which personal financial gain is the undisguised

---

[2] Catherine Steel gives a succinct account of these developments in her introduction to *The End of the Roman Republic, 146 to 44 BC. Conquest and Crisis* (Edinburgh: Edinburgh University Press, 2013), 3–6.

impetus for political engagement. Caesar could be thought of as 'progressive', in the way Brecht's comment to Korsch suggests, because he is regarded as instrumental in shifting power from the feudal families of the Senate to a new moneyed class of merchants and speculators.

The problem of debunking the idea that Caesar is one of the great men of history, while simultaneously indicating a trajectory that points towards developments in the modern period, perhaps leads to the shortcomings in Brecht's presentation that classicists and ancient historians have pointed out. Karl Christ in his major study of the historiographical and literary reception of Julius Caesar in the twentieth century suggests that Brecht fails to resolve the contradiction between the Caesar who appears as a buffoon, constantly falling into traps of his own making, and the Caesar who achieves his ends by means of subtle political calculation and personal manipulation.[3] Yet the provocatively contradictory nature of the central figure is surely part of the point of *The Business Affairs of Mr Julius Caesar*.

The contradictions of the figure are carefully held in suspension by the narrative framework Brecht creates. Far from giving a single, coherent, systematic and objective version of Caesar's life and interests, Brecht distributes the many stories and anecdotes about him across a number of different voices and points of view. The novel begins with the first-person account of a scholarly young man who is setting out to compile a biography of Julius Caesar about 30 years after his death. In seeking authentic historical materials, he wishes to have sight of a manuscript called 'the diaries of Rarus', who was one of Caesar's domestic slaves and made notes on Caesar's career at first hand. The document the young biographer needs to consult is in the possession of one Mummlius Spicer (his Latin name is an impossible form). Spicer insists that Rarus' comments on Caesar's career will be incomprehensible without his specialist explanations of the financial issues involved: as he says to the aspiring biographer, 'This fellow Rarus

---

[3] Karl Christ, *Caesar: Annäherungen an einen Diktator* (Munich: C. H. Beck, 1994), 253.

was concerned with the commercial aspect of the enterprises and, as you know, our historians are not very interested in that side of things. They haven't got the faintest idea what short selling means. They think things like that are only of minor importance' (p. 21). In addition to this double perspective, Brecht introduces other voices. In the first book we encounter the figure of Afranius Carbo, a lawyer who is very keen that the young scholar should produce a biography reflecting a heroic view of Caesar's achievements – though not without its own ideological spin:

> 'And I hear you're approaching your subject from the right angle. *The concept of empire! Democracy! The ideas of progress!* At last a book written with a scientific foundation that the common man *and* the man in the City can read. His success, their success! Facts!' (p. 44)

Facts would be the last thing that such a construction of Caesar's career would reveal, let alone a corporatist sense of common purpose between the common man and the speculators in 'the City'. As it turns out, the young biographer is unnerved by Carbo's panegyric to the virtues of trade – 'We're perfectly capable of presenting Syrian scents, Egyptian linen and Samnian wines to their best advantage, but we have never understood how to present commerce itself, its ideals, in the best light. The great, democratic ideals!' – which in his view are the true substance of Caesar's imperial conquests.

From the outset, then, the ideological point of view represented by the informants available to the young biographer challenge his assumptions about writing the monumental life of a great man. If Mummlius Spicer presents the cynical view of a former bailiff turned banker, and Afranius Carbo wants to turn Caesar's life into a manifesto for the commercial and financial sector, the biographer's task is further complicated by his interview with one of Caesar's legionaries, who happens to live near Spicer's estate. 'Convinced that this simple legionary, one of the old-fashioned, valiant warriors' will demonstrate the 'fanatical devotion to the great general' (p. 40) that he has encountered in previous historical monographs, the biographer is frustrated when he is given only the legionary's financial reasons for preferring conscription to working on a family farm too small to sustain him and his three brothers. The conversation gradually sketches in the economic consequences of slave labour, cheap food handouts (the corn dole), and an artificially depressed wheat market ('Growing corn on a small scale simply isn't profitable', p. 80). By means of the legionary's account of his family's fortunes, Brecht adds Friedrich Engels's perspective in the *Anti-Dühring* on the agricultural crisis in ancient Italy, that land reforms attempted to address, as well as some aspects of Marx's *18th Brumaire* with its analysis of the under-lying rural economy in Napoleonic France.

Rarus' diaries in Book Two, dated in the Roman fashion from the foundation of the city – *ab urbe condita* –, cover the period from August 63 BC to the end of the year, and introduce further perspectives on the biographer's subject and his background. Here too the problems of unemployment occasioned among Roman citizens by the growth of the slave economy are emphasized, alongside Caesar's position in the political manoeuvrings and plots afoot in public life, in particular the Catilinarian conspiracy. Many other voices are heard, of aristocrats such as the historical figure of Clodius Pulcher and of leading mercantile figures like the fictional Pomponius Celer, 'head of the leather syndicate' and thus making his profits from equipping Pompey's army. As Brecht had planned, Caesar is seen moving enigmatically between the representatives of various political tendencies and financial interests in pursuit of his own venal ends. The last of the unreliable witnesses to Caesar's career encountered by his biographer is the preening poet Vastius Alder, who reopens the question of Caesar's involvement in the Catilinarian conspiracy just before Mummlius Spicer, with Machiavellian cynicism, glosses the historical value of Rarus's account.

Among and across these different stories and their differing evaluations of Caesar's motivation in the political and economic life of Rome, Brecht contrasts the monuments of imperial progress with the reality of grasping self-interest – the inside story. This conforms to the ironic and critical conception of the novel as a kind of antibiography: the young biographer who arrives at Spicer's villa hoping to find authentic evidence for his heroic assumptions about Caesar in fact writes an account of his frustration: the authoritative voices of the novel – Spicer, Afranius Carbo, Caesar's legionnaire, and finally Vastius Alder – constantly contest the glorious projections of the 'official history' in Plutarch and Sallust, and force him *and* Brecht's modern readers to ask what motives we imagine can have carried forward Caesar's imperial career towards dictatorship. In a fragment from Brecht's working notes probably written when he was still planning a dramatic version of the material, the political interest of a Caesar biography is canvassed by an animateur drumming up an audience: 'If it is true, ladies and gentlemen, that a new age of Caesars lies before us, then we are in no doubt that you will be profoundly interested by the life and doings of the great Julius Caesar' (*BFA* 10.2, p. 808). Perhaps, writing during the ascendancy of the Third Reich, Brecht intends his novel as a satirical booby trap: after all, 30 years on a young biographer might well be setting about a life of Adolf Hitler – but the role played by money and the violent pursuit of power would be no different than in 63 BC.

Antiquity and the Modern World

When Brecht was still intending to write a play, he insisted in a note that if his Caesar character came eventually to believe in his own legendary status, the alienation effect would be invoked (*BFA* 10.2, p. 804: A 20). The same principle of distancing is evident in the transformation of a biography of Caesar into an account of its fictional author's *failure* to get to grips with authentic documents and eyewitness accounts that challenge the published authorities. At the same time, as in Brecht's plays, the process of literary construction itself can be displayed through the ideological struggle to get the image of Caesar 'right'. Above all, the novel distances the reader from a heroic idea of Julius Caesar, paradoxically, by making him seem more accessible. The novel rewrites Roman history in colloquial forms and presents the problems of antiquity in terms of an extremely modern conceptual framework.

Brecht presents the rise of Caesar the dictator amid conflicting political and economic interests and against the background of a definable crisis, as Crassus' Epicurean librarian Alexander summarizes it: '"Catilina," he said quietly, "is the unemployment question, and the unemployment question is the land question." ...' (p. 61). Grain production, speculative hoarding, land reform, and the unemployment of Pompey's veterans are the critical details in the materialist history Brecht insinuates. Caesar's political machinations are closely related, as told here, to the conflict between the still feudal Senate and *arriviste* new money in the ongoing social crisis to which Pompey returned after his victory in the Eastern Mediterranean. This symptomatic modernization of Roman history is part of a kind of historical transparency that Brecht makes space for. This doesn't make *The Business Affairs of Mr Julius Caesar* a *roman à clef* or a strict allegory; but it does mean that the imaginative process of the fiction is more than an attempt at modern-day realism.

In September 1934, Walter Benjamin noted in the diary he kept during his visit to Svendborg that Brecht was faced by a number of alternatives for his next literary projects. Some were in narrative prose, including 'the smaller one about Ui – a satire on Hitler in the style of Renaissance historiography'.[4] The work Benjamin referred to eventually took shape as *The History of Giacomo Ui*, though it remained a fragment. The larger project was the TUI novel, a satire on intellectuals in the service of the status quo. Brecht sketched a list of names for *Giacomo Ui* which makes it clear that the Italian renaissance costume is a thin disguise for political figures of the interwar years: an 'Emilio Bertone' stands for Friedrich Ebert, the first President of the Weimar Republic; and, more scurrilously, Philip Scheidemann, the SPD politician who proclaimed the Weimar Republic in 1919, is encoded by taking the two parts of the German name, 'Scheide' (which can mean 'vagina') and 'Mann', and translating them directly to give 'Vaginuomo'.[5]

This kind of satirical allegory was developed in Brecht's play *The Resistible Rise of Arturo Ui*, in which the allusion to Shakespeare's

---

[4] 'Notes from Svendborg', in Walter Benjamin, *Selected Writings*, ed. Michael W. Jennings with Marcus Bullock, Howard Eiland and Gary Smith, trans. Howard Eiland, Edmund Jephcott, Rodney Livingstone and others, vol. 2: 1927–34 (Cambridge, MA and London: Belknap Press of Harvard University, 1999), 788.
[5] Brecht Archive (Akademie der Künste, Berlin): BBA 2943/17.

Julius Caesar nevertheless makes clear the imaginative continuity between the satirical novel and the comic political allegory. Yet the novel tries for something more complex. Both Brecht's own productive process and the dialectical tension between ancient history and the modern world are apparent when, towards the end of Book Three, Spicer explains what Caesar got out of the Spanish campaigns:

> C.'s reward for the pacification of the province was also suitably gratifying. The historians disagree as to the actual source of his earnings. Brandus is of the opinion that he only accepted money at all because he was anxious to have tangible proof of the Spaniards' great gratitude for his unselfishness. He emphasises that C. refused all but voluntary donations. (p. 164)

The Latinized name Brandus is a thinly disguised version of the Danish writer Georg Brandes, whose study of Caesar was one of the books consulted by Brecht, with Margarete Steffin's help, in his historical research. The technique of Latinization is close to the Italian translations of politicians' names in the Ui prose text. Through the allusion to Brandes, Brecht's engagement with and critique of the traditional historiography through which we are obliged to understand Caesar are written into the narrative itself. The same allusive technique generates other moments of transparency with a more political perspective. The minor character Cruppulus, for instance, is presented as a simple wool dealer; yet his name obviously evokes Krupp, the arms manufacturer, and it can hardly be a coincidence that Rarus records his remark, 'Whatever happens in politics, weapons decide things, short term and long term' (p. 185).

In one or two cases Brecht seems keen to allow for a more precise identification. We learn, for instance, that the poet Vastius Alder, who appears at dinner with Spicer in Book Three, has had the front part of a small warship brought to his estate as a permanent monument to his prowess as a naval commander in taking the city of Acme. This apparently absurd detail in fact alludes to the gunboat, commanded by the Italian nationalist poet Gabriele D'Annunzio during the First World War, which his friend Mussolini had set up in the park of D'Annunzio's villa on Lake

Garda. The taking of Acme is designed to recall D'Annunzio's grand gesture of declaring a sovereign state in Fiume (now in Croatia), subject to the Italian crown. For the aristocratically minded Alder, in any event, Caesar is incapable of acquiring the patina required for true heroic memory: instead he remains the great 'dealer'. As this dismissive term for him ('diese Usance') – derived from the technical terminology of international currency exchange – suggests, Caesar is himself the *currency* of a deal done through him by other forces. Finally, alongside D'Annunzio's appearance in the Alder figure, it has been suggested that the lawyer Afranius Carbo, who asserts the importance of Caesar's achievements for the economy, conceals a caricature of the legal theorist Carl Schmitt, whose physical appearance has been identified in the 'thickset man of about 50 with heavy jowls and watery eyes' described by Brecht (p. 43). By condensing and superimposing different political and intellectual positions adopted by Schmitt, the figure of Carbo becomes an absurd parody of the conservative legal theorist who became one of the leading ideologists of National Socialism.[6]

In this way both major set pieces and minor figures in the novel suggest the figurative relationship Brecht has in mind. In an often quite nuanced way, the novel is designed to *allow* the parallel history of the Weimar Republic and its decline into dictatorship to come into view through the prism of the late Republic in Rome and its similar movement towards dictatorship. This double image of the two republics emerges within the broader framework of a stylistic – and often highly amusing – modernization of the historical material. Brecht's interpretation of Rome in the first century BC as a kind of mirror image of contemporary politics is far from unprecedented. As we have seen, Mommsen projected an image of ancient Rome as similar to the modern capitals of Europe, but the rather racy style that marks the political terminology of *The Business Affairs of Mr Julius Caesar* also gains from what Brecht had noted in Eduard Meyer's study of Pompey and Caesar, where the style is briskly contemporary. Meyer regarded the struggle

---

[6] See Niklaus Müller-Schöll, *Das Theater des 'konstruktiven Defaitismus'* (Frankfurt am Main: Stroemfeld, 2002), 381.

---

between the two men as the conflict between three distinct forma-
tions of the state – 'the old republic in the form of the rule of the
senate; so-called democracy, i.e. the rule of the capitalists; and in
competition with them, the rule of the metropolitan rabble'.[7]

In a similar way, the street politics of Republican Rome are
exploited in the novel as the ambiguous reflection of the struggles
fought out on the streets of German cities in the course of the
Weimar Republic. When Crassus' library slave enters with Clodius
Pulcher, for example, the two appear as 'the rather battered
nobleman – former leader of the Democratic Street Clubs, the
armed wing of democracy – and Crassus' slave, democracy's theoretician!' (p. 71). The political vocabulary of 'democracy' serves to
disguise the groups of violent thugs which Publius Clodius Pulcher
– who was tribune of the people in 58 BC, and was murdered in
52 BC – set up; on the other hand, the vocabulary of armed struggle
also alludes to the storm troopers ('Sturmabteilung') of the Nazi
Party. The street riots that follow the election of Nepos and Cato as
tribunes of the people are 'commanded by some young chaps who
were later revealed to be members of Catilina's stormtroops and
the Democratic Street Clubs retreated into the house doorways
again and again' (p. 93). The vocabulary here is ambiguous: the
Nazi associations evoked by these 'stormtroops' (Brecht's original
has the word 'Sturmrotten', alluding to the 'Rotte' or squad that was
the basic organizational unit of the Storm Troopers) suggest that
the Catilinarian party can be deciphered as an emblem of fascism.
On the other hand, the democratic clubs, 'in which the masses of
the capital were organized by street and district' (p. 64), seem to
represent working class organizations, whether in Communist or
Socialist form. Brecht's imprecise allegory seems simply to have
confused the opposed forces of right and left. Caesar toys with the
strategies of political extremism – armed revolt and putschism –
yet he emerges from all these political complications as a merely
self-interested fellow traveller, dedicated ultimately to autocracy
and personal power.

[7] Eduard Meyer, *Caesars Monarchie und das Principat des Pompeius* (Stuttgart and
Berlin: J. G. Cotta'sche Buchhandlung Nachfolger, 1919), 5.

However, Brecht's method in *The Business Affairs of Mr Julius Caesar* does not simply fail to offer a straightforward allegory of the rise of Hitler through Caesar's career. The different ideological contexts on offer, as the budding biographer sets about his task, provide for the possibility of political readings, but not without ambiguity. Rarus' notebooks constantly stress the *enigmatic* character of Caesar's strategy and personality; Brecht does not try to resolve this enigma – instead he gives scope for different readings. Caesar's political clear-sightedness itself exemplifies such a practice of political interpretation – perhaps as a further clue to the reader in deciphering the historical configuration. The conversations that follow a physical attack on him raise the question of whether a genuinely popular movement should seize power, independently of the Catilinarian ideology, and led by an alliance with Cicero – and therefore associated with the old ruling class. Caesar says nothing after this proposal has been made, and Rarus identifies in his silence a moment of political reassessment: '[...] how quickly his sharp gaze had discerned behind the few malicious rioters last night the powerful figure of the Roman citizen who had become restless and remembered his own strength' (p. 100). It seems that the otherwise cynical Rarus himself falls prey here to the temptations of political myth: even *his* insight into Caesar's political analysis has to be questioned. Although Caesar, not without all irony, quite openly admits to him his belief that political convictions can be bought 'just like every other commodity' (p. 82), Rarus fails to apply his own words about Caesar's flexibility – 'His mind works incredibly quickly, and he's so adaptable!' (p. 68).

Pompey seems to have a far better understanding of Caesar when he is reported as saying 'the man (C.) was a chameleon' (p. 187). When a 'simple district election manager' expresses doubts about Caesar with the words 'He's a great man, but unfortunately he isn't always himself', Rarus highlights the truth the grassroots activist has stumbled on:

> If the man in the street knew more about the infinite complications of political struggles, if he had any idea of all the factors which dictate the decisions taken even by the man in charge,

who *isn't always himself* because he in turn is at the mercy of others, the man in the street definitely wouldn't talk like that. (p. 77)

Rarus not only draws attention to Caesar's systematic unreliability here; he provides a clue to the method of open allegory that guides Brecht's entire strategy. The instability and ambiguity of Caesar's identity is based not only on the infinite complexity of political struggle, as Rarus suggests, but on the way the novel encourages the reader to see his ideological posture in the context of a more contemporary reading: Caesar and Crassus, trade guilds and street clubs, Alexander the plebeian theoretician of class struggle and Cornelius Lentulus Sura, nicknamed the Shins, who is the chief sponsor of the Catilinarian conspiracy – all of them must be freed of their historical identity if they are to serve as ideological figures in relation to the politics and political style of the late Thirties.

Putting on the style
Reading *The Business Affairs of Mr Julius Caesar* we move continuously between the modernization of Roman history and a reflection of contemporary capitalism, as it evolved after the First World War. The notion of a Roman merchant class, perhaps moving towards a form of 'industrial capitalism' represented by the *City* (which is Brecht's word, but borrowed from existing historical writing) and in an alliance with the 'democrats' against the aristocratic senatorial families, can be seen as a satire on German history from the second Reich through the political instability of the Weimar Republic and into the Nazi dictatorship.

The novel's fundamental insight illuminates the 'return' of motifs from antiquity in the whole military repertoire of the Nazi spectacle. Although the accoutrements of Nazi uniforms are generally 'Germanic', the SA paramilitary groups with their 'Germany Awake' insignia during the Third Reich aped in design the standards of the Roman legions. Similarly, official Nazi architecture was designed to suggest monumentality and permanence – the 'Tribune of Honour' at the Nuremberg Zeppelin Field, where the Nazi Party Rallies were held, and the 'House of Art' in Munich together with other buildings by Paul Troost, are well-known examples. Even the 'Hitler salute' of the raised right arm was supposed to derive from a Roman original, popularized in early Italian cinema epics and adopted by the Fascist party of Mussolini. Amid all this Roman paraphernalia, Caesar himself embodies a conception of dictatorship, in the form of 'Caesarism', as it was sometimes called in the Thirties. The Italian political theorist Antonio Gramsci, responding to the analogy often drawn between Caesar and Mussolini, comments that such a political formation 'expresses the particular solution in which a great personality is entrusted with the task of "arbitration" over a historico-political situation characterized by an equilibrium of forces heading towards catastrophe'.[8]

Brecht can't have read this, but in the late Thirties he recognized a similar dynamic. Caesar's position between the old families of the Senate and the new money-aristocracy of the 'City' uncannily mirrors Gramsci's analysis. The title page of one set of drafts for *The Business Affairs of Mr Julius Caesar* is adorned with an image of Napoleon I, a political leader cited by Gramsci in the passage quoted above and often thought of as the classic instance of modern Caesarism.[9] Napoleon styled himself on Caesar and promoted the 'empire style', derived from a more luxurious version of the clear lines associated with the Roman Republic in earlier phases of the French Revolution. It is this identification of Caesar as the paradigm of dictatorial style that makes the use of Mark Antony's speech from Shakespeare's play so revealing in *Arturo Ui*. In a famous scene, an actor has been brought in to coach Ui for his public speeches: in consequence the rhetorical gestures of a demagogue are taught through a rehearsal of Mark Antony's eulogy after the death of Caesar. In the play, the satirical effect reveals the artificiality of this repertoire of postures and gestures, and an ironic gap opens up between the aspiring but culturally inadequate Ui and the tacit model of Hitler's projection of power. The Caesar novel works in the same ideological framework, but offers a broader critical range. Through its focus on the corruption,

[8] Antonio Gramsci, *Selections from the Prison Notebooks*, eds and trans. Quintin Hoare and Geoffrey Nowell Smith (London: Lawrence & Wishart, 1971), 219.
[9] Brecht Archive: BBA 187/01.

financial speculation, and jockeying for power that accompany Caesar's career in business and politics, Brecht undermines the propaganda effect that can be derived from the Nazi self-identification with the Roman world.

The flash of recognition

In 1936 Brecht helped to edit and then submitted his friend Walter Benjamin's text 'The Work of Art in the Age of its Technological Reproducibility' to *The Word*, the exile publication of German writers in Moscow. It was rejected; but Benjamin's description of his own contribution to art theory is suggestive in relation to Brecht's novel: 'In what follows, the concepts which are introduced [...] differ from those now current in that they are completely useless for the purposes of fascism.'[10] By dismantling the monumental image of Caesar and replacing it with the wheeler-dealer of Rarus' diaries, Brecht renders a whole world of imperial fantasy 'useless for the purposes of fascism'.

When Brecht heard of Benjamin's suicide, his journal for August 1941 returns to the Caesar novel. The entry records that he has just read Benjamin's last work:

> the little treatise deals with historical research, and could have been written after reading my CAESAR (which b[enjamin] could not make much of when he read it in svendborg). b[enjamin] rejects the notion of history as a continuum, the notion of progress as a mighty enterprise undertaken by cool, clear heads [...].[11]

Benjamin was like many readers of early drafts in the late Thirties, and of the first published editions 20 years later, in finding Brecht's narrative too schematic or merely diligent – which may account for the fact that a modern English version is appearing over 50 years after the original publication. Yet Benjamin had understood the strategy of the book perfectly well, as Brecht recognized. In 18

[10] Walter Benjamin, 'The Work of Art in the Age of its Technological Reproducibility', in *Selected Writings*, vol. 3: 1935–8 (2002), 102.
[11] Bertolt Brecht, *Journals 1934–1955*, trans. Hugh Rorrison, ed. John Willett (London: Methuen, 1993), 159.

discrete, numbered paragraphs, 'On the Concept of History' sets out a radical reworking of the idea of history, not as a continuum along which humanity progresses under the leadership of great men, but as a flash of intuition connecting a critical moment in the past with a current crisis:

> Articulating the past historically does not mean recognizing it "the way it really was." It means appropriating a memory as it flashes up in a moment of danger. Historical materialism wishes to hold fast that image of the past which unexpectedly appears to the historical subject in a moment of danger. The danger threatens both the content of the tradition and those who inherit it. For both, it is one and the same thing: the danger of becoming a tool of the ruling classes. Every age must strive anew to wrest tradition away from the conformism that is working to overpower it.[12]

For Brecht in the late Thirties, the moment of danger was only too apparent. The identification of the Nazis' self-image with Caesar's dictatorship and of the *Reich* with the Roman *imperium* could be subverted in the course of his own enigmatic reading of Roman history. Brecht's *Caesar* does not *impose* allegory to illuminate some already fixed common structure in the European dictatorships; rather his sceptical reconstruction comes alive, in a flash of recognition, as we see afresh and with wry familiarity the corruption and violence that keep great men in power.

A. Phelan

[12] Benjamin, *Selected Writings*, vol. 4: 1938–40 (2003), 391.

Book One
The Career of a Distinguished Young Man

The path which had been pointed out to us was narrow and climbed quite steeply in zigzags through the olive groves as they rose from the coast in terraces, supported by low stone walls. It was a bright morning. We had probably arrived during the second meal break, since only a few slaves were in sight on the plantation, and smoke was rising from several of the farm buildings.

Soon the villa could be made out, or at least we could see parts of it glimmering through the olive trees. It was situated halfway up the hillside.

As we were climbing I began to wonder once again whether the old man would really grant us an insight into the priceless documents. The letters of introduction my man Sempronius was carrying were not exactly weighty. I'd rather have seen him sweating under a heavier load.

As so often when the effort, and ultimately also the expense, had become altogether too tiresome I comforted myself once again with the thought that the great politician whose biography I had undertaken to write had placed greater obstacles in the way of his biographers – sometimes deliberately, sometimes inadvertently – than a difficult journey. There was the legend, which obscured everything. He had even written some books himself, to deceive us. And he had spent money: considerable sums, too! Great men have made discovering the true motives behind their actions a laborious task.

The villa proved to be only one storey high but very extensive. It was built in the simplest style, quite unlike the awful architecture favoured by the nouveaux riches in our capital. And the master of the house, who came to meet us in the library, had nothing in common with our new Senators.

Mummlius Spicer, who was first a bailiff and subsequently a banker, is a tall, gaunt old man with a rather grey face distinguished by a heavy jaw. He tends to stoop forwards, but this does not appear to be due to the weakness of old age.

He stood at the window, inspecting our letters of introduction very attentively. The way he handled the papers was indicative of his profession. Financiers read documents more thoroughly than lovers of literature. They are more conscious of the negative consequences a cursory glance can produce.

Nothing in his roughly hewn face gave me any indication of his opinion on the various letters, or of the value he placed on their recommendations. At the time I thought he must have been most impressed by the words of the Imperial Quaestor, Tullius Varro, a very influential man. Later, when I knew Spicer better, I changed my mind and deduced that the short letter from Cavella, a freedman, which contained a reference to my legal practice, prompted him to support my project. For his part, he never referred to the matter. After having read the documents he returned them to me without a word and proceeded to address me in precisely the same tone he had used to receive me.

To some extent the letters indicated the purpose of my visit, and the old man began to inquire into my studies and interests. His questions were brief, and he accepted my replies without any signs of approval or disapproval. He wanted to know whether I had published any books yet. I mentioned my 'Solon'. Then he asked me about my party affiliations, to which I replied that I did not belong to any of the parties. Next, quite nonchalantly as it seemed to me, he turned to the question of my private means, and I gradually realized that he intended to demand payment for any information he might provide.

I must admit that I was slightly shocked by this. The library where we were sitting was that of a very wealthy man. Later I realized that the collection must have consisted of gifts – there was no connection between the individual works – but they were expensive presents appropriate to a rich man. I also knew that his properties were extremely profitable, and that his house, which was by no means humble, could be considered modest in relation to his income from Sardinian silver mines alone. My project, and also the request which it necessitated, was of a purely scholarly nature. No financial reward of any kind could be expected from it. It really was not customary to purchase historical accounts in the same way as crockery.

He could not help but notice my reticence. There was a short and not entirely comfortable pause. Then he asked, brusquely: 'What is it you actually want from me?' I said something about it being assumed that Rarus' diaries were in his possession. 'I haven't got them any longer,' he said, calmly. I kept silent once again. If he thought that after travelling for eleven days I was going to haggle with him for a few rolls of parchment as one would for an orchard or a slave, he was mistaken. However, he seemed quite unmoved as he slowly continued: 'And they wouldn't be any use to you, in any case. I assume you intend to write a biography. That's a matter of politics.' – 'Diaries kept by a politician's secretary are of political relevance, whatever else they may also be,' I said, quite sharply. 'Perhaps so,' he said, gazing into a corner of the room, 'but I haven't got them.'

A short Gallic slave entered the room; he was apparently the estate foreman. The old man gave him some very detailed instructions concerning the repair of an irrigation plant. The conversation lasted for more than a quarter of an hour, and during the whole of that time the old man did not look over in my direction once. Then the Gaul left, and the master of the house resumed our conversation.

'The material would also be absolutely useless to you without comprehensive annotations,' he said, calmly, 'and who is supposed to provide you with them? Of course, if all you want are a few intimate details ... but I doubt whether the diaries really contain the sort of things that would interest the general public: whether the gentleman in question had fish for breakfast, and so on. This fellow Rarus was concerned with the commercial aspect of the enterprises and, as you know, our historians are not very interested in that side of things. They haven't got the faintest idea what short selling means. They think things like that are only of minor importance.'

'I hardly imagine that the diaries only contain a record of the price of corn,' I said.

'And what if they did?' he asked, and although his face remained as impassive as ever, I thought I perceived a gleam of amusement there. 'Then something could be learnt from that,' I shot back at him.

'Really?' he asked in turn.

I began to think he was one of those people who got no fun from a hurried encounter, like most women when it came to intercourse, and I decided to prolong his pleasure.

'It's a pity that you've thrown the things away,' I said, regretfully. 'After all, they were concerned with nothing less than the foundation of the Empire.'

He thought for quite a while before speaking again.

'You mean, if you can deduce X's character from the nature of his breakfast, you can do the same from his relationship to the price of corn. Have you rented anywhere to stay yet?' The question came as rather a surprise, and it was only after some hesitation that I told him I had rented a small house down by the lake for a whole month: an unforgivably rash thing to do, since it provided him with a good opportunity to make the most extortionate demands.

He studied me closely for a few minutes. Then he stood up, crossed to the wall and rapped his knuckles on a brass plate hanging there by a cord. Stepping over to a beautiful low desk, he took a piece of parchment out of a leather folder and pointed out one of the items marked there to the slave who entered. Silence prevailed until the man returned with a small ashwood box under his arm.

The old man took the box casually and put it on the bookshelf behind his chair.

'There are the diaries,' he said, dryly. 'What are they worth to you?'

I laughed.

'They wouldn't make any sense without detailed annotations,' I said.

'And they are not for sale without those annotations,' he replied impassively. 'I shall provide them for you. And, of course, you cannot purchase the documents themselves; only the right to inspect them.'

'8,000 sesterces,' I said.

He hesitated perceptibly.

'It's taken you two weeks to get here, and you've rented a house for a month, so you're hardly likely to want to return empty handed,' he growled. '12,000 sesterces isn't very much at all. A good cook costs 100,000.'

I was annoyed. He was definitely not well-born. I resolved to deny him his lengthy encounter.

'Fine,' I snapped.

'But I have drawn your attention,' he said, carefully, 'to the fact that there may well be very little material which would be of use to someone like you.'

'You certainly have,' I answered, impatiently.

12,000 sesterces was a large sum of money. I still did not know whether the diaries were worth that much. And by that time I was too angry to consider the idea of my host providing annotations.

He, however, appeared to regard it as part of the arrangement we had concluded and invited me to return that very evening.

The great Gaius Julius Caesar, details of whose private life I hoped to learn from the notes kept by his secretary for so many years, had been dead for just twenty years. He had inaugurated a new era. Before him Rome had been a city with a few scattered colonies. He was the one who founded the Empire. He had codified the law, reformed the currency and even modified the calendar on the basis of scientific knowledge. His Gallic campaigns, which had taken the Roman flag as far as distant Britain, had opened up a new continent to trade and civilization. His statue had its place with those of the Gods, he had given his name to cities as well as a month in the calendar, and the monarchs added his illustrious name to their own. The history of Rome had found its Alexander. It was already apparent that he would become the unattainable model for every dictator. All lesser mortals were left with was the task of describing his achievements. That was the purpose of my planned biography. Now I had the material to base it upon.

When I made my appearance in the villa belonging to my idol's banker, towards evening time, I had already taken steps to arrange financial matters. In the afternoon I had sailed to the next town, and the bank there had assured me that they would process my letter of credit immediately. It would only take a few days for the sum of 12,000 sesterces to be transferred.

Mummlius Spicer had apparently been waiting for me before dining. He led me to the table at once. We dined alone, and the meal was simple; in fact, the old man only ate a few figs, excusing himself with references to his weak stomach. A cask of Black Sea sardines was opened for me, however: a delicacy which, as I was quite aware, cost 1,600 sesterces in Rome.

Naturally this lavish hospitality, after the awkward events of the morning, caused me no little surprise. I would like to state straight away that the banker continued to treat me with such hospitality for the length of my stay. I must have cost him many times more than my 12,000 sesterces; the original manuscript of Hortensius' speeches, which he presented me with when I left, was alone worth a far greater sum.

However, Spicer did not yet refer to the object of my visit during that first evening, except for making some very vague comments on the writing of history, which, incidentally, were extremely disparaging. Rarus' diaries were not mentioned, either; the ashwood box was no longer on the bookshelf.

I could only attribute this reticence on the old man's part to the fact that I had not yet concluded the financial aspect of our arrangement, and this rekindled my anger.

We parted rather coolly.

The money arrived the next morning, and I set off at the same time as on the first day. The old man was sitting in his library, and a slave was taking dictation. He finished his dictation while I examined his collection of books. Then he took receipt of the money, counted it and passed it to the slave for safekeeping. He behaved precisely as if it were the everyday sale of a pig. The most tactless thing, it seemed to me, was that immediately afterwards he instructed the slave to fetch the box. Which he did. It was again pushed casually on to the bookshelf.

Then the old man began speaking, in a deep, level voice. Without any preliminaries, as if merely fulfilling a contractual duty, he said:

'As you may know, during the nineties I was working as a bailiff in the Fourth District. As such, I came into possession of all manner of promissory notes against C.,* who lived in that district: most of them for very large sums, but also an incredible number for small amounts, from bakers for example, or tailors. This indicated that his estate in Campania was already incapable of providing the supplies he needed for his town house; it was in the hands of the receivers. C. was very well known for the elaborate games and sports meetings he had organized as Aedile and Quaestor. The ordinary people were impressed by the size of his debts, which were the subject of fantastic rumours. The first time I saw him, if I remember correctly, was in his bedroom, where a tailor was fitting him with a tunic. I still recall noticing how exact his demands about the collar fitting were. He actually employed the technical terms tailors use. It wasn't the first time I had been inside his house. Usually his secretary, this same Rarus, received me. It had been arranged that I should only turn up there in the mornings, so C.'s mother would not encounter me; apparently everyone in the house was terrified of her, not least C. himself. She was a friendly little old lady, but she could let you feel the cutting edge of her tongue. Later I got to know her quite well.

C. treated me with the utmost candour, by the way, and it was without any irony that he pointed out the most valuable pieces of antique furniture, asking me whether I intended to take them with me. He didn't seem at all embarrassed by the presence of the tailor, though the man must have begun to wonder about his chances of being paid when he saw me.

And I think even at our very first meeting he made some inquiries about the circumstances in which I lived. They were not auspicious. I had a small floor in one of Crassus' houses, for my wife and six children, and I had some difficulty paying the rent. Almost all the conversations I had with him referred to these problems of mine, in one way or another. There he was, advising me, sitting on a chair which I had no intention of leaving behind.

---

* Spicer always referred to Caesar only as C.; initially I thought he was doing so in order to emphasize the secret nature of our dealings. But Rarus never used any other name than C., either.

After that I met him more often, and I can certainly say that I enjoyed going to see him. Our acquaintanceship lasted, in fact, until his death.'

He stopped talking. We heard voices and the shuffling of many feet on the paving stones outside. The second meal break had finished. The short Gallic slave from yesterday came in, and Spicer signed a huge 'S' in the order book that the slave held out for him. Through the open door I could see the sky with scattered clouds. The laurel hedge, planted as a windbreak, trembled in the wind. The room was narrow but high, the whitewashed walls were covered with comfortable, leather bookcases, and it was agreeably warm. A couple of enormous logs crackled in the hearth. I was still relishing the old man's straightforward narrative.

I could see Spicer in my mind's eye, a younger, but otherwise probably not very different Spicer – people like that change very little, because anxiety and adversity make them look old at an early age – and the indebted aristocrat with the great name. It amused me to think that this rough-looking fellow with his heavy jaw probably performed his duty to the letter despite any trust which may have developed, and did not fail to take the chair with him. I remembered my 12,000 sesterces.

The old man took a sip of the wine that had been served to us before continuing:

'As far as I know he had given up doing anything at all by this stage. He had attempted to learn a profession and earn his own living at one point in his life. He tried his hand at being a lawyer for the Democratic Clubs in two cases they brought against senior Senate officials for extortion and other abuses of office perpetrated in the provinces.'

When I went through my notes about the conversation at the end and discovered that Spicer had conferred upon the young Caesar the profession of lawyer, I raised the subject with him again. He insisted upon employing this term. He did concede that the word lawyer could not be employed for all the noble young people who went to the Forum with their clients – i.e. leaseholders, debtors, freedmen from the plebeian branch of the family or anyone who had approached them for help – to lend their support in obtaining concessions or in other legal matters. This activity had been pursued since ancient times for no fee and could only secure political influence. But Spicer maintained that a transformation had taken place at precisely this time. And that the young C. had been engaged just as any lawyer today would be.

'The City paid young lawyers from good families very decently in cases like that. It was the old struggle between the City and the Senate. Since time immemorial 300 families had distributed all the important government posts inside and outside Rome among themselves. The Senate was their stock exchange. That's where they negotiated who of them should sit on the benches of the Senate, who should sit in the courts of law, who should be mounted on battle chargers and who should just stay on their country seats. They were major landowners who treated the other citizens of Rome like servants and their servants like vermin. They treated merchants like thieves and the inhabitants of the conquered provinces like their enemies. One of them was the elder Cato, a great-grandfather of our Cato, who was the leader of the Senate party when C. and I were in Rome. He commended the second-century law whereby a thief had to repay double the amount he had stolen, while anyone caught charging interest on a loan had to repay four times what he had "taken". Only one generation before mine they passed a law which prohibited Senators from engaging in commercial activity. The law came too late, and immediately ways were found to get around it – laws can accomplish anything except stop trade – and it even led to expansion of the trading companies with each partner in a group of fifty owning a fiftieth of a ship, thus controlling fifty ships rather than just one; but anyway, you can see the way those gentlemen's minds worked. They were outstanding generals and quite able to conquer provinces; they just didn't know what to do with them afterwards.

But as our trade grew out of its infancy and we began to export oil, wool and wine in larger quantities, and to import grain and many other commodities, and especially when we wanted to take money out of Rome and invest it in the provinces, those gentlemen revealed their completely aristocratic inability to move with the times; the younger element in the City realized that they were suffering from a lack of sensible leadership. We had no urge whatsoever to go off and be generals ourselves, you understand, or to waste our time, which was money, sitting in musty offices; the gentlemen were quite welcome to stay where they were, just as long as they were under proper control from the City. If you take the Punic War as an example you'll see what I mean. We had waged war from the best of all motives, which was to eliminate competition from Africa, but what was the result? Our armed forces didn't capture produce and tributes from Carthage; they removed its walls and warships instead. Rather than bring the corn, they brought the plough. Our generals proudly proclaimed: "Not a blade of grass remains where my legions have been." But this grass was exactly what we were after; one of these types of grass can be used to make bread, you know. What had been conquered in the Punic War, at immense cost, was wasteland. The land could have easily provided food for the whole of our peninsula, but everything the people would have needed to enable them to work for us, from the agricultural tools to the slaves who wielded them, was taken away from them for the triumphal procession in Rome. And a conquest like that was followed by a similar administration. The only place the governors kept any track of figures was in their personal account books. Everyone knows that a general's tunic has more pockets than any other coat – but the governors' clothes consisted entirely of pockets. When those gentlemen returned home they were rattling as if they were wearing suits of armour. Cornelius Dolabella and Publius Antonius, the characters C. prosecuted when he was younger, had loaded half of Macedonia on to their ships.

Of course, it was impossible to establish in that way anything you could really call trade. Every war was followed by bankruptcies and suspended payments in Rome. Every victory for the army was a defeat for the City. The triumphs celebrated by the generals were triumphs over the people. News of the Battle of Zama, which ended the Punic War, was greeted with cries of horror in two languages. Both the Punic *and* the Roman banks were horrified. The Senate was slaughtering the cash cow. The system was rotten to the core.

All this was on everybody's lips in Rome. There was gossip in every barber's shop about the moral decay of the Senate. Even in the Senate itself they went on about the "necessity for thorough moral reform". Cato the younger saw a bleak future ahead for the 300 families. He decided to do something to improve their reputation, so he set out on foot to visit all the towns under his jurisdiction as Governor of Sardinia, with only one servant to carry his clothes and sacrificial bowls, and when he returned from his governorship he sold his warhorse before he sailed, because he didn't feel justified in claiming the transport costs from the state. Unfortunately his ship was hit by a storm; he was shipwrecked, lost his account books, and lamented to the end of his days that he couldn't prove to anybody how honestly he had conducted himself. He knew his behaviour had been quite beyond belief. The City didn't think much of "setting good examples" and making moralistic speeches. They were certain what the problem was; the officials had to be paid.

The fact was that the gentlemen in question performed their duties from a sense of obligation. To have taken money for their services would have seemed dishonourable to them. Of course, with such high ideals they had no alternative but to steal. And they stole from the corn paid as tributes, from the funds assigned to the construction of roads; they even stole water from the public supply.

As I said, the City was not unreasonable. It liaised with the merchants in the conquered provinces and encouraged them to take legal action. That's how the trials came about. Cicero himself, the City's main spokesman, conducted a few on behalf of Sicilian companies.

But as time went by those gentlemen of ours in the Senate got used to legal cases the way you get used to rain; you put a coat on. From that point on, rather than stealing a lot from a few people they stole a little from everyone. And if a legal case was threatening nevertheless, they stole everything. It costs money to take legal action. So they also stole the money to pay for possible lawsuits from the people they fleeced.

Then a couple of wealthy Democratic Clubs in Rome began to finance cases against the thieves in the Senate; or rather, against the most shameless among them, those who even made it impossible for Roman merchants in the provinces to go about their business. These prosecutions did discredit the accused to some extent and, perhaps more importantly, gave young lawyers the opportunity to learn their trade. Because this involved more than just making a couple of witty speeches. The lawyer had to procure and coach his own witnesses, and he needed to distribute the cash wisely, so the judicial mechanism was well oiled. We even got young lawyers from Senatorial families. There was no better way for them to learn how the administrative system worked. You have to have bribed people yourself in order to let yourself be bribed properly.

C. lost both cases. Some people said it was because he was incompetent – I think it was because he was too competent. This is suggested by the fact that he had to leave Rome afterwards, in order (as he put it to me himself on one occasion) to escape from the hostile mood which had built up towards him. He went to Rhodes, ostensibly to perfect his rhetorical skills. Since this reason for a young lawyer's rather precipitous departure doesn't exactly cast credit upon him, it's reasonable to assume there were other reasons for his journey which would have sounded even less creditable.

It's true that a lawyer can make more money by losing a case than by winning it, under certain circumstances. But he shouldn't do so with the first few cases he accepts. It was one of this young man's weaknesses that he didn't do anything by half. He probably wanted to be a proper lawyer from the very beginning. He had exactly the same attitude later on, towards making war. That's what turned my hair white.'

The old man related all this, the whole story of the trials, quite neutrally and without any trace of humour. He hardly seemed aware that the picture he was painting of the great statesman in his first public appearances was not a very appealing one. It implied nothing less than that he had accepted bribes from the other side. After all, both cases had been accorded a certain place in the biographies. They were cited as the first, though not particularly successful, attempts on the part of the young Caesar to raise the flag of young democracy in opposition to the corruption of the conservative Senators. He was descended from a family, which despite being patrician, had long-standing connections with democracy. His aunt was the widow of Marius, the people's general, and his wife was the daughter of Cinna, the rebel. Spicer was clearly revealing a certain disapproval of Caesar's first appearance, but from an odd perspective.

'But at quite an early stage he was regarded as one of the rising men in the Democratic Party,' I said, casually.

Spicer fixed me with his impassive gaze.

'Yes,' he then replied, dryly, 'he was regarded as a rising man. And he rose when money was the bait. They were keen on names. His family was one of the 15 or 16 oldest patrician families in the city.'

I decided to restore a little tone to the conversation.

'You can't deny that it indicated a democratic spirit when he absolutely rejected Sulla's demand that he should divorce his first wife, Cornelia, because she was Cinna's daughter. Are you trying to tell me that he wasn't serious about that, either?'

'Why shouldn't he have been serious about it?' the old man asked, patiently. 'Cinna had made a fine fortune in Spain.'

'That was confiscated,' I retorted.

'Not C.'s share. And when they threatened to do so, he took it and Cornelia to Asia.'

'So you think this refusal to leave Cornelia had nothing to do with political convictions. And no doubt love didn't come into it, either?'

Spicer was giving me a curious look, but nevertheless I continued:

'I suppose he wasn't capable of loving at all, according to you?'

'Why should I believe anything of the sort?' he said, calmly. 'He was in love at precisely that time. With a freed slave, a Syrian: I can't remember his name. Cornelia was quite furious about it, if what I heard was true. It led to some unpleasant scenes even before they got off the ship, and the Syrian insisted that C. should get a divorce. Like Sulla. But C. didn't give in to him, either. He wouldn't let his heart rule his head, although it may disappoint you to hear it.'

He was completely serious as he spoke, and even exhibited a certain reserve, which isn't conveyed by the coarse words when they are put in writing; it was some sort of consideration for me.

He seemed to want to express by his tone of voice that it was up to me whether to continue listening to him or not, and whether to make use of the explanations which were part of our contract, but that he was unable either to alter the truth or change his opinions on my account. His opinion on C.'s capacity for genuine love was surprising, however, since the man in question had had six children and no doubt been a perfectly correct father. I angrily forestalled any further irrelevancies by saying simply:

'And the funeral he arranged for her and his aunt?'

'That was a matter of politics. He had wax masks of Marius and Cinna worn in the funeral procession. The Democratic Party paid him 200,000 sesterces to do so. His family, and especially his mother – I've mentioned her to you already, a very sensible woman – wouldn't forgive him for a long time. 200,000 sesterces was less than you'd pay for two good cooks. But the clubs thought the figure was high enough, since there was no longer any danger attached to the demonstration; the Praetor was already a Democrat by then.'

He also showed me something of how the estate functioned before I went back down to the lake. It was primarily devoted to vine cultivation, with a few olive fields. We headed in the direction of the slaves' quarters, which consisted of two clean, whitewashed stone huts with a large number of narrow window slits high above the ground.

Two donkeys were turning a millwheel on the tidy, paved courtyard, supervised by an unchained slave. Another slave was sitting on a small wooden bench next to the doorway, not working. He was an elderly man, and he seemed very restless. There was a preoccupied expression on his face, and he was moving his head incessantly, as if straining to hear something.

'They're coming to fetch him at lunchtime,' remarked Spicer. 'He'll be taken down to the market. He's over forty and no use any more.'

'What's bothering him so much?' I asked.

The old man questioned the slave who was leading the donkeys round in a circle. We discovered the news that he was to be sold had come as a surprise. He had been brought in from the fields and only told when he got here, so he hadn't been able to say goodbye to the others. What was tormenting him was the thought that the agent might arrive to take him away before the others came in from the fields for their midday break.

'He may have friends among them,' said Spicer, 'or even sons. You know, you can never tell with them who the father is. I'm not opposed to them having sexual relations in captivity; in fact, I encourage it. The women are set free after the third child.'

We slowly went on our way. The overseer's wife had gone up to the man and given him a loaf and some salted fish for the journey. When I looked back again I could see that he was holding these provisions under his arm and staring out over the fields, even more restless than before.

'He always needed money. Once he even had a go at the slave trade,' said the old man as we walked on. 'You're bound to have heard the story about the pirates?'

I realized that he was talking about 'C.' again and nodded, surprised. The delightful anecdote was to be found in every schoolbook.

'Would you be prepared to repeat what you know about it?' he asked.

'Quite prepared,' I said, and I recounted the story as I knew it. I gave my voice something of the cadence I was accustomed to using when reciting material for my Greek teacher as I quoted the famous anecdote.

'The young Caesar was captured by pirates just off the island of Pharmacusa. They operated fleets of considerable size and dominated the seas with a large number of vessels. At first he taunted the pirates because they only asked for a ransom of 20 talents. Didn't they know who they had caught? And he offered to pay them 50 of his own free will. So he immediately sent some companions to various towns to raise the money. He stayed behind with his doctor, his cook and two manservants, and he remained unperturbed by these murderous denizens of Asia Minor. He continued to treat them with such contempt that he would order them to be quiet when he wanted to go to sleep. For 38 days he behaved as if the ship's crew were his bodyguards rather than his captors. He joked and made fun of them without any sign of fear whatsoever. Now and then he even wrote poems and speeches, which he read to them; he called anyone who failed to admire his works a fool and a barbarian, and he would often threaten, with laughter in his voice, to have them hanged in the end. The pirates found him very amusing and thought his free speeches highly entertaining.

But as soon as the ransom had arrived from Miletus and he was released he recruited enough armed men to fill several ships in Miletus harbour and set off after the pirates. He found them still at anchor off the island and managed to overpower most of them. He regarded their property as legitimate plunder, but he delivered the pirates to the prison at Pergamum before proceeding to arrange their punishment with Junius, the Governor of Asia. But since Junius was only concerned with the property confiscated from the pirates, which admittedly comprised a sizeable sum, he merely replied vaguely that he was unable to deal with the prisoners at that time. So Caesar, without bothering to raise the matter with Junius again, returned to Pergamum and had all the pirates nailed to the cross on his own authority, as he had so often jokingly promised to do when he was on the island.'

The old man had nodded at almost every sentence. He made a mark with one of his large feet in the soft earth of a row of radishes, to point something out to his men. As he walked on he started speaking:

'These days almost everything about his life looks that way. I'll tell you what was going on. It was slave trading. That little deal was made during the period when C. made democratic capital out of the funerals of his first wife and his aunt, and immediately after he had brought the cases against the Senators' abuses in the provinces. It was all connected with his journey to Rhodes, where he was to learn the art of public speaking from a Greek. Our young lawyer loved to do several things at the same time. And, as I mentioned, he needed money. So he took a shipload of slaves with him, skilled tanners from Gaul, if I remember correctly; you could sell them for a profit down there. Of course, it was smuggling.

The major slave traders from Asia Minor had long-standing agreements with our ports, and with those in Greece and Syria, which assured them a monopoly of slave transport in both directions. You see, the slave trade was a highly organized line of business, backed by a great deal of money, some of which was from Rome. Sometimes up to ten thousand head were sold on the slave market in Delos on a single day. The slave traders enjoyed a close and well-regulated relationship with the businessmen in the capital. There was only friction with the Export Trust of Asia Minor later on, when the City set up its own slave trading operation. Our tax contractors started organizing regular slave hunts in the provinces of Asia Minor, in times of total peace, under the protection of the Roman Eagle. The Cilician and Syrian firms defended themselves against this competition, which they regarded as unfair, as best they could. Soon the struggle for a monopoly of the slave trade led to a quite sizeable war at sea. Transport ships were being captured and slave cargoes confiscated all over the place. The firms in Rome and Asia Minor cursed each other, and called each other pirates.

C. sailed in winter, when there was less danger from the patrol boats there, due to the storms. But they still caught him. His cargo was confiscated and he was detained. As you know from the history books, he was treated with great courtesy. They left him his doctor and his manservants, and even listened patiently to his poems. Those good people of Asia Minor even tolerated that brutality and remained polite.* He was only required to pay a fine, which was calculated according to the size of the cargo. It was 20 talents.

I heard the rest of what I'm going to tell you from the Proconsul Junius; he was in office down there at the time, and I got to know him when he was an old man. He investigated the whole business, because it blew up into a big scandal.

First of all C. sent messengers to raise the money from the cities of Asia Minor. He concealed the fact that the money was to pay a fine for slave trading and maintained that it was for a ransom set by pirates. And he demanded 50 talents, instead of 20. The money

---

* I do not know what to make of Spicer's description of the pirates as law-abiding merchants, but the ancient writers certainly did report that they lived in a civilized manner. Their literature was said to be of a very high standard. To quote: 'Neither before nor since has such beautiful singing been heard on the coast of the Mediterranean, never did such elegant and intellectual discussions take place, as during this time when slavery was in full bloom.'

was raised. He never paid it back. When he had been released he went to Miletus, filled a couple of ships with gladiator slaves, and took his "ransom" back from his captors, as well as his cargo of slaves. And what's more, he not only seized the crew of the patrol boat; he also took some of the slave traders who had dispatched it back to Pergamum, along with their entire stock of slaves. When summoned by Junius to explain himself he demanded that each and every one of the people from Asia Minor be treated as pirates, and when Junius refused and began to enquire too closely into the details of the case, he stole back to Pergamum under cover of darkness and had them nailed to the cross by forged orders, so they wouldn't be able to testify against him.

Incidentally, the historians – convinced that C. had the last laugh by actually having the awful "pirates" crucified after having jokingly threatened to do so – have also bestowed upon him a sense of humour; that claim is completely unfounded. There wasn't a trace of humour about him. But he did have a nose for business.'

'I don't understand how he already had the power to do all that in those days,' I said.

'He had no more power than any other young cub from a Senatorial family. They did whatever they wanted to.'

We were obliged to step to one side. An ox cart came jolting down the path behind us. The elderly slave was sitting on it, a small box at his side. He was being taken to market.

He waved to a team of slaves who were working in a vineyard to one side of the path. They waved back but did not call out to him, probably because their boss was in sight.

The slave who was being taken away peered desperately at the team, searching for someone, but the man or woman he was looking for appeared to be absent.

'You mustn't lose sight of the fact,' continued Spicer, 'that C. had had merchants hanged, if you want to gauge the problems Junius was faced with as a result. At that time the firms in Asia Minor hadn't officially been designated pirates. That's what they are called in our history books today. Of course, since we write the books, we can bring our version of events to bear.

However, even in those days a moral campaign against the firms in Asia Minor had been started in Rome, with a lot of money behind it; it was claimed that they obtained their merchandise by unlawful means, and people even went so far as to accuse them of treating their goods inhumanely. Actually, it's obvious that goods captured by governors in military campaigns suffered a lot more in transit, since it was all the same to the armed forces how many individuals reached their destination. The traders, on the other hand, lost money with every man, so they arranged sanitary shipping facilities. But the Roman firms only succeeded in getting the state to adopt their cause officially years after the little incident we are talking about. They encouraged the mood in the Forum to a certain extent by occasionally having a Roman corn transport ship or two captured by some sort of Greek buccaneer. That enabled them to scream for help from the state and demand that the law against piracy be enforced. But the City didn't get the Roman Navy's help in their struggle against competition from Asia Minor without a fight. And C. played a part in this, too – although a very modest one.

In the year 87, when Gabinius, the People's Tribune, demanded on behalf of the City that the Senate should give Pompey command of the Roman Navy to fight the "pirates", he was nearly lynched by those well-bred, landowning gentlemen. They had long-term contracts with the traders of Asia Minor and couldn't tolerate any reduction or interruption in slave imports; they couldn't run their vast estates without slaves. And they had no desire to give the City a monopoly of slave imports. They were afraid of monopoly prices.

The City appealed to the people. The Democratic Clubs went into action. Of course, it wouldn't have been any good without a little demagogy. You've got to speak to the common people in a populist style. The speakers (and C. was one of them) emphasized the low prices for slaves charged by the firms in Asia Minor, which would bring starvation to the craftsmen of Rome.

Before long the resentment of the Senate's opposition among small farmers was quite widespread. The use of slaves on the large estates put immense pressure on the small agricultural concerns. They hoped that the slave trade in general, and not only that based in Asia Minor, would be quashed. In Etruria the Senate had to use the army to control rioting peasant farmers.

The urban proletariat also suffered because employers were pushing down wages for craftsmen by using cheap slave labour. But what tipped the balance was that the recently established slave import firms, with a lot of capital at their disposal, engineered a slight rise in the price of corn and spread the word that pirates were obstructing imports of corn. And, of course, cash was being scattered around in all directions. Pompey was always preceded by people handing out sealed envelopes, just like lictors preceding officials. So when old Catulus from the Senate, after giving a glowing account of Pompey's merits, begged the People's Assembly not to expose such a man to the dangers of war, the people just laughed; and when he shouted, in despair: "Who will you have left if you lose him?", they grinned and yelled back: "You!" And when another speaker warned of the danger of handing over so much power to one man they sent up such a scream that a raven flying over the market place was stunned and fell on top of the crowd. It was probably on its way to pick up some of the public money that was being handed out. But the whole bag of tricks wouldn't have been any use if they hadn't pressed piles of shares in the slave import firms into the hands of a dozen or so senators. It was only then that the affair became a matter of national concern, and Pompey got the use of the Roman Navy to serve the City.

The price of corn was halved, the seas were cleared of the competition from Asia Minor in three months, and immediately afterwards Pompey was made supreme commander in Asia, by means of what might be called a mere amendment to his contract. *He fetched slaves.*

You see, the common man voted for the same person twice in a row. But he didn't behave the same way twice. His war at sea could pass as a blow against slavery, but his war on land meant slave trading on the largest scale. Six months later the slave market in Rome was absolutely flooded, this time by Roman firms. Incidentally, Cicero made his maiden speech at that time. He spoke in favour of conferring supreme command on Pompey. You can work out for yourself who paid his honorarium.'

We walked on for a while in silence.

I must admit that I was revolted to no little extent by the irreverent way the old man described this manoeuvre.

He seemed to guess what I was thinking. The notorious bankers' talent for being able to see into people's souls was developed to the highest degree in him. He said dryly:

'You're taken aback that I approve of things like that. I'll tell you why. I approve of the way we obtain our slaves because we need slaves.'

I did not reply. His views on our City with its slave trading, which seemed to interest him much more than Gaius Julius Caesar, left me completely cold.

As we descended to the lake we came across a team of slaves, shackled by heavy chains, who were working on vines.

'Don't the chains get in the way while they're working?' I asked.

'No,' he replied. 'Not with vines. They are ex-convicts. Working with vines requires more intelligence than working in the fields. This type are the best for work like that. They've got more brains than the others, and at the same time they're cheaper.'

Before I took my farewell of him he showed me some young cherry trees he had had delivered, a new variety of fruit. Some of the small trees had already been planted, and the rest were still lying on the newly ploughed land, wrapped in straw.

'I'm always trying new techniques here,' he said. 'The return I get is no higher than 12 per cent. Columela boasts 17 per cent, but his calculations don't include maintenance costs, slaves and the wooden frames.'

My impression was that he ran his estate, which was not actually so large, less for profit than for his own amusement. At the same time, the thought that he was not showing a good return for his capital would have been unbearable.

In any case, it was a model farm.

When I returned to my little villa I found my Sempronius in the kitchen, talking to a short, stocky man with a powerful head whose clothes were almost in tatters. As I entered he left with a swift salute.

I discovered that he had brought us some firewood.

Sempronius, who as usual had found out everything about the neighbourhood in a couple of hours, told me in his gossiping way that he had chosen the man, who tended a few acres of olive trees on the other side of the hill, to deliver the firewood because he had been one of Caesar's legionaries.

I was delighted by this discovery and decided to question him. This seemed like a good opportunity to get over the rather dejected mood which had descended upon me while listening to the old man's stories.

It was amazing how little I had discovered about the real Caesar from Mummlius Spicer, who had known him for so many years and had even been his financial advisor throughout the entire Gallic campaign. I was convinced that this simple legionary, one of the old-fashioned, valiant warriors whose fanatical devotion to the great general is evident from so many moving passages in the monographs, would tell me more.

After I had refreshed myself a little, we set off.

Caesar's former legionary was sitting with his slave at the fireplace in the only room of his very dilapidated hut. The bare walls built from large, irregular lumps of stone had been blackened by smoke from the fire. A huge fishing net hung in one corner of the room. He probably did a little fishing down at the lake occasionally.

The man nodded to us in silence as we entered. He was just eating his evening meal. While the slave brought an old wooden bench in for us from outside the hut, his master carried on eating, spooning up lumps of bread from a pan. The slave, an old chap with insipid red hair, sat back down with him and started spooning his own food into his mouth. Sempronius set the conversation in motion by asking where thrushes could be found in the area.

When he had obtained that information he introduced the subject of the book which I, his master, was going to write about the great Julius Caesar. The stocky man turned his head, with its shock of grey hair, in my direction and threw me a brief glance but said nothing. He remained silent until he had finished mopping up the scraps of cheese in his bowl with a piece of bread: then he spoke slowly:

'I only saw him twice in ten years.'

While the redheaded slave bustled around, taking the bowl and spoon to the back of the room and starting to wash the dishes in a bucket, his master sat so far back on his stool that he was leaning against the wall and, thrusting out his incredibly broad chest, blinked from me to Sempronius.

'What do you want to know about him?' he asked, not particularly cordially.

'Were you with him in Gaul?' I asked, in response.

'Yes, sir,' he said, 'we were with him. Three legions, sir.'

I was slightly puzzled, so my next question turned out to be rather banal:

'Did you see him at close quarters?'

'Once from 500 paces, the other time from 1,000 paces,' was the answer. 'The first time, if you want to know exactly, was at a parade in Luca, which meant four hours extra drill. The other time was at the embarkation for Britain.'

'He was very popular?' I asked.

He remained silent for a while, staring at me with an almost dubious expression. Then he said:

'He was supposed to be smart.'

'But the common man had confidence in him?'

'The rations weren't bad. They said he saw to that.'

'Were you with him in the Civil War?'

'Yes, sir. On Pompey's side.'

'Why was that?'

'I belonged to the legion he borrowed from Pompey. He gave it back before the Civil War broke out.'

'I see,' I said.

'It was tough luck,' he said. 'I lost my pension. And he paid very decent pensions. But I didn't have any choice.'

I thought for a while. How could I get anything out of him? I tried a new approach.

'Why did you become a soldier?'

'Long time ago, sir.'

'Don't you know any more?'

He laughed. His massive chest lent a powerful note to the short man's laughter. But it was not malicious laughter, and I joined in.

'You're a stubborn one,' he went on. 'I joined the army because I was conscripted. I come from the area around Setia, if that means anything to you. A Latin. If I hadn't been a Roman citizen they wouldn't have been able to conscript me.'

'Would you have preferred to stay in your home town?'

'No, I wouldn't. I was one of four boys as it was. That was too many for a few acres of land. And we couldn't go to work on one of the larger estates, either, because they preferred freed slaves, who couldn't be conscripted, and besides, they had their slaves.'

'Are your brothers still on the farm?'

The stocky man shrugged his shoulders.

'How should I know? It isn't very likely, sir. With the price of corn what it is. You get Sicilian corn in Italy, see, and it's much cheaper. Even the army was fed solely with corn from Sicily, back in my day.'

'And you haven't tried to get some land for yourself again until now?'

'That's right. You can't carry on as a soldier once you reach my age. Yes, the land question wasn't solved then, and it never will be. It's impossible.'

'Your farm isn't really that big, is it?'

'Just a few olives. But little men like us can't compete. You need slaves for that.'

He looked over at the redheaded slave, who was taking the bucket outside. But he could still hear what followed. The former legionary said:

'He's from Rhaetia, that one. He isn't much use any more; hardly earns his keep.'

The conversation was getting bogged down. And it was getting dark.

'Did you ever hear of the Democratic Clubs during your youth?' I asked, suddenly.

'I think so,' he said. 'When I was in the capital. I did vote once. But I don't remember whether it was for the Democratic Praetor. I got 50 sesterces. A lot of cash.'

'I think the Democrats were in favour of solving the land question?' I ventured.

'Really?' he said. He thought this over for a while, and then added:

'Didn't they want corn handouts for the unemployed?'

'Yes, that too,' I said.

'But that's exactly what ruined the price of corn.'

'But for people who were living in the city, like you were at that time, it was good to be able to get cheap bread, wasn't it?' I asked, astonished.

'Yes, there was a need for it in the city,' he replied. 'That's where the unemployment was.'

'But it was a bad thing for your people in Latium, you mean, because the low price of corn ruined everything?'

'Yes, that – and all the slaves. By that time we were importing them ourselves. From Gaul, and so on. Difficult, huh? Politics.'

I got to my feet, since I still wanted to see Mummlius Spicer.

'And how did Caesar look?'

He thought for a while and then answered, vaguely:

'Exhausted.'

I was very thoughtful as we left. I was finding man's inability to recognize greatness when faced with it more depressing than ever.

Spicer had a visitor. Afranius Carbo, the lawyer I knew as the writer of numerous works on constitutional law, was interrupting his long journey from the capital to distant Belgium, where he was to study the prospects for the export of Nervian cloth and Menapian ham on behalf of a trust, to consult the old banker and authority on Gaul.

The great legal expert, a thickset man of about 50 with heavy jowls and watery eyes, greeted me jovially as a young colleague.

'It's a fine subject you've chosen for yourself there,' he said loudly as soon as I had sat down. 'An excellent, heroic subject, if tackled properly. And you've come to the right source.'

I confess I was flattered that such an indubitably distinguished man seemed to approve of my literary project, which Spicer must have outlined to him. As his very first sentences indicated, at last I could expect from him attention that was focused on greatness and ideals. He seemed inclined to discuss the subject with me, which he rightly described as heroic.

He had stood up, as if to make room to air his feelings, and he marched to and fro between the table and the wall with short, stamping steps. 'And I hear you're approaching your subject from the right angle. *The concept of empire! Democracy! The ideas of progress!* At last a book written with a scientific foundation that the common man *and* the man in the City can read. His success, their success! Facts!'

At this last word he leant over the table and banged the top hard with the flat of his hand. Then he ploughed on again.

'A book like this should have been written long ago; we should have written down our history – a history as heroic as any! What a terrible omission! I must say, a typical omission! Inadequate appreciation of history. The old, fatal indifference towards our own history. The opposition is allowed to express the dominant viewpoint while we devote ourselves to business, taking pride in our sobriety, without taking into account that by doing so we're abandoning the younger generation to the opposition. We're perfectly capable of presenting Syrian scents, Egyptian linen and Samnian wines to their best advantage, but we have never understood how to present commerce itself, its ideals, in the best light. The great, democratic ideals!'

Afranius Carbo came to rest briefly by the table to fortify himself with a sip of red wine. He rolled it around his tongue like a connoisseur.

A slight sense of disappointment had descended upon me. His point of view struck me as open to question. I found my host's behaviour disturbing, too. Spicer was leaning back comfortably in his chair, his enormous chin resting on his chest, reaching out for a fig now and then. Between figs he would reach into his mouth to extract a seed from his yellowing teeth. My attention was divided between this procedure and the jurist's speech.

'We keep Scipio Africanus' catapults in our military museums, in places of honour,' he continued. 'But where are the covered wagons of our first merchants? Aren't they worth putting on display? Is it a lesser feat to conquer the world with a pen than with a sword? Of course, you don't find any pens in the halls of fame! Why not, I ask. What gives the sword priority? You can see a sword being wielded in every butcher's shop; there's nothing particularly honourable about it. Why should genealogy books be preserved in preference to account books? You young people have a rotten habit of laughing when the subject of the ideals that commerce has

brought into the world is raised. You simply imitate the contemp-
tuous attitude of so many upper-class pickpockets. Is heroism only
seen during a war? And if so, isn't commerce a type of war? Words
like 'peaceful trading' may appeal to ambitious young people. They
have no place in history. Trading is never peaceful. Borders that
cannot be crossed by goods will be crossed by armies. A catapult
is as important a tool for a weaver as a loom. And there's another
sense in which trade constitutes a war in itself. Blood isn't shed in
this war, it's true, but I maintain that it's still a fight to the death.
This bloodless war rages through every shopping street during
business hours. Every handful of wool sold at one end of the street
produces a cry of pain at the other end. A carpenter will put a roof
on your house for you, but you'll suffer from exposure to pay his
bill. The need for bread kills those who experience it and those
who don't. And it isn't just the need for bread that kills but also the
appetite for oysters.'

The great man had reached the end of whatever furrow he was
ploughing. He stood with his back against the wall, his legs spread
in warlike fashion.

'Nevertheless,' he said, somewhat more calmly, 'it is true to
say that trade has brought a certain humane influence to bear on
human relations. It must have been in the brain of a merchant that
the first peaceful thought arose – the idea that a milder approach
might be useful. You see, the inspiration was that peaceful methods
could yield greater advantages than violent ones. In fact, being
condemned to death by starvation is a slightly milder fate than
being condemned to death by the sword. In the same way that the
fate of the dairy cow is pleasanter than that of the fatted pig. It must
have been a man of commerce who first realized you could get
more out of a man than just his guts. But still, don't ever forget that
the great, civilized slogan "live and let live", really means *live* for the
man who drinks the milk and *let live* for the cow. And when you
consider history, what conclusion do you reach? If ideals can only
be taken seriously when blood has been shed for them, then our
ideals, the ideals of democracy and the City, should be taken very
seriously. A great deal of blood has been shed for them. Tiberius
Gracchus was murdered for them, along with 300 of our followers,
by Senators' sons wielding chair legs. The dead showed no sign of

having been touched by metal weapons. The corpses were thrown into the Tiber. An entire province of Asia Minor had been offered for sale to the King of Pontus or the King of Bithynia by Manius Aquillius, the Senatorial general. The King of Pontus offered a higher price, and the Senate ratified the sale. "The Senate is divided into three groups", said Gracchus. "The first is in favour of the sale. It has been bribed by the King of Pontus. The second is against the sale. It has been bribed by the King of Bithynia. The third group is silent. It has accepted bribes from both kings." The Senate answered him with the chair legs. That was in 620, more than a century ago. Thirteen years later Gaius Gracchus demanded that grain requisitioned from the Spanish provinces should be paid for, peasants should be sent as colonizers to the areas of Africa which had been conquered, Italians should be accepted as citizens, taxes rather than tributes should be imposed in the provinces, and state revenue should be checked by businesspeople; a horde of Senators chased him down to the banks of the Tiber. He sprained his ankle and ordered his slave to stab him in a suburban grove, so he wouldn't fall into their hands. His head was cut off, and a Senator paid for it. Twenty-one years passed, during which the Italian peasant and the Roman craftsman defeated the slave gangs of Sicily, Jugurtha's Numidian troops, the Cimbri, and the Teutons, and one December day in the year 654 all the Democrats were rounded up in the market and then driven up to the Capitol, where the water supplies were cut off, to force them to surrender. They were crammed into the town hall, and the noble youth of the city climbed up to the roof, tore off the tiles and smashed the prisoners' heads with them. Then the Italian peasant and the Roman craftsman conquered half of Asia and Egypt too, and it was time for some more bloodletting. Sulla took charge of the proceedings, and this time he did the job properly. 4,000 of our followers, at a conservative estimate – that is, only counting the prosperous ones, only those who belonged to the City. I'm not talking about massacres like the one after the battle of Porta Collina, when 3,000 prisoners were taken to the city dairy on Campus Martius and slaughtered down to the last man; so they could hear the clanking of weapons and the groans of the dying in the nearby Temple of Bellona, where Sulla was chairing a meeting of the Senate at that very moment. And that wasn't the end, either of the unrest or of the suppression of that unrest. Less than eight years before Catilina's rebellion Sertorius, the Democratic General, was butchered by Senators as he was dining. Two of them held his arms and one pushed a sword through his throat.

That was all in the past, but none of it had been forgotten when Gaius Julius raised the Democratic flags again. Every paving stone in Rome had been saturated with the people's blood. My father could still show me the place where they had hunted down Gaius Gracchus. Two stunted cypress trees were growing there; I can see them in front of me even now.'

The lawyer's educated voice had taken on a not unpleasant, almost human tone. But when he shaded his eyes with a hand on which his Equestrian ring was clearly visible, the effect was spoilt. I was not sure which I was yearning for more urgently; that he would find his last words or Spicer would find his last fig seed.

But Afranius Carbo continued:

'We have forgotten that we are plebeians. You are, Spicer is, and I am. Don't tell me that it doesn't matter any more these days. That's exactly what was accomplished: that it doesn't matter any more. That's Caesar for you. What are the other things he achieved – a few old-fashioned battles, a few shady treaties with a few chiefs of native tribes – compared to that!

The City was a creation of the Gracchi. They were the ones who handed over the collection of taxes and customs duties in both Asias to commercial interests. And it was the ideas of the Gracchi that Gaius Julius adopted. The result was: the Empire.'

I was almost tempted to add out loud: 'And me, Afranius Carbo.' As far as those two gentlemen were concerned, my book had already been written.

By the time the great legal expert took his leave, excusing himself on the grounds that the exertions of the journey had exhausted him, I had hardly said another word. Spicer indicated that he would like me to stay a while longer.

I followed him into the library in silence. He insisted that I should be provided with one of his bulbous bottles of red table wine, wrapped in straw, and procured another plate of his beloved figs for himself. Then he began:

'In accordance with our agreement, before handing over the manuscripts in question for your inspection this evening, I should outline for you the situation in which C. found himself when the diaries were started. The first entries refer to the beginning of the year 91, when the great Catilinarian affair was just gathering momentum.

It was a source of satisfaction to me that our friend gave you a brief account of Democratic ideas, which is something I should hardly have been able to do. My activities were of a more practical nature; you know what my profession was. Nevertheless, when C. did become involved in mainstream politics, through a combination of circumstances which you can see from his secretary's diaries, it was the Democratic Party with which he was associated.'

'Hardly a glorious association,' I interjected, unable to contain myself. I had gradually succumbed to a mood of annoyance. The old man's account up to that point, the tone he adopted with reference to my idol, had upset me more than I can say. It was inconceivable that he had not noticed that. He had, however, paid not the slightest attention to it. On top of all that he had obliged me to endure an interminable lecture about the massacres of the Senate and the disreputable ideals of trade. The little he had revealed about the founder of the Empire, one of the greatest men in the history of the world, was apparently intended to portray him as the particularly decadent offspring of an ancient family.

My patience was exhausted. Had it been anything less than essential for me to obtain a glimpse of the invaluable documents, I should have left long before this point. My sole intention was to wait until I had them and then leave, so I could finally discover something about the real Caesar.

But the old man was stubborn, as one would have to be to haggle over a vineyard for half its value. He was still not ready.

He pushed his plate of figs to one side (I noted with some relief that his teeth also appeared quite clean), and said in a leisurely manner:

'Glorious or inglorious, in any case C. was also a Democrat. What this actually meant, you understand, was that when it was a matter of official positions, he had the Democratic Clubs nominate

him. They lent him their support because there were certain tradi-
tions which linked members of his family with the party. The City
put up some tidy sums to enable him to stand for elections, and
they financed his candidature for High Priest after 91, but people
weren't exactly enthusiastic about him.

They turned to him when they needed him, and then they sent
him an envelope with a cheque. If it was somehow possible to
manage without him, they left him well alone. People basically had
the impression that backing him was putting money on the wrong
horse. They didn't bother him with important political issues. And
he, in turn, didn't concern himself initially with either the two
Asias or Catilina.

I can still remember quite clearly the conversations I had
with him almost every day at that stage, which really were not
political. He saw his bailiff more frequently than anyone else.
He had served in two of the Curial positions in the past, Aedile
and Quaestor, and he was up to his ears in debt. Those positions
were not connected with politics in the slightest. The gentlemen
served in these offices in order to get a province in the end, after
the position of Praetor. So Quaestor and Aedile were under his
belt, but those elections had swallowed up a fortune, and now
there was no more money available for the Praetorship. Which
would mean all the money he had invested in his career would
be wasted. Good God, he had debts of 25 million sesterces! That
was more money in those days. A craftsman in Rome earned
3 sesterces a day.

On more than one occasion he said to me: "This Catilina is the
ruin of me. Who would want to lend me money when that man is
arming the rabble of Italy to push through a general cancellation
of debts! Half the City has packed its bags!"

The man was forty years old!

It's really no wonder that a man in his position should be
amenable to any proposition, political or non-political, which
might enable him to keep his head above water. He had always
taken money wherever he could find it. A glance in his secretary's
diary will show you that by now, and not before time, he had finally
begun to realize the situation he was in. Don't expect to find heroic
deeds described in a classical style, but if you read it with an open

mind perhaps you'll find some clues as to how dictatorships are established and empires founded.'

And he raised himself ponderously, reached for the ashwood box on the bookshelf, and handed me the Diaries of Rarus, the Slave.

Book Two
Our Mr C.

Diaries of Rarus

11 August 691

After twelve years the war in the East is coming to an end. Twenty-two kings have been defeated, among them the three most powerful in Asia; twelve million people have been subjugated, 1,538 towns and fortresses captured. The Roman Eagles have been planted on the Maeotic, Caspian and Red Sea coasts. Rome is opening up a new continent.

The plans have arrived for the new riding school which C. wants to build at the bottom of the garden, opposite the gymnasium. 40,000 sesterces. This time the contractors are demanding an advance payment of 25,000 sesterces. They won't give any exact reasons. But when I pointed out that it was not usual to treat men like C. in that way, one of the bosses laughed.

It doesn't make any sense to build this riding school when we're only staying here in the Subura until we can move into the big house in the Via Sacra; for months now they have been renovating it for him, since he was elected High Priest. He just can't bear waiting. I daren't even think about the cost of the building work over there. Whenever he's presented with the bills he gets angry. And then, every time, he starts cutting back on the staff's food. As if the money spent on that would make any difference!

Went to the Tiber Gardens with my one and only darling Caebio this evening. He simply can't find a job anywhere. He is a perfume worker, and that's another industry that employs slaves almost exclusively these days. Pompey has been sending thousands of them back from Syria, skilled people who had their own shops there. Everyone Caebio approaches just says it wouldn't make any sense to hire people who might be called up tomorrow. Caebio is a Roman citizen. He's really desperate.

He says he doesn't know what he'd do if I didn't support him.

13 August
None of the best people back in town yet. Hot and dusty. Trying not to think about the morning breeze in the mountains of Alba. We're only staying in Rome because of Cynthia, not 'due to the political situation', as C. puts it. He hasn't seen anyone except her for days.

14 August
Glaucos, the new fencing instructor Pompeya bought in Capua for 15,000 sesterces, tells me that C. is in outstanding condition. 38 years old, and not an ounce of fat on him! The climate in the city doesn't bother him at all. It's a disgrace that a person of his calibre is hanging around virtually unused. With his abilities, he should really have been taken up long ago. It would be understandable that he hasn't been made use of if he had made any sort of definite political commitment. But even though he's a Democrat he's completely open to any suggestion that holds out the slightest chance of a profit; his principles are so flexible and he's so unprejudiced about every political issue that the way he is treated defies comprehension. A man from one of the oldest families, with a seat in the Senate!

Glaucos is a charming person, by the way: cultured. Saw him doing his morning exercises. Wiry chap. Perhaps I'll take fencing lessons with him, to counteract the effect of the climate, which is really unhealthy at this time of year.

I don't feel on top of the world, physically: overworked.

Seeing the clients is a dreadful business. They're admitted at nine o'clock. But they gather in the street from as early as seven o'clock and make a racket like the herds of sheep that are driven down the Appian Way to the slaughterhouse at five in the morning. C. receives them in the hall, over breakfast. They enter trailing dirt from their boots and gossip from their mouths. They want to know whether they should mortgage their property, beat their wives and change their lawyers. They want jobs and loans. A lot of them are down at heel, but some are richer than us; they're accompanied by bodyguards who don't let me out of their sight, as if I were a potential assassin. War veterans want licences for taverns or certificates as bathhouse keepers, perfume merchants bring samples of their goods, writers bring books, burglars bring their summonses, and civil servants bring office secrets. Hardly any of them bring envelopes with cheques. C. talks to everyone in a different way, but he's always C., while Crassus, who I once saw dealing with his clients, tries to speak in every dialect and conducts himself in a thousand ways, but never as Crassus. Cicero is said to come out with sentences that last five minutes (but not one drachma).

16 August
First fencing lesson. Tiring.

Strangely enough, the city isn't as empty as one would expect, considering the time of year. Quite a lot of people are already back. Some gentlemen from the Senate are here for dinner. Subject of conversation: the war in the East.

The Chamber of Commerce has submitted a memorandum to the Senate, via Cicero, proposing that Pompey should be given a 'statement of gratitude'. Apparently expressions of praise for his achievement in 'leading the Roman Eagles to victory in darkest Asia' were carefully but unmistakably interwoven with certain demands that the City should be allowed to participate in the Asian trade. The gentlemen made copious jokes about that. They harbour an extremely healthy distrust for the conqueror of the East. If their gratitude created too many waves, it could encourage him to set his ever victorious legions at their throats. The ominous phrase 'Pompey's lust for dictatorship' has been whispered in the Palace on the Aventine Hill for a couple of years now.

17 August
Unbearable heat.

Pomponius Celer here. He has come back from Baiae to settle his commercial transactions with the East. As head of the leather syndicate he's Pompey's military supplier. The leather syndicate represents 34 tanneries, and during the war it devoted its efforts to the production of belts and backpacks. Celer laughed about the 'statement of gratitude', too. He had some interesting information about the City's position with regard to the war in the East. Despite the army supply business, the City has never been able to work up any real enthusiasm for the campaign. Before Pompey took over supreme command several Roman divisions had been defeated. But everything we heard at the time, like 'the generals are incompetent', 'the Roman army isn't what it used to be' and 'legionaries are running away like frightened rabbits', was nonsense. The real reason for the defeats, according to Celer, was simply that the City didn't invest any money in the campaign at first. The Senate had deprived them of the concessions to collect taxes and duties. Not until these concessions were reintroduced, at least in their present modest form, did the City drum up a certain amount of enthusiasm for the war in the East and approve financial support for Pompey. Asia is *the* business of the City. Without tax farming in Asia there'll be no democracy in Rome, says Celer. Pompey has been allowed to earn 20 million so far. And now he won't lift a finger for the banks, which will no longer be satisfied with the tiny profit margins from taxes and duties under any circumstances. Apart from all that, the enormous business of financing war reparations lies ahead! Of course, the Roman banks want to advance the money which the newly colonized provinces need to pay as reparations to the State of Rome as high interest loans. Pompey is only moving very sluggishly on that front, too. So: a lot of resentment against Pompey in the City.

C. went red behind the ears when he heard about the 20 million.

18 August
Our financial situation is hopeless. The fights with the bailiffs have started again. Made an inventory of the smaller debts today, which are now also mounting up alarmingly. C. completely surprised by the total.

Meditated on the mystery of love. Can't understand how I can love Caebio and still not be immune to purely sensual, base, physical impulses (Glaucos!). Perhaps the two things aren't connected? Odd.

Pompey the Great's stubborn attitude towards the City has even had its effect on yours truly, by the way. My few shares in the Cilician tax farming operations of the Asian Commerce Bank have dropped considerably in value.

19 August

The slaves Pompey sends back from Asia are usually brought into town to be auctioned in the early hours of the morning, to avoid unnecessary commotion. I saw one of those processions today. About 2,000 of them were trotting down the Subura in a pitiful condition, their shoes much too flimsy for the bad paving in our streets. Despite it being so early I found myself surrounded by small shopkeepers and unemployed people (the former start work early to make the most of every hour of daylight, while the latter set off early for the market halls, to look for rotten food being sold off cheap). Everyone was scowling at the long procession. They knew that every slave meant one less job or one fewer customer.

19 August (evening)

Went with C. to a social evening held by *Lucullus*. He stays in his cool gardens next to the Tiber, even in summer. The gentlemen from the Senate who had been invited came up especially from their country estates. I saw the host in his atrium, a small, wizened man who limps along with a stick. He's still very powerful; it's been pointed out with particular emphasis in the Senate recently that he had actually conquered the East even before Pompey arrived to take over command with new authorization and fresh funds. As Cicero is supposed to have said, the fame of his banquets now overshadows the glory of his battles.

C. wanted to talk to the city Praetor, who had also been invited, and I waited in the atrium with some papers. The cupola is so high that it's quite impossible to light it up at night. The palace actually consists of five palaces, one behind the other; you would need a chariot and four to get to the other end.

I listened to the servants for a short time while their masters were inside, eating. For two whole hours all they could talk about were the new acquisitions that people in Senatorial circles have bought this summer (country estates, villas, horses, statues). All the Asian loot is going straight into the pockets of these gentlemen once again. Which makes the discontent in the City understandable.

Only about 40 people had been invited, all of them landowners, military men, senior officials. In spite of this, C. was apparently unable to engage the Praetor in conversation about business. We wanted to get a building contract with the city water department for a client who had promised us a tidy commission. The Praetor's secretary told me, as bold as you like: 'You may as well take your portfolio home. We don't do business over meals.' And then I saw him making jokes about C. with the others. The situation we are in is common knowledge.

I began to wonder why C. has so much less success with men than with women. Half the Senators didn't even greet him.

Sure enough, I wasn't sent for, and when everyone left at the end of the evening I discovered C. had already gone.

20 August
Uncomfortable scene during the clients' surgery. The office is next to the hall. The hall was full of people who wanted to speak to C. when Horus the delicatessen merchant appeared in the doorway, shouting wild threats because nobody showed any sign of paying him his 4,000 sesterces. C. still hadn't come down. I went up to ask him what to do. His response was to ask me whether I could lend him the money. I lent him the 4,000 sesterces. (That is, I only had 3,200, so I borrowed the remaining 800 from Glaucos.)

21 August
The casualties in the war in Asia are awful. The lists of the dead are posted in the Forum, between two banks. People shuffle past in a narrow line. Women leading children by the hand look through the long rows of names for their relatives. A lot of them have made the journey from the countryside. When they have finished, if they haven't found their relatives' names on the list they sit down in a corner of the Forum and eat the bread they have brought with them. Most of them go back home before nightfall, since they can't afford to stay overnight in the city, and in any case they have

to be back at work again early in the morning. They have started threshing the corn in Campania.

24 August
As if sent from the gods, our merchants from the Po towns turned up today. Good old fat Favella from Cremona leading the way. For the consular elections this autumn the commercial groups on the Po are determined to launch a new campaign to have rights of citizenship extended to the Po plain. Three years ago C. made speeches in all the major towns of the area, as a guest of each Chamber of Commerce, and it was a well-paid venture. Crassus was Censor then, and C. instilled new hope in those good people, who are so keen to become Roman citizens. They paid up. With their unfortunate desire for papers of citizenship they have been a regular and reliable source of income for Democracy for quite some time. Then the good people were disgruntled for a while, because Crassus didn't manage to have them put on the Citizens' List immediately, and they claimed that C. had promised them too much. But C. was innocent. If Crassus had paid enough to old Catulus, his fellow Censor, he never would have objected – not with his huge debts. When his cut turned out to be too small he naturally exposed the fraud, and that was the end of Roman citizenships for the Po towns. And now they are back again. Nobody really gives a damn about them, apart from the Democrats; ideas like that are too brazenly democratic. Now they want to put a considerable sum at C.'s disposal for the campaign. When the people had left he said cheerfully: 'Humane politics are sometimes worthwhile, after all!'

We went over the plans for the riding school again. They really are excellent. Contract concluded.

29 August
What a time for Caebio to admit he hasn't got a single assarius left from the money I gave him last month. And he has to pay six months' rent if he doesn't want to be thrown out on the street. His mother is very unhappy. And I've used all my savings to keep that delicatessen owner quiet – who's already starting to make more trouble, by the way. And he's not the only one. I can't really push C. for the money! What is to be done?

1 September
The bricklayers who are sweating away in the garden building the new riding school talk of nothing but the Catilinarian combat squads that are springing up all over town. Everyone who joins up gets a little badge with his number on it. They have completely taken over certain taverns on the outskirts of town. People thought Catilina was completely finished after his defeat in the Consular elections last year. All over the place people were babbling on about his combat squads being disbanded due to lack of funds. They really did vanish from the streets during that summer. But now they are back again. The workmen in the courtyard are divided in their opinions. The building work has been commissioned from a large firm which employs slaves but also uses a few skilled craftsmen for specialized work. On the whole the latter are in favour of Catilina, since he's promising cheap corn and a cancellation of debts, and they're master builders in a small way, with bank debts. The slaves don't care.

Caebio here again this evening: couldn't I manage to raise the money for his rent? Awkward. I really have to keep a few sesterces in the house, too. But I gave him half the rent at least (60 sesterces). People really are starving. In the old days the unemployed used to get corn from the market halls at very low prices. What are they going to live on now? *Must* get the 4,000 back from C.

Mr Cicero, the Consul, is also said to be back in town already.

2 September
For the last fortnight or so I've heard people talking about Catilina here and there, but now people suddenly aren't talking about anything else. I find out that he held a meeting in the Third District, and they say he spoke out against profiteers and speculators, to great applause. He demands that every last Roman citizen, not only the Senate and the City, should get a share of the Asian loot.

Pompeya suddenly back from the Alban Hills. Big scene on the first floor. She seems to have heard about Cynthia. That is, I don't think she knows the name, only that there is someone again. C. was able to calm her down by showing her the new riding school under construction. I saw them both in the garden, clambering over stones. Of course, he told her he was building it for her, and that's why he's stayed in town. Good job we started to build it. (The blessings of the gods on our merchants from the Po!) C. can't afford a quarrel with his wife just now. If it weren't for her family connections we'd be struck off the roll of Senators because of our debts. Pompeya is going back tomorrow.

4 September

Old Mouldy* is already back in town, too. He had a long talk with C. in the library. Just as C. was showing him out, Cruppulus the wool merchant arrived. When Cruppulus asked Crassus what he thought of Catilina I heard him reply: 'Catilina is a talented man from one of our oldest families, so he's completely bankrupt. The City has saved him five times. He signs every promissory note that's put in front of him, and if he were head of state he'd sign every new decree they put in front of him, too. Unfortunately he's remarkably eloquent. Those of my tenants in the poorer quarters who have heard him speak don't pay their rent any more. He's going to make trouble for us.'

Later C. said scornfully that the poorer classes were being driven to rebellion less by Catilina's eloquence than by the eloquent nature of the damp patches in Crassus' tenement blocks. And he added: 'Not to mention the eloquently high prices our Cruppulus charges for his cloth.' He gets such modes of speech from Alexander, Crassus' librarian.

Unfortunately, the money from the Po merchants still hasn't arrived. And of course the envelope that good old Favella handed over to us in person was emptied long ago. Mummlius Spicer, the bailiff, threatened to impound the furniture today. During the clients' surgery, too. C. talked to him for a whole quarter of an hour. He talks to people like that as if they were his equal, quite shamelessly. If any sort of reference is made to it, he says: 'Now, don't be so undemocratic, my dear Rarus.'

The affair with the slim Cynthia seems to be tailing off fast. Met a rather showy woman (red powdered hair) in the vestibule.

---

*Old Mouldy is the nickname of Crassus, who owns a lot of tenement blocks in the city. People identify him with the mould rampant in most of those buildings.

Wanted to find out who she was, so I went outside for a look at her sedan chair. A quite common rented chair (!). The meal lasted three hours.

5 September
Rising prices and flight of capital. A bushel of corn costs a denarius and a half now, compared to one denarius in June. Every ship that sets sail transports gold and silver away from Rome. Although the harvest in Sicily was excellent this year.

With regard to the flight of capital, the following comment was made by one of our top shipbrokers during the clients' surgery: 'The gold ingots are tightening their belts around their plump bodies, and they look very grim when they are boarding the ships. They have no confidence in this government.'

Though the government is the City itself: Mr Cicero.

But Asian shares are going up slightly.

6 September
Glaucos is a Catilinarian! He admitted it today. He joined a year ago. That's why his last master sold him. He says he really just teaches the combat squads how to fence, but he does subscribe to their views. The squads are organized in military style and hold regular meetings in certain taverns. He says they want a firmer government and are against corruption. Discussed it with him until the early hours of the morning. They say the 'Democratic' Consul Cicero has been working for the corn companies since he was Proquaestor in Sicily. And that Catilina is an idealist with great love for the people.

Decided to go and see Crassus' librarian. He usually knows better than anyone else what the common man is thinking. He's a Greek, one of Crassus' slaves (they say he cost Crassus 80,000 sesterces), and he has more integrity than anyone else in Rome.

Went to see him this evening.

He lives on the Palatine Hill, in an incredible house you can get lost in. A beehive of offices! A seething mass of secretaries, visitors and messengers hurry around the corridors, shouting to each other in every language of the world! I had to go through several court-yards with schools for the craftsmen. The doors were open, because it was so hot and sultry, and I saw the slaves crouching on their low benches, staring at the teachers. Old Mouldy makes a fortune with these craftsmen, by having them trained by architects or engineers bought in Greece or Asia and then selling them or hiring them out.

A squad of Gauls he had trained as firemen were practising in one of the courtyards. He has lookouts posted in every district of the city, and as soon as a fire breaks out the Gauls set off with their fire engines. An agent goes in front of them, though, and buys the house that's on fire for a tenth of its value, but in cash, and usually the houses on each side, too. Only then do they put out the fire.

Alexander's tiny whitewashed room has no furniture except a bed with leather webbing, an old table and two chairs, and it's in semi-darkness since the window, which looks out on to the courtyard, is barred. Books are piled up on the floor, and they form another wall which is three-quarters as high as the brick one.

Alexander is a sturdy fellow of medium build with a big ruddy face, a fleshy nose and quiet round eyes that seem to be made of tortoise shell. He's a follower of the philosopher Epicurus, and C. – who often summons him under the pretext of needing a book from Crassus' library and argues with him for hours on end – calls him the only real democrat on Italian soil.

I immediately raised the subject of Catilina.

'Catilina,' he said quietly, 'is the unemployment question, and the unemployment question is the land question. Do you know what Tiberius Gracchus said seventy years ago?' He teased a slim volume out from his paper wall, not without some difficulty, and read me the words of the great People's Tribune.

'The wild animals that live in Italy have their burrows; every one of them knows its lair, its den. Only the people who fight and perish for Italy have nothing but light and air to count on; they sit in the streets with their wives and children, instead of on their land. Before a battle, when the generals exhort their men to defend their homes and the graves of their ancestors from the enemy, they are lying; the majority of Romans have no home and do not know where their ancestors are buried. It is for the luxury and fame of others that they must spill their blood and perish. They are called the masters of the world, yet they are unable to call a single patch of earth their own.'

He put the little book back in its place.

'The peasant,' he continued, 'who was taken from his fields to defeat the Carthaginians, the Spaniards and the Syrians, returns home to find himself defeated by the enemy, who has been transformed by his actions into slaves. His land is forfeited to the big landowners, and he wanders into the city in the vain hope that some Sicilian corn may be trickled into his little bag, out of charity. Half a million people are suffocating on the 500 hectares of land within the Servian Walls of the city. And it was only this spring that Mr Cicero sabotaged the Democratic proposal to permit the unemployed of the capital to settle on land outside the city by reminding the jobless that as settlers they would not receive the bribes they get now as voters. And these degraded, hopeless people, always living in fear of what tomorrow may bring, actually voted against the settlement programme. I heard Cicero's speech myself. It was as though he warned the whores in the Subura not to accept wineshops as gifts, because then they wouldn't have any time left to sell their own bodies. But that's the way it is; he knows the people, even if he has five villas to live in. For a handful of copper coins these masters of the world will vote for a law that is to their disadvantage, and they'll only vote for a law to their advantage for a handful of copper coins, too. For them the future means only their next meal. Catilina will be elected, not if he promises land, but if he can meet the expenses of the election campaign, which means the cost of the bribes.'

'So you don't think the land question is the really decisive factor?' I asked.

'Oh yes I do,' he said with a smile. 'I just don't think it can be solved by elections.'

I was in a pensive mood when I left. Alexander has a lot of influence with the craftsmen's trade guilds.

This evening Caebio, still beaming with joy, told me that his landlord has deferred half the rent. We went to the dice games at the Porta Trigemina. He threw his arms around me in the middle of the street, in a cloud of dust! He's the old, excitable, affectionate Caebio again.

7 September
Surprised Spicer in the garden this afternoon, he was having an argument with the foreman in front of the new riding school. He

was threatening, in a loud voice, to have the timber seized for the creditors. The foreman saved the situation by declaring that the timber was still his company's property! The bricklayers stood around, grinning.

That woman with the red powdered hair is Mucia, Pompey's wife! What a conquest! Cheeky of her, to come here, to our house.

9 September
In the barbers' shops the wealthier people are talking of the threat posed to the Republic by Catilina. I heard one well-heeled cloth merchant, apparently a sensible man, saying: 'The chap wouldn't be winning people over if the gentlemen in the Senate weren't once again trying to divert all the Asian war loot, which each one of us has paid for with blood or money, into their own pockets!' The barber mentioned Cicero in an attempt to console him. 'As long as Cicero has anything to do with what goes on in Rome,' he said confidently, 'there won't be a dictatorship of the right or the left. Cicero *is* the Republic. And the City is behind him.' All the customers, including the cloth merchant, agreed with him.

10 September
The flight of capital assumes larger proportions each day. The interest rate has climbed from six to ten per cent. So people in the City really are afraid of Catilina! Pomponius Celer (skins and leather) said something odd, though: 'Perhaps the City is moving out its capital so people will start to be scared of Catilina.'

We talked about this comment for another hour.

12 September
Caebio rather odd recently. Does he suspect about Glaucos? He's so touchy. Or could he be ill? Very worried about him.

Difficult to break things off with Glaucos at the moment, since he keeps me informed about the Catilinarian movement, which could become very important any day now.

C. constantly in a bad mood. He says he knows something is happening at the Forum, but he doesn't know what. Apparently the City clubs still can't agree on how the Democratic side should behave in the Consular elections. C. and Crassus, working together, have quite often run the Democratic election campaign for the clubs in the past. This year they still haven't made any approach to him at all. Of course, he pretends not to care, and the most he says is that he's really tired of being called on by the clubs to deal with the petty little jobs at the last moment, without being told what game is being played. And on top of all that, his creditors are plaguing him.

At times like these C. just makes fun of the City. Then he enjoys acting like a Senator. Admittedly, these moods never last long. Unfortunately he always lets himself be drawn back into their politics. Remarks like the latest one from Pomponius Celer (skins and leather) about the 20 million sesterces Pompey made in the East are sheer poison to him. And now, despite his professed disgust for politics, he sits in the library with Clodius once again, and they talk for hour after hour about the City's enigmatic game. Last year they were happy to have got Cicero in as Consul; a 'new man' from a non-patrician family. He has turned out to be worse than the Senate itself. The first thing he did was to dissolve the Democratic Street Clubs in which the masses of the capital were organized by street and district. His justification was the claim that the activities of gangs had to be brought under control. The same law for the left and the right, preached the new man, who is a former schoolmaster. (I am quoting Clodius): 'You shouldn't put up with half of what goes on,' he says, in his provocative way. 'Your name is very familiar to the man in the street. Your Quaestor games haven't been forgotten. Everyone, from the lowest workman up to the building contractors and the money-changers, has thought of you at one time or another. The City clubs use you like casual labour – whenever they want. Who else have they got from such an old family? Defend yourself, man!' C. paces up and down with his long strides, and I can see the poison beginning to work. That Clodius really gets up my nose, despite the scented pomade on his boyish head, and even though Pompeya is always praising him for his 'wit'. He's just dragging C. back into his own brand of politics again. (Although he comes from a patrician family himself, he was head of the street clubs.) I think our famous Quaestor games have left us quite broke enough.

16 September
Now I've got positive proof that there's something going on between Caebio and Rufus, that fat warehouseman from the Second District. He's accepted a ring from him. I said as much to him, to his face. He coloured visibly and started stammering! He promised not to meet him any more, but I can't really believe that until I get him to give back the ring. He *must* send back the ring.

Slept badly. Took a sleeping powder.

17 September
The other day Mummlius Spicer suggested as bold as brass that I should point out to him some sizeable property which could readily be impounded: he would show his gratitude. What does he take me for?

18 September
Caebio got the ring from his mother, who confirmed it to me herself. It belonged to his father, a legionary. I'm too suspicious.

Listened in on a conversation between C. and Alexander from the writing room. The librarian said: 'These struggles are of the greatest significance. A politician who fails to involve himself here is no politician; a democracy which doesn't fight now is no democracy. The fine clubs up on the Palatine Hill, where Mr Cicero dines, listen so smugly to his witty, elegant speeches about the despondency in the Senate caused by the flight of capital and the Catilinarian agitation. But the man in the street is getting restless. He knows it's now or never, if he's to gain anything at all. Why don't you seize the opportunity? Go over to Catilina, if you want, transform his movement into a serious political programme, and expel the adventurers from that movement! Or set yourself against Catilina, talk to the trade guilds and demand Mr Cicero's resignation and the forceful execution of the Democratic programme, particularly concerning the land question! You can do anything except for one thing: keep yourself out of all this.' C. made close enquiries about the mood in the electoral districts. The price of corn (high and still rising), increasing unemployment, and debts to the bank – everything combined is stirring up the poorer people to a considerable extent, and according to Alexander there is a great danger that people will go over to Catilina. C. seemed pensive after their conversation, but not inclined to take action. Still, there was conviction in his voice as he said: 'The land question is the key problem, the man's right there. There won't be any peace until the land question has been resolved.'

The second attempt to draw him back into politics already!

19 September
C. always makes a point of taking me along when he dines with Fulvia. Either because he wants to demonstrate his democratic principles (she moves in Catilinarian circles), or because he doesn't want any really intimate relationship to develop between them again. She's very amusing and always knows the latest news. She gave C. a veritable lecture on the astonishing similarity she sees between the situations of politicians like him and ladies like her. 'You've got to be able to bide your time,' she said, 'just like us. However expensive that may be. How much do you think my gowns cost me? And the cost of being well groomed! Do you think I wear my jewels just for the fun of it? It's no more fun than you get from staging fencing matches in the arena! But one has to make an impression. And to be expensive: that's why I admire you, darling. I always say: Gaius Julius doesn't waste his money, though it very likely isn't yours, anyway. But patience is everything. Just don't back the wrong horse! Of course, it doesn't do to be too particular, either. Neither you nor I can be that. Have a look at everything and then choose the best; that's the way. You'll get your chance yet, I've no doubt about it.' A chicken leg seemed to get stuck in C.'s throat.

22 September
Spicer has struck. He managed to find out about the stud farm in Praeneste, and he's seized the horses. I have no sympathy. C. told me over lunch that he reproached Spicer for this mean trick, and the bailiff couldn't look him in the eye. Seemed amused by it all. He can't fool me.

He alternates between moods of real depression, when he sits hunched up on a stone bench in the garden for hours, staring at the ground, and periods of elated optimism.

26 September

Crassus is for Catilina! Today he was talking to C. about the possibility of the City placing considerable means at Catilina's disposal, since Pompey is still siding with the Senate as far as Asian tax farming is concerned. Catilina has provided assurance that he will combat radicalism in his movement and cease agitating against the banks. On these conditions the Democratic side is prepared to support him when he stands for the post of Consul this year. We are to handle the election campaign. C. acted immediately. By late tonight at least twenty people had gathered in our house. All of them district managers of election committees.

Crassus left before they arrived. C. received them in the riding school, which still isn't quite finished. They are shop owners, craftsmen in a small way, house owners, veterans of Marius and so on: quiet men. They have connections with the hundreds of religious sects and craftsmen's trade guilds. When they get a commission to prepare for an election they go out and get the voters to sign up on their lists, or pass on the lists (and money) to the separate organizations, who take over from there. They know C. from similar occasions in the past; he's regarded as Crassus' lieutenant, and Crassus has enormous influence due to his wealth.

C. apologized for receiving them in the as yet unfinished hall, and showed them the only half completed mural, *Diana on a Blue Horse*. They inspected it in silence; it is a little modern.

C. questioned them about the attitude of the man in the street towards the Catilinarian agitation, and a little man with a limp, himself the head of the ropemakers' guild, reported that the guilds could no longer keep the increasing number of their members who were unemployed. Anyone who was turned out on to the streets once became a Catilinarian as a matter of course. The suspension of supplies of military equipment to Asia was having catastrophic results. Hatred of the banks, who were collecting rents and recovering debts with great harshness, was mounting steadily. The return of the army from Asia could only be expected to increase the suffering further. Peace in Asia was having a double-edged effect. A woman, returning home in tears after having found her son's name on the list of casualties in Asia, might well meet her sister-in-law, also in tears, in her case because their small saddler's shop hasn't had its contract for military supplies renewed. So the family would be mourning the consequences of both the war and the peace simultaneously.

C.'s announcement that 'one' would require their support for Catilina in the forthcoming consular elections was received with visible consternation.

C. immediately started talking about the slogans. I had total admiration for the way he pulled from his toga a complete programme, worked out in every detail, without having made the slightest preparation. He hadn't discussed anything but the financial side of the affair with Crassus or had more than half an hour to make a few notes about the political aspects before the district managers arrived. His mind works incredibly quickly, and he's so adaptable! He spoke for over twenty minutes about new settlements which would give the capital room to breathe, as well as providing work for craftsmen. Corn handouts, not only for the unemployed, but also for everyone who needs them. 'It's ridiculous,' he exclaimed, 'to maintain that a ropemaker or a baker who has two or three miserable slaves, who is crushed by bank debts and tormented by the need to find the high rent for his shop, doesn't need cheap corn!' He spoke at length (and with figures!) about the cancellation of bank debts, and especially about the need for the state to provide the craftsman with credit for the purchase and upkeep of slaves. 'Why are his sons conquering both Asias?' he demanded. 'Where are the innumerable hordes of slaves sent? Only to the estates of 300 families, only to a few bronze factories? Hand over the slaves!'

You could see that the people were very satisfied. They called it the most far-reaching Democratic programme ever to be presented at a Consular election. It would be a pleasure to present it to the trade guilds. Slogans like that would make all their mouths water. Then a minor note of discord was struck.

A man with a cheesy complexion and a flabby neck croaked: 'I'm positive that Catilina accepts slaves in his combat squads. What about that?' The meeting grew lively. This was a crucial point. Now other people also spoke up. An elderly man with a friendly face – the head of a burial society, I later discovered – called out amidst considerable commotion: 'Are we supposed to aid and abet a slave rebellion?' And the ropemaker from earlier, now with red blotches in his cheeks, said loudly but without looking at C.: 'That's out of the question. Two-thirds of our members employ slaves in their workshops.'

C. didn't permit the uproar to continue. He said a few words which were drowned out by the raised voices, since he spoke rather quietly. As a result silence was quickly restored. His next sentences could be understood. He said: 'This is the first I've heard of it. I shall make immediate enquiries, but I think it can safely be ruled out.' He paused and then continued in a lighter tone: 'Gentlemen, refreshments are now being served in the garden; they are being served by slaves. My secretary, who will later itemize the financial formalities of our little agreement,' (he smiled over at me) 'is also a slave. I don't think we need discuss the slave question any further. There is no such question.'

He quickly turned to the purely commercial considerations. They discussed the electoral sporting events to be arranged for the individual voters.

Then the refreshments were served, and yet again I had to admire C.'s skill in dealing with simple people. He pays attention to them but doesn't permit any intimacy to develop. I saw him discussing *Diana on a Blue Horse* with a master baker for a whole five minutes!

The whole new development strikes me as very sinister.

I discussed it at some length with Caebio, who came out with some very smart opinions. He hasn't seen Rufus for three weeks now.

27 September
This afternoon three gentlemen called, and C. shut himself in the library with them. As they were leaving I recognized one of them as the former Consul Cornelius Lentulus Sura (the 'Shins'), who is now Praetor again, one of Catilina's main sponsors. He looked at me, completely unabashed.

We have come a very long way.

Today C. asked me quite casually to find out the price of land in Campania (?). Three days ago we were so broke we couldn't afford to have the drains fixed!

2 October
Today Fulvia, who is surely one of the most charming coquettes in
the capital, told us very amusing stories about the headaches that
the uncertain political situation has given the ladies. Although the
season hasn't finished in the spas, they have all returned to hot,
dusty Rome. They are doing everything they can to squeeze some
information out of the politicians about what's going on behind the
scenes. She asked C. with a smile: 'Will he get in as Consul? I've
made a bet that he will.' – 'Who?' asked C. – 'Catilina, of course.'
– 'You certainly shouldn't put too much money on him,' said C.
slowly, 'and anyway, what gives you that idea?' She explained to us.
The young and even the not-so-young Catilinarians are rated very
highly at the moment. The fashion is for simple, popular outfits.
Jewellery – just a little amber. Toenails are no longer painted.
Topic of conversation – the land question. Fulvia says: 'When it
comes down to it, we're all being exploited, aren't we?' However,
her friend Fonia is remaining faithful to her Senator, and says:
'My fatty will come out on top in the end. He's so brutal.' ('She's a
reactionary!') Democracy is the watchword of the day. Cicero is
admired for his democratic ideals, and because he wants to buy
Crassus' town house (four and a half million sesterces). But only
since Catilina came along has it been considered chic to show
sympathy for the wounded of the war in Asia. At more than a
few society evenings people have gone so far as to hold collections for war cripples. Tertulla donated a piece of beryl jewellery
(Corinthian workmanship) to men blinded in the war – she got it
from Pulcher, who is involved in tax farming in Asia. In return two
young aristocratic Catilinarians took her on a tour of the slums by
the Tiber. One of them is very handsome, apparently. Of course,
everyone is ordering a new wardrobe, hoping that Catilina will
bring about a cancellation of debts.

6 October
The first election posters have been stuck up. Everywhere, on
house walls, in the markets, even on monuments, you can see
Catilina's big *Questions: Why is the price of bread going up? Who's
pocketing the loot from Asia? Why don't the fields of Rome belong to
the citizens of Rome?* etc.

As we were crossing the Forum together C. pointed out that this last slogan is particularly effective.

7 October

Today the following dialogue took place during the clients' surgery between C. and a tall, powerful man with the battered ears of a wrestler. The chap: 'I wanna start a school for orators.' C.: 'Have you got the money?' The chap: 'No sweat.' (He put a sealed envelope on the table in front of me). C.: 'References?' The chap: 'Got 'em from the Colosseum, your excellency.' C.: 'Is the orators' school going to be for athletes?' The chap: 'Nar. For the nobs.' C.: '?' The chap: 'Common talk is the new fashion. Big one, too. I'm selling individual expressions as well. Got five lads out on the street, collecting swearwords. Putting 20,000 sesterces into it.' Publius Mucer, our election agent, was standing next to me and remarked under his breath when the chap left with his letter of recommendation: 'Democracy marches on.'

8 October

Clodius here, along with Alexander. An extremely unequal pair! The rather battered nobleman – former leader of the Democratic Street Clubs, the armed wing of democracy – and Crassus' slave, democracy's theoretician!

The conversation was about the involvement of the Democrats in the election, on Catilina's side. In a long speech Alexander explained that one should only get involved in the whole thing if one intends to follow it through to the end; otherwise the election machinery would be destroyed. C. asked what gave him the idea that anyone might not want to follow it through to the end. Alexander seemed rather embarrassed and mumbled that although some of the banks closely associated with Crassus were providing funds to support Catilina's candidature, he had heard something about a group of influential businessmen who were secretly negotiating with the Senate Party about adopting a quite different stance towards the election. And that Cicero was trying hard to bring about some sort of reconciliation between the City and the Senate. Apparently he was issuing warnings about Catilina every day. C. absolutely refused to accept that any such negotiations were being held. In the end Clodius, in a bad mood, said: 'If those racketeers in the City really want to side with the Senate against the people, under Mr Cicero, I'll become a Catilinarian.' When the gentlemen were already on their feet and about to leave, Alexander casually remarked: 'They might also want to act with Pompey against the people, instead of with Cicero.' C. made no reply, although Alexander did seem to be waiting for one. In fact, he wasn't saying very much at all. Perhaps he was dismayed by the rumours of the City negotiating in secret with the Senate. Perhaps he just didn't want to reveal to the other two how little he really knows. His position appears rather undecided. He has been given a job, but he doesn't receive any information. In any case, you can't really talk about reasonably unified policies with the Democrats, like those pursued by the Senate Party, where Cato and Catulus have a firm hand on the reins. The Democrats don't work well together, particularly since the City itself often has conflicting interests.

Alexander sounds bitter when he talks about the City. He says they haven't adopted any policy at all. They simply shift their fat behinds around restlessly, because they have a vague feeling they aren't sitting comfortably yet, so the pressure they exert is sometimes increased in one place, sometimes in another. No trace whatsoever of any meaningful activity.

Incidentally, C. asked me today whether I had found anything out about the price of land. I gave him some figures. He put the sheet of paper in his pocket.

11 October
Four district election managers here. They were quite despondent as they described the curious indifference they had encountered in the trade guilds with regard to Catilina's election. People weren't saying anything openly, but they shrugged their shoulders a bit too often. The sailmakers' guild 'will not prevent its members' from voting for Catilina but won't recommend it either. The silversmiths expressed doubts about the soundness of the election agreement and were very disparaging about C., as were the saddlers. The bakers went even further; they consider the programme untrustworthy. And people everywhere are against a dictatorship.

Conclusion: the Election Committee is to appeal direct to the voters, using lists from previous elections.

13 October

The money from the Po merchants has also arrived. C. and Crassus have earmarked it for Catilina's election fund. At least, that's what I heard from the moneychangers in the Forum. The Po merchants have been promised that Catilina will have them put on the Citizens' List. I myself still can't believe that Crassus is entirely serious in his support for Catilina. Of course, he must share the Senate's fear of a dictatorship under Pompey – they are personal enemies – and above all he will be hoping that Catilina as Consul, kept under strict control, represents his best option of accessing the Asian revenues. He's gone to Sicily on business, incidentally.

It's obviously sensible of C. to put the money from the Po towns into Catilina's election fund. Election debts are always settled very generously.

Some good luck; suddenly the value of Asian shares has increased considerably. I'm a good 700 sesterces better off today. Took Caebio out.

14 October

C. is now on good form, as always when there's cash around. He told Pomponius Celer (skins and leather): 'The fate of democracy will be decided by this election. You only have to talk to the common people to discover that resentment is seething in the poor districts. My agent' (he meant Mummlius Spicer, the bailiff) 'told me where he lives. Out of his six children, two of them have got bad lungs. The walls are so damp that the salt in the saltcellars goes lumpy. They can't keep the rats away any longer. Not so much as one sesterce has been spent on the sewerage system for a hundred years. Asia has to be conquered!'

The elections are on the 20th. We're in for some interesting (and dangerous) weeks. I hope C. isn't getting too deeply involved with Catilina. Glaucos absolutely insists that he was here, in this house, last night. Must check up on that.

15 October

I'm beside myself, can't think straight at all. Caebio has been deceiving me. When I called round to his apartment today, since I happened to have the afternoon off, I noticed straight away that his mother was very embarrassed. She said Caebio had gone to a dog race with his uncle. Right away I told her, straight to her face, that he had gone off with some chap or other. She tried to deny it, but then she confessed. It's Rufus. He's been there almost every night for weeks. I had a fit of crying but controlled myself enough to get to the Fourth District, where the dog race was supposed to be, accompanied by Caebio's little brother. Of course Caebio wasn't there. I walked round the stalls and fairgrounds for the whole afternoon and half the night. Then I went to the granaries on the Tiber, with the little boy. He knew where this Rufus lives; he's taken him messages. (No shame!) We stood in the yard until two in the morning. No lights in the warehouse.

16 October

Caebio won't speak to me. His mother said she appealed to his conscience; she respects me. A new blow: the warehouse manager has *forbidden* him to see me again! The child slipped me a message. Caebio has got a job as a clerk in the granary! So that's his idea of love! He sells me out for a job as a clerk! For two sesterces a day. When I read that I went ice cold. I immediately resolved to let that animal finally fall where he belongs; in the dirt. He really isn't worth getting upset about. Sacrificial fees collected from the Capitol (of course they tried to cheat us), desk tidied, inventory made of interest due in January. While doing this I came across a letter between the pages of Hermina's Chronicle, which C. is reading in the evenings these days; apparently he's made considerable purchases of land. Acres and acres of arable land in Campania. What can he have in mind for that property?

17 October

Went to the granaries on the Tiber today. Had someone fetch Caebio and confronted him in a corridor. He can't look me in the eye. What's become of my Caebio?

18 October

Miserable days. Can't work up any interest in anything. Hardly eating a thing.

19 October
Horrible scene at the granary. Only wanted to ask Caebio whether I should renew the lease (his mother asked me to). Then that Rufus appeared and had two slaves throw me out! He's a completely uneducated person, and the way he speaks is awful. Three against one. Caebio stood in the office doorway and said *nothing*! I've taken to my bed. What's going to happen?

20 October
Been wondering whether I couldn't approach the grain firm through Pomponius Celer (skins and leather). That Rufus simply has to be sacked. Perhaps it would be better to have a word with the Shins. If there's any sort of revolution, that Rufus must be one of the first to be rubbed out. Couldn't do anything about the rent for the whole day, as the banks were closed. Cicero made a speech in the Senate disclosing Catilina's assassination plans.

It's raining.

21 October
Lethargic.

The Consular elections have been postponed for eight days. Great excitement in town. The streets are full of former soldiers of Sulla, who have come to vote for Catilina. It seems certain that if the election had been held today, Catilina would have been elected. That's probably why it didn't take place today. Is Cicero making deals in the City? Is he trying to destabilize the financiers who are behind Catilina? Is he promising the banks influence in Asian business through administration of the province, is he again agreeing to City courts which will exercise control over Senatorial measures in Asia? It's bad that Crassus has left Rome.

The suburbs are full of police patrols.

22 October
Got a letter from Alexander asking me to call on him 'at my convenience'. When I arrived he was working on a speech for Crassus, who is away, about a legal matter. He told me that increasingly strident rumours are circulating the Forum to the effect that certain banks are negotiating their position on the Consular

elections with the Senate, through Cicero. It's said that in return for certain concessions (in Asia?) the City would be prepared to ensure that the funds being supplied to Catilina from somewhere or other would dry up quickly. But apparently the Senate Party refuses to grant any concessions at all, because Cato doesn't believe the City really wants to see Catilina as Consul. What's almost more important is that the trade guilds are taking a stand which is more and more clearly opposed to Catilina's election. He's heard references to 'serious' negotiations being conducted with the Senate about 'genuine concessions', which will result in a 'surprise'. It's said that Cato even led the leaders of the cabinet makers to understand that 'a gentleman in the administration of Catilina's Election Committee' had called on him and 'made some strange offers'.

Alexander asked me straight out whether I knew anything about C. holding talks with Cato and Catulus, the leaders of the Senate Party. If Alexander's informer is telling the truth, C. assured the Senate Party that he would sabotage Catilina's election from his position, no matter how the City behaves, as long as the Senate actually does set up the ten-man committee proposed by the Democrats in the spring, on the instigation of Alexander, to provide land for the unemployed (a solution to the land question!). Apparently Cato hasn't responded to this offer yet. I didn't know anything about talks like that, although I did take a letter from C. to Cato yesterday, during his clients' surgery. I was shown in immediately, although the atrium was very crowded. Our business is nothing compared to his. There there's a whole city district milling around, kept under control by a dozen secretaries, and among them I saw businessmen who had brought along several secretaries themselves. The short, portly man, who everyone in Rome knows as the kind of drunk who gets five bottles of red wine down by lunchtime, read the letter in my presence, muttered something incomprehensible and handed it to his head secretary, who read it himself, whereupon they exchanged glances. I was notified that C. would receive a reply in writing. As I was leaving I heard Cato murmur: 'That gentleman seems to be getting pretty nervous.'

When I told Alexander all this he seemed horrified. Should I not have told him?

23 October
Went to see Caebio's mother again. She said if he loses the job he's got now, he'll go over to the Catilinarians. They're promising to take people on. My delicate Caebio, a soldier!

The people really are living in awful misery. It's an eight-storey house that's constantly on the verge of collapse, propped up from the street by three thick wooden beams. Over two hundred people live in the house, if you can call it living. Children with diseased eyes tumble down the rotting stairs. What those poor people eat (and they can't get enough of it) is what we would throw away.

Can't help thinking that maybe I'm being unfair to Caebio. He simply couldn't stand the financial strain. He felt I was betraying him. Suddenly I had even stopped paying his rent. How could I have explained to him that I had lent C. my savings? What good would that have done him? I've been dropping hints to C. constantly ever since. He doesn't react at all. But he buys Cynthia a pearl bracelet! (And not on credit. I know for a fact that no jeweller would give him any more credit.) He *does* have money again at the moment.

24 October
Trying to deaden the pain by concentrating on politics again. Often hard to work with C. Usually he spends days on end doing nothing at all; he won't see anybody, he doesn't make any decisions or give any instructions. Then you hear the simple district election managers expressing doubts about C., his determination, his consistency, etc.: 'He swings one way and then the other, he talks so vaguely, he doesn't know what he wants. For weeks on end you can't speak to him, everything is at sixes and sevens, and nobody knows what he's going to decide. He's a great man, but unfortunately he isn't always himself.' If the man in the street knew more about the infinite complications of political struggles, if he had any idea of all the factors which dictate the decisions taken even by the man in charge, who '*isn't always himself*' because he in turn is at the mercy of others, the man in the street definitely wouldn't talk like that. C. started being very active again today, for example. There's something fishy about the attitude the Democrats have adopted towards this election. Shares in the Asian tax farming companies

have gone up again, by twelve points. What's been going on behind the scenes there? Has an agreement been reached? By whom and with whom? Cicero's warning that Catilina would let the mob loose on the Forum if he got to power is certainly not being received with a shrug of the shoulders, as it was last week. The trade guilds are already against Catilina; are the banks dropping out, too? Now C. wants to get to the bottom of the matter, it seems. I discovered from the sedan chair porters, who were completely worn out by the evening, that they spent all day taking him from company to company in the City. This evening he told Clodius, in my presence, that he had demanded political concessions from Cato. (I had made a report to him about Alexander's mistrustful questions.) 'What kind of political concessions?' asked Clodius, visibly suspicious. 'The usual,' replied C. But Pomade-head dug deeper. 'Corn handouts?' – 'Yes, that too,' said C., nervously. 'But of course I put more emphasis on the land question. If the unemployed men of Rome had land to cultivate, they wouldn't need charity.' – 'But at the moment they're starving,' said Clodius obstinately. C. became quite wild. 'You simply can't engage in politics,' he said angrily, 'with people who are always thinking of their stomachs. You can't take Rome with an army that's always getting lost in the granaries. The problems are either going to be solved comprehensively or not at all. If that rabble doesn't want anything more than a loaf of bread, it'll remain a rabble. I'm a politician, not a baker. Anyway, I haven't been making deals, I've only been fishing for information.' – 'And what was Cato's reply?' asked Clodius, quite calmly. 'He wanted to think about it but didn't seem averse to moving in our direction.' – 'How far?' asked Clodius. 'I told him that the entire Democratic election machinery, to the last man,' related C. rather more calmly, 'would be brought into action for Catilina if no concessions were made.' – 'But you know that's not true. The City has already stopped funding him.' C.: 'That's why I spent all day in the City. It *must* threaten to get Catilina elected.' Clodius: 'And it *daren't* let him be elected. That would mean a cancellation of debts. And the Senate knows that, too.' C.: 'And we could obstruct the City's activities, as you well know; and Cato knows it too, my dear man. And as from today, the City also knows it. I've seen to that. We could have the electorate vote for Catilina and promise to pay them when he's in.' Clodius: 'And is that what you want?' C.: 'Under certain circumstances.' Clodius: 'Which circumstances?' C.: 'If no concessions are forthcoming. Don't ask such stupid questions.' Clodius stood up. 'And when will you find out whether the concessions will be made?' C.: 'I'll be having more talks this evening.' Clodius: 'And when will we hear the result?' C.: 'As soon as I know definitely, of course.' – 'Fine,' said Clodius, his tone curt and not very friendly. He left soon afterwards.

The worst thing is that C. didn't have any more talks; he went to see Mucia, instead, though only after a rather thick envelope had been delivered from Cato. There could hardly have been concessions in it; political concessions don't come in wads. The outlook for the next few days is bleak.

Irony of fate; now I have the 4,000 sesterces that caused me to lose my Caebio! Mummlius Spicer lent it to me. Too late ...

25 October

C. isn't at home to the election managers today. He even cancelled the clients' surgery, so he wouldn't have to speak to anybody.

On the other hand he was continually receiving people, and I recognized some of them as members of the Chamber of Commerce. He seems to be fishing for information wherever he can.

And he is associating with the conspirators again. At night I encountered a thin person in the atrium flanked by two huge Nubians, a man with jaundiced features and a nervous twitch in the muscles on the left side of his face. Catilina! I recognized him immediately from his description.

26 October

C. has gone to one of the sea spas in the middle of the election campaign. He told nobody but me which one, because he needs complete rest, he's very nervous, and he's beginning to suffer from insomnia again. That's what he told Pompeya. But I know he's meeting Mucia. I wonder whether she's also written to her husband to say she's very nervous, and whether Pompey believes it as much as Pompeya does? What's more, she happened to come in and see him packing his Hercules, the dreadful hexameter he's been writing for the last fifteen years, which he always reads aloud to the ladies when he can't find anything to talk about. He even told me that bit about needing a rest, and he made sure to raise his hand to his head as if it were aching.

It'll be interesting to hear what Clodius and the election committee have to say when it becomes known that C. has left town … and Old Mouldy has gone away, too!

For myself, I'm pleased C. isn't here. I'm looking around for a little shop at the moment. I'm determined to set up a perfume shop for Caebio. I want him to be free to make up his own mind. I simply can't stand by and watch him sell himself.

Rents are comparatively low, since there are more and more auction sales after foreclosures. The banks are being quite ruthless. Loans to craftsmen are being terminated, and owners are renting out property for next to nothing, if they don't install their slaves in the shops, or freed slaves who then have to pay them commission. The names of the shopkeepers show that the number of foreigners in Rome is increasing. They are the slaves imported from Asia. Alexander's comment on all this: Pompey is defeating the Romans.

27 October

At about 11 o'clock in the morning squads of young people with white armbands paraded down the Subura. That's Mr Cicero's Civil Guard, hastily assembled in the last couple of days from members of the 'merchant classes'. The populace watched the battalions curiously and in silence. I saw a few astonished faces at the little windows, between the bits of washing hanging on lines above the street to dry. Mr Cicero is protecting his republic.

At lunchtime we received an explanation for this warlike demonstration in the form of sudden and very convincing rumours to the effect that the Catilinarians have raised Catilinarian Eagles in Etruria. Is this the beginning of civil war? They are said to have assembled a legion of former Sullan legionaries, all experienced soldiers, ready for combat. A lot of veterans of Sulla's campaigns did settle in Etruria, actually, and of course their farms are burdened by mortgages. Growing corn on a small scale simply isn't profitable.

28 October

The election. The town has been in complete uproar since early this morning. Everywhere there are parades, street orators, posters, wagons with voters. Lots of police.

Campus Martius is packed to the brim with Cicero's bodyguard, the new Civil Guard. He's overseeing the election himself, and they say he's wearing a cuirass under his toga. I saw him sitting on the platform, surrounded by armed men, when I went to Campus Martius at lunchtime in the hope of glimpsing my Caebio, at least from a distance. Grey, stormy weather. An incredible noise. Impossible to get anywhere near the gangways along which the members of each Century are led to the boxes for their voting tablets. Caebio wasn't to be seen in the crowd. Once I thought I saw him; a young man walked along next to the ropes without stopping, and his bearing was similar to Caebio's, but the way he held his head was different. My heart was beating like a drum for a few minutes. But I was standing much too far away. It couldn't really have been him.

I encountered the first drunks even before I got home. The whole election circus disgusts me.

The night before Election Day was awful. Deputations from the districts arrived every few minutes, angrily demanding to see C., because the money hadn't been paid out. Of course, no one believed that he had left town. There is enormous resentment against him. He has been stalling the district managers the whole time, and the voters were still waiting for their money this morning, so they had to sell their votes at the very last minute, when they hardly got anything for them. After all, the other party just needs 51 per cent of the total votes. So it bought up a small number of the Democratic stock of votes, just to be on the safe side. They got those votes for a bowl of soup, as the voters undercut each other in the last few hours before the election; they were sitting around with votes which had been ordered but not collected. The vast majority left empty handed.

Catilina's opponents are both candidates from the Senate Party.

Did C. really make a deal with the Senate? Will there be a peaceful transition to democracy? C.'s behaviour is incomprehensible otherwise. Surely it wasn't just Cato's envelope?

29 October
Catilina lost. He's said to be incredibly depressed.

On the other hand, nobody regards his cause as lost. The general feeling is that he could implement a decision by the use of armed force. He's done for on the Capitol. The election of the two People's Tribunes, which is still to take place, won't change a thing. The candidates haven't even been nominated; in view of the Senate Party's gigantic victory there just isn't enough interest in the matter.

It's rumoured that the tax farming companies have now got Pompey where they want him. But whether the new Consuls will honour the contract a few banks have made with Pompey is a different question.

C. still in Campania. Is he really there? Or is he in Etruria? Pompeya and his mother are very nervous. Came across the old lady in tears today. Someone has written *Beware, Swindler!* on the wall of our house in black paint, three metres off the ground. Right next to the gate, so nobody attending the clients' surgery could miss it.

Went back to the barber's for the first time. Everyone's talking about Catilina's army in Etruria. People are expecting a great deal from his programme for a cancellation of debts. Only good things are said about him, only bad things about Cicero; one tall, fat man – some kind of butcher – called him a traitor to democracy.

30 October
We'll have to cope with a great deal in the immediate future, too, due to the seething rage of the electorate. Yesterday it was the writing on the wall, today stones as big as your fist were lying around in the atrium.

C. has come back. He *wasn't* in Etruria. When I told him his mother had been worried he was quite astonished.

When I reported to him that Clodius was furious, he just laughed. 'He'll get his share,' he said. He doesn't regard it as particularly tragic that the Democratic voters are outraged. 'If you want to sell your convictions,' he said, 'you've got to unload them at exactly the right time, just like every other commodity. Of course, now these good people's votes have gone bad on them, like fish that have been kept back too long to try to force the price up. Serves them right. It might even teach them that you have to think with your head, not with your stomach.' It's so incredibly easy for him to be reassuring, if only he wants to. Then he can adopt wider points of view.

He also talked about the terrible situation of the small farmers. In some cases they can't bring in the harvest these days, because the men and their sons are at war. They are hoping for an increase in the price of corn; otherwise they're ruined. When Catilina promised corn handouts for the unemployed in Rome, it turned many of the small farmers against him. C. found a warm reception for the Democratic programme, which would provide a solution to the completely intolerable land question.

So he apparently doesn't think the victory of the Senate Party, which absolutely everyone's talking about, is quite so certain yet.

Was in a good mood until Caebio's brother turned up and, without a word, handed me a small packet containing the gold medallion I once gave Caebio.

Sank into the deepest despair.

31 October
Pomponius Celer (skins and leather) reports that in the City everybody is at each other's throats. Huge discontent. There are still significant groups which support Catilina. He just can't explain to me why that is. Now, when the movement is becoming incredibly radical! My butcher from the barber's shop, yes. But Oppius, the banker? Baffling.

C. had a short conversation with Alexander and Clodius. Alexander was totally depressed when he greeted C. (for the first time since the disastrous election). As a decent man he was disconcerted because he felt C.'s behaviour had been deeply improper. Pomade-head, on the other hand, was remarkably civil about it; C. must have already given him 'his share'.

Nevertheless, he made a detailed report about the deep resentment of the mass of the voters. The top men of the street clubs, which have now been disbanded, had been to see him. Now life is returning to this organization quite of its own accord. Apparently, although Clodius was very vague about this, the top men have been demanding that he should distance himself from C., who is of course being cursed by the majority of people these days.

C. was quite taken aback.

He told us some details about how the banks changed sides just before the election.

He said he had been going to pick up the actual money for the election from Mr X, the banker. He had hardly sat down when the man told him, quite calmly, that his services were no longer needed, and he should specify his expenses, etc. C. was thunderstruck. After beating about the bush a little X calmly announced that he had tried everything but hadn't been able to secure the money which had been promised from any of the larger firms. Everyone was complaining about the extraordinary shortage of funds, the big banks were involved in business in Asia, which was as uncertain as ever, Catilina's election slogans had upset people by their aggressive tone, etc., etc. C. asked him what Crassus would have to say about it. X answered slowly, choosing each word with care: 'I haven't heard from Mr Crassus for the last two weeks. However, yesterday he issued written instructions to the effect that his contribution was only to be paid to the election management if the other contributions which had been promised were also forthcoming.'

C. was naturally incensed and insisted he had been wilfully misled; now he would lose face before the Democratic Election Committee. The banker had simply gazed at him, unabashed, and repeated: 'State your expenses; I'm authorized to compensate you for them.'

After a rather uncomfortable silence Clodius remarked, quite listlessly, that it looked as though they would have to wait for Old Mouldy to return: everything depended on him now.

At this point Alexander became very embarrassed, and after skirting the subject for a while he came out with the news that Crassus was already back.

C. and Clodius stared at each other in surprise.

Alexander quickly said he was sure Crassus would call a meeting 'certainly within the next few days'.

They were all rather depressed when they parted.

1 November

The price of bread has gone up again. The corn firms have gone mad. What are they trying to provoke? An uprising of the starving people? This is all playing into Catilina's hands. Although perhaps that's the intention? But why? If that's the case, why was his election sabotaged?

While Cicero pushes useless decrees through the Senate against the flight of capital, the police raid departing ships to stop the transportation of gold, and a few steps further away, at the Forum, turmoil rages among the corn speculators. The world has gone insane.

It's becoming increasingly apparent that Rome needs a *strong man* more desperately than anything else! It's tearing itself to pieces over the Asian loot.

2 November

C. has restocked the stud farm in Praeneste. He and Pompeya take great pleasure in breaking in the new thoroughbred horses. It wasn't just Cato's envelope. There must have been envelopes from the City too.

Still no word from Crassus.

Instead, an official from the Praetor was here. He reported that the disbanded street clubs are once again displaying considerable underground activity. It has come to the attention of the Praetor that extremely vitriolic speeches have been made against C. He shouldn't go out without an escort.

2 November (evening)

Informed Caebio's brother that I'm in negotiations for a shop. Assured him explicitly that I wasn't attaching any conditions to it.

Glaucos is greatly agitated. All gladiator slaves are being sent away from Rome. Glaucos himself received an order from the police to make his way to Capua. Evidently Mr Cicero is afraid that the Catilinarian movement will now be radicalized, following the election defeat. Cicero believes that Catilina is now quite capable of recruiting supporters even from among the slaves. In this respect he isn't entirely on the wrong track; Glaucos did admit to me that he isn't only a fencing instructor but also a squad leader.

Of course, that doesn't mean that the people in the Catilinarian camp are actually in favour of equality for slaves. Glaucos is only counting on making enough money in the general upheaval to buy his freedom. No plebeian wants to be faced with a general uprising of slaves. Ultimately, the right to vote – and not *only* because of the financial benefits attached to it – would be meaningless if it were suddenly extended to everybody. Therefore, as Glaucos remarked with some bitterness, everything is done in the squads to 'keep the slaves in their place'. He's certainly been quite depressed about it on occasion.

C. sent him to the Praetor with a letter. The order was revoked.

3 November

Crassus has been in touch at last! Oddly enough, he sent word that he would be coming with some gentlemen from the Senate.

C. showed his guests the new riding school. His painting *Diana on the Blue Horse* made them shake their heads as well. General opinion; horses aren't blue. By way of apologising for the artist, C. said: 'And these days it seems that politicians are sometimes not politicians, financiers don't have any money, and priests don't believe in the Goddesses.'

There was some laughter, as he is High Priest himself.

Appreciation of modern art is only found in the City.

The gentlemen from the Senate still don't take the 'Catilinarian commotion' seriously. 'The City will get cold feet quickly enough,' somebody said, 'the first time all the scum of the 34 districts flock up to the moneychangers' offices at the Forum with rucksacks.' And a particularly fat squire said with a sneer as he stuffed himself with our delicious quails: 'When the trade guilds wanted free corn for their idle members they threatened to elect Catilina as Consul. Well, there wasn't any free corn, and Catilina wasn't elected.' – 'But negotiations were conducted with the trade guilds,' said Old Mouldy, angrily. 'To keep them from behaving stupidly. There won't be any more negotiations.'

These gentlemen's sense of security is maddening.

The real, immense power of the Senate shouldn't be underestimated. It is, purely and simply, the state. 300 families, almost all with vast estates. You see these people riding through the streets on golden wagons during the triumphal processions, recruiting soldiers, officiating as judges. Anyone who wants to build a water pipeline has to go and see one of them. Every one of these families has a clientele of thousands in the city: small merchants, craftsmen, leaseholders, military suppliers. They get married and divorced, they give letters of recommendation for the provinces and little notes to officials which open every door.

Old Mouldy stayed after the others had left. The conversation had annoyed him considerably. 'They're not budging at all, are they?' he said. 'The pressure must be increased. Perhaps we really should have got Catilina elected. Then they wouldn't be talking this way.' C. stared at him in surprise and then asked, apparently casually: 'Why did you let the election go to the dogs, anyway?' – 'There was no chance at all,' said Old Mouldy lazily, 'once even the trade guilds refused their support.' And after a while he added, apparently addressing the ceiling: 'What's Catilina going to do now?' – 'Resign, presumably, or attack.' – 'An uprising? I wouldn't give five assaria for his chances in Rome. Mr Cicero would put it down with his miserable Civil Guard and a few thousand gladiator slaves borrowed from Lucullus.' – 'But he's got an army, too. In Etruria.' – 'Yes, and no money for it.' C. was looking at him closely. 'Well, are you still interested at all?' Old Mouldy returned his gaze. 'Why not?' he said. 'Perhaps he has to come up with something else. Up to now he's only brought chaos to the salons. Why isn't he with his army?' – 'Do you want me to ask him?' asked C., as if he were making a joke. 'Then he'd ask me why you stopped the money.' – 'What do you mean, I stopped the money? It just hasn't been collected, my dear Gaius.' – 'That's extremely interesting,' said C.

4 November

I heard from Paestus, Clodius' secretary, that the intention is to draw Catilina out of his apathy (he's still in Rome, and seems to be more afraid of an uprising than his financial backers). Clodius had a long talk with Fulvia, who is the mistress of Quintus Curius, a Catilinarian. The idea is to send her to Cicero with secrets to reveal. Clodius: 'Cicero is an old goat, and he can't resist getting something for nothing. She'll reveal everything, including herself, of course. His immense cowardice will take care of the rest.'

Paestus is pursuing me quite insufferably with his affections, but small items of news like that are worth one evening.

5 November
C.'s involvement in land speculation, which is more and more prevalent around town in general these days, really does disturb me.

I pointedly tidied up his maps after the dictation. He looked at me with a smile, and said: 'Mucia asked me to acquire some land for her. I gave her a little advice. If I had any money, I'd buy some, too.'

Well, he doesn't fool me. If I had any money! Apparently Mucia does have some money. After all, she is Pompey's wife.

The sums involved in the property purchases are immense; at least 5 million. Prices have risen sharply just recently.

C. is clearly on excellent terms with high finance at the moment. Otherwise he would hardly have been permitted to get involved in their property speculation. It's become known that he accepted a cheque from Cato to sabotage Catilina's election when he already knew the City would never permit it anyway, but nobody holds it against him; in fact, people are amused by it.

6 November
Once again secret meetings are being held here, in the library. Usually they feature Curius, Lentulus and Statilius, well-known Catilinarians from the radical wing. Lentulus, a former Consul and one of the most dashing and bankrupt men about town in the capital, was given the nickname 'The Shins' because, after having been convicted of outrageous corruption by the entire Senate, he retorted dryly that he couldn't account for the missing money but would extend his leg, the way little boys do when they make a mistake in a ball game, so the ball can be hurled against it as painfully as possible in punishment. Statilius, a tall thin man whose father lost all his money when a bank collapsed, is highly educated and discusses grammar with C. for hours on end. He is uncomfortable with the Shins' brutal, libertine behaviour. He emphasizes that he is only taking part in the coup because he is opposed to 'the tyrants'. Curius is insignificant.

As soon as they've had something to drink all three of them start complaining about Catilina's hesitation in taking the only path still open to him. He absolutely refuses to leave the city and abandon the futile negotiations. And while this is going on, the army in Etruria is dispersing. They're mad about money; even the smell of it gets them going. On the other hand, they're suspicious. The Shins constantly makes jokes about the City playing with fire, and about the 'Clubs for Friends of Armed Uprising.'

Have decided, incidentally, not to make any more attempts to meet Caebio before his shop is completely fitted out. I chose blue for the walls, very light. After some hesitation I decided on the Egyptian bottles with cut glass stoppers: expensive but beautiful. When I showed Caebio's brother the perfume shop, which is almost finished now, he just stood there for a while with his mouth open. Then he simply said: 'He's really stupid.'

8 November

Cicero made a 'sensational speech' in the Senate. He exposed a plot of the Catilinarians to assassinate him. He kept on shouting: 'I know all about it!' So Fulvia did her job.

I went to the Temple of Jupiter Stator, where the Senate was in session, to take Crassus a letter. In front of it, in the Via Sacra, there was a veritable forest of sedan chairs, waiting for the Senators. Lots of excited secretaries bustling to and fro. The sedan chair porters, mostly supporters of Catilina, were making jokes about the Senate and laughing at the secretaries, who were telling them to keep quiet.

Catilina was present at the session. His chair porter was the star in front of the temple. The others formed a ring around him and lapped up his every word. A big, good-looking chap.

I was able to get a glimpse of the Senate, too. The immense room seemed full to the brim. The Senators who don't live in Rome had been fetched from their country estates during the night by special couriers. The session was already in progress, but Cicero hadn't appeared yet. Nobody was listening to the speaker, who was talking monotonously about Macedonia. Conversations were being held at high volume, across several benches. People were laughing at jokes in here, too, but the laughter was oilier than outside. I did see one group in earnest conversation near one of the walls, gathered around a brazier; it was probably about business.

I heard later that Cicero's grave accusation hadn't caused any particular sensation. But when Catilina defended himself the people sitting nearby visibly edged away, as if he had a contagious disease. The benches around him were empty by the end of his speech.

The Senate has been astonishingly patient with him for a long time. On the other hand, those gentlemen have only benefited from him up to now. Look at the elections! Cicero's hysterical attacks alone would hardly have moved the Senate, but apparently there has been unrest among the slaves on some of the larger estates recently. Nobody knows any details about it, but the session today showed that they are trying to pin something like that on him. Now he really is facing arrest. Is he going to strike first?

9 November
Catilina has left Rome with two hundred of his supporters, many of them members of the aristocracy! He's on his way to Etruria now. This is finally civil war.

10 November
Catilina's departure is completely overshadowed by the latest news around town; acting on Pompey's instructions, his brother-in-law Quintus Metellus Nepos has arrived in the capital to stand for election as People's Tribune on the 13th. They say the news that Nepos was standing for election met with a cool reception in the Senate. Cato himself intends to become the other People's Tribune, certainly not in order to support Nepos. The gentleman from Asia is sure to be elected, of course. He must have brought whole baskets of 'envelopes' ashore with him in Brundisium. He has already been a guest of the Chamber of Commerce. C. is expecting him to call, too.

11 November
Fulvia: 'This Colonel Nepos is charming! Quite different from those youngsters who are always babbling about revolution, unless they happen to have a headache. How bored I am with my Curius

and his "if only we could"! Incidentally, Nepos assured me quite seriously that Pompey (he always says "the boss") has absolutely democratic convictions. He calls him the only democrat among all the Romans. Of course (to C.), you're one, too. It's simply shameless, the way our ladies are throwing themselves at him; they're tearing each other to bits! But he's displaying restraint. After all, there are women where he comes from, too. A Roman from one of the old families, hardened and victorious, over there in Asia where they've only got those fat, fastidious men – oh yes! His hips are so incredibly slender, you know. I told him: "You could use a bracelet as a belt; not one of mine, of course, but one of Mucia's!" He had a good laugh.'

Big debate in the barber's shop about the 'gentleman from Asia', who will no doubt convey all sorts of 'little desires of great Pompey', and whose activities 'will soon be felt' in Rome. However, some people also maintained that Catilina's movement might well cause him some headaches.

There's no doubt that Catilina's following has grown considerably since he left Rome. Everyone knows that he left his main conspirators behind, in town. In fact, some of them are still in their places in the Senate, quite unperturbed, such as Lentulus (the Shins), who has control of the police in his position as Praetor. The most capable of them, Cethegus, was one of the two gentlemen who appeared in Cicero's house on the morning of the 8th to bump him off, according to Cicero. Nevertheless, he daren't make any move at all against Cethegus. All the conspirators still move around the city in complete freedom, hold secret meetings and correspond with Catilina. And their squads are filling up more and more with slaves. Cicero won't go out without a cuirass under his toga, apparently. (He made a slit in his toga, so people can see how threatened he feels!) The Senate is showing the utmost negligence in the task of raising armies to deal with Catilina.

I heard this evening that the Forum was given quite a shock today. Two moneychangers' stalls were stormed by the crowd! Someone or other wanted to pay back a reclaimed loan to a bank and suddenly discovered that the interest was too high. Of course, he had been told the interest rate, but when he was informed of the total that had accumulated he remembered that his sister's son, who had taken out the loan, had fallen in the Asian campaign, and he made such a racket about it that he had to be shown the door. In an instant the whole Forum was packed with a raging crowd: nobody really knows where they came from. Since they couldn't get into the bank itself – it has excellent bronze doors and is adequately guarded – they stormed two small moneychangers' stalls next to it, destroyed all the furniture and raided the cashboxes. Everybody in the City is talking about it. In certain circles people are mainly perturbed by the fact that, according to the reports, the crowd *distributed* the money fairly (and, what's more, among those people present who had lost relatives in Asia or suffered some other losses as a result of the Asian campaign). Normal plundering would not have been so upsetting by a long chalk.

12 November

Wonderful autumn days. In the evenings I pay sad visits to all the places where I used to sit with my Caebio last year, when the leaves were falling. Miss him immensely, but resolved to remain strong and not to see him for the time being. Still, I often stand in front of the little shop at night and gaze through the window at the crucible and the colourful pots that have already been installed. Doesn't he ever go to look at the place? His brother must have told him the address.

Incidentally, when you see all the shops in this lane that have closed it's obvious how the war in Asia, bringing about the import of slaves, and the peace in Asia, bringing about a drop in demand for military supplies, have both devastated small businesses.

13 November

So Nepos and Cato have been elected People's Tribunes. And thus the conqueror of the East, the mighty Pompey, is becoming actively involved in politics. However, his man Nepos has been assigned a braking mechanism, in the person of Cato, which shouldn't be underestimated. Asian money has been flowing in torrents today (and some Roman money too, it seems). C. still hasn't had a glimpse of Nepos, the man with the slender hips. 'Someone' in Asia appears to be annoyed by the policies of the Democratic leadership.

Just today more disturbances broke out, which introduced an ugly note of discord in the elections for People's Tribunes. In the Lower Subura district some families were to be turned out of their homes because they hadn't paid the rent. But the district came together, and when Crassus' bailiff and slaves arrived (the tenements belong to him), they found the narrow lane, one of the steep, winding lanes that leads up to the Esquiline Hill, blocked by angry women, and ... donkeys. The crowd had fetched the animals from the stables of a haulage contractor who was at the election. At first the crowd, which incidentally included many slaves, was merely amused by the situation, and the inevitable exchange of words was met with resounding laughter, though not without anger as well. There were already a lot of drunks in the crowd as well, as always on Election Day. But when some mounted police arrived, the fun quickly turned into fury. It became a regular battle. The crowd, commanded by some young chaps who were later revealed to be members of Catilina's stormtroops and the Democratic Street Clubs, retreated into the house doorways again and again, so the inhabitants of the upper floors could empty all sorts of pots on the policemen, and soon roof tiles were raining down, accompanied by shouts of 'Spare the donkeys!' Strangely enough, this continued for quite some time without any bloodshed, but then there was a terrible incident. The police were just riding up the lane again when an old woman, a salted fish seller, dropped her basket of fish as she was running into a doorway. It rolled down the bumpy cobbles towards the riders. The fish couldn't have been worth more than a couple of assaria, but the old woman instinctively ran after her basket, in among the hooves of the horses as they charged towards her. Nothing left of her but a bloody mass. That was bad enough, but one aspect of the event which didn't appear to have any particular significance at the time proved to be even worse. The basket itself remained undamaged, which was, it must be said, a piece of bad luck, so the crowd discovered that it contained no more than three wretched salted fish. This news spread with incredible speed throughout the whole of the inner city within a few hours. Everyone grasped the point: it was a terrible comment on the authorities if the people were so badly off that they had to risk their lives for three salted fish. In the evening the Catilinarians declared that they wanted to hold a civic funeral for the woman and called upon the public to take part.

And it was only yesterday that the moneychangers' stalls in the Forum were stormed!

14 November

By utter coincidence I learnt something about the financial problems which are said to have arisen quite suddenly in the Catilinarian camp. Since I hadn't had any response to the offer I had made (without conditions) to Caebio (his brother could only tell me that he had looked incredulous), I decided to get in touch with him through Glaucos after all. Of course, I couldn't be completely open with Glaucos, so I just said Caebio owed me some money. Glaucos took me with him to the bar in Sandlemakers' Lane which is frequented by the squad Caebio belongs to. He didn't come, but I heard the people sitting around, most of them unemployed, say that they hadn't been paid for three days. The mood was rather dejected.

Glaucos curses the 'leadership' with all his might. He doesn't understand how there can be no money in the party funds. They are paid for their services, but they pay contributions, too. And they hold house and street collections. The events they organize bring in something, too. He would understand if he knew that these collections of petty cash, which seem so tangible to him, have no other purpose than to conceal the source of the large sums of money, which come from somewhere else entirely. But Glaucos just says dismally: 'Our bigwigs around the party cashbox live a little too well, that's all. Someone should let Catilina know what's happening. He doesn't know a thing about it.'

15 November

We're suffering from financial embarrassment again, too. The banks really do seem to have stopped their contributions. Has that Nepos had a hand in it? Is 'Pompey the Great' reaching out from Asia and slamming safes shut in the banks? It's obvious that he must be opposed to the uprising. Or is it really, as will certainly be claimed, that the ludicrous affair with the two moneychangers' stalls that were stormed has driven the banks to take such radical decisions? And Old Mouldy is in Sicily again!

Incidentally, you can see how unswervingly people 'at the bottom' still believe in Catilina and the victory of his cause from a very disagreeable argument I had today with Spicer, that most obstinate of bailiffs. He has a whole host of claims against us, mainly small ones like tailor's and butcher's bills, apart from the larger ones (objets d'art). It's interesting that the little people are now as bloodthirsty as horseflies before a storm. They are all confident that Catilina will win, which would mean a cancellation of debts, and of course they think, ridiculously enough, that butcher's bills would be included.

We're trying to sell the villa in Praeneste without our creditors getting wind of it. It's a matter of cash. I was able to sell a couple of Greek statues by roundabout means which were, incidentally, quite costly. But of course, that's nothing.

Spicer had a beautiful Hermes collected.

Things like that do get about!

Just before she set off for the country with Pompeya the old lady asked, for about the sixth time, to be repaid the 400 sesterces that she lent C. last month. Afterwards I told him: 'You have to repay your lady mother before you pay Spicer a thing.' He looked really worried for a minute. Luckily, he suddenly brought 20,000 sesterces home this evening. That's something, at least. Now I'm rather more prepared to face Spicer, who always gets here at eight in the morning.

Now, at a curiously late stage, Catilina has been declared a public enemy for having had himself proclaimed Consul in Etruria. A price has been put on his head, and the same applies to his followers, while Cicero's colleague, the Consul Antonius, has been dispatched against him with two legions. The Forum responded favourably to the appointment of Antonius. Shares, which had fallen ten points or more before Antonius was appointed, are rallying again, oddly enough. The slump is only continuing on the grain market. Heavy selling of corn.

The days pass unbearably slowly. C. spends a lot of time in the Forum on business. The property he owns is giving him a bellyache. He's terribly depressed. Says again that he'll keep away from any sort of politics.

16 November

Glaucos says you wouldn't believe some of the people who are in his organization. Senators, too. I appeared doubtful, in order to find out more, and he asked me whether I thought it possible that one of the two Consuls, for example, could be with them. That can only be Antonius, who certainly is said to be heavily in debt.

Two election district managers here. Would we like to stand for the post of Praetor next year? Ridiculous! Who's still going to trust us with the money to stand for Praetor? People only buy the position because of the province you get afterwards, but you really kill yourself buying it, and if you want to get a little something out of the province, to cover expenses at least, you face lawsuits for abuse of the position – if you're known as a Democrat in the Senate. C. was right today when he said: 'New villas, juicy positions, and Caelia,' (a pretty coquette he's after just now) 'we've got to put them out of our minds for the time being, Rarus.'

I know he's doing everything he can to shed some light on the abrupt and almost complete drying up of the money supply. As Alexander says, the banks closely associated with Crassus offer completely contradictory explanations. The only thing that's clear is that the City is moving further and further towards Cicero. And therefore towards reconciliation with the Senate, which is incidentally supposed to be showing some signs of flexibility. (?) Some banks are telling C.: 'Are you really still hoping for a moderate dictatorship headed by Catilina, moderated by you and your friends? Or do you think people are waiting for you to emerge as dictator, Mr Caesar of the Forum Café? Who will make the mob see reason again the minute he gets up there on the Capitol? Don't be naive!' And everyone's still talking about the unfortunate storming of the moneychangers' stalls.

16 November (night)

When I came home tonight there was a crowd gathered in the Subura, in front of our house. Riff-raff from the suburbs, a lot of youths among them, low-class elements. At least 200 people. They were shouting curses at C. A half-starved person, with traces of mud from the banks of the Tiber on his shoulders, scrambled up on to the statue of Prometheus next to the main entrance and yelled out the ridiculous old accusations; that they had been swindled in the elections, and so on. I had to go round the back to get into the house. I was coming through the atrium when I heard the main doors crash down and the mob storm in. C. was standing on the first floor landing – there was nobody else in sight, incidentally – wearing a kimono, as white as a sheet. At first he didn't register at all what I said to him. He was just listening to the terrible row downstairs. They were smashing up the atrium. I led him away, and he followed, looking back over his shoulder. Caelia was standing in the doorway to his bedroom, also very pale. We ran on past her; they were on the stairs by now. Still no trace of the servants to be seen. Down the back stairs. Through the colonnade. When we reached my room we could hear the crowd raging through the front garden. A terrible five minutes. Then they're outside the door. In the darkness I shove C. behind a filing cabinet. Then they're inside the room, waving storm lanterns from the atrium. He came in here, says a voice. He must be here. They kick the amphora over, and it smashes. Then they push the filing cabinet to one side. C. is standing there, cringing, with his kimono open at the front. Laughter, idiotic jokes. Not until now do I get punched.

'What have you done with the election money, you filthy cheat?' They've already dragged him out; the kimono is ripped to pieces. They spit at him. A bloke as tall as a tree holds him tightly with both hands and pushes him down, another pulls his clothes off, and then they beat him systematically. 'This'll – teach – you – to – steal,' they say, over and over again, always the same sentence, while they beat him.

Then they're gone at last. C. is crouching on the floor, wiping off the spittle with a scrap of his yellow kimono. I run out to get some smelling salts. In the meantime Caelia has put some clothes on; she wasn't touched, but I won't let her come down with me to see him. She goes, reluctantly. He won't go back upstairs for a long time, until I tell him she's gone. Officers come from the Praetor half an hour later. We don't want to press charges. I push some cash into the good people's hands, so they don't press charges.

And during the whole show not one of the slaves was to be seen; none of them stood by their master, none of them asked about him. In the morning I hear that they ran off into the riding school and waited there until the mob had gone. What times!

17 November
The atrium is completely wrecked. The slaves who were clearing up looked bewildered. We cancelled the clients' surgery, of course.

I took Caelia a letter before we ate. One can only hope she keeps her mouth shut.

Clodius came early in the afternoon to convey a formal apology on the part of the street clubs. He hasn't been here for weeks; he probably thinks it would compromise him to visit C. I led him through the devastated halls; he didn't look round.

He and C. spoke in private for two hours. Then I had to go and fetch Alexander. I went in with him.

C. was pacing up and down restlessly. Clodius was eating ginger from a small clay pot and only glanced up when Alexander entered. I had related the events of the previous night to Alexander; there was no further mention of them. What followed was one of the most astonishing scenes I have ever experienced.

C. initiated the discussion with the blunt statement that the people of Rome had had enough of the Forum's activities and were tired of ineffectual, deceitful electioneering. Entirely new forces were stirring in the bosom of the population. The revival of the street clubs proved that the Roman citizen was starting to take governance of the state into his own hands. The rampant disturbances in the capital might still lack methodical organization by an intelligent leadership, and wild, irresponsible elements might have become involved in the real people's movement here and there, but even the occasional excesses indicated that new life was breaking through here. This power had been underestimated in the leading Democratic circles, since they had only been concerned with the banks' activities or, at the most, with the intermediary role of the trade guilds, which had proved impotent. But the City and the trade guilds were not Rome. 'For too long we have persisted in the view,' he said, earnestly, 'that votes are weapons. It's true: votes are weapons, but not for the voter. For the voter, his vote is a commodity. It's a weapon for him the way a sword is a weapon for a blacksmith. He doesn't use it; he sells it. Once the customer has bought the sword, he can run the salesman through with it immediately. The election process is corrupt, through and through. It is of no more use to democracy.'

Alexander listened, speechless with amazement, as his old assertion – that the points of the Democratic programme could not be carried through by mere elections – emerged from C.'s mouth.

C. spoke with extraordinary firmness and clarity. The moment had arrived, he said, when the citizen of Rome, pushed to the edge of the abyss, would have to engage in politics for himself. The brute electorate could not engage in politics. The electoral herds would have to be shaped into a Democratic military unit. The street clubs, which Clodius had under control in any case, should comprise the shock troops. Alexander should try to round up the unemployed members of the trade guilds. The lists of the election district managers should be made use of. The managers themselves would still be furious. At the moment they were probably obliged to withstand mocking comments from the bigwigs of the trade guilds. Those gentlemen would stress that when election agreements are made they usually insist that the bribes for their members are paid in advance. But it was necessary to take advantage of precisely this indignation, felt by the simple voters at the fraudulent election system, and to explain to them how unscrupulously the fine City clubs, those Democratic gentlemen of the Forum, had cheated them. The treachery of the banks had to be mercilessly exposed. It was of the utmost importance not to be left behind by the Catilinarians. C. himself would establish contact with them. He informed Clodius and Alexander that he still had a very close relationship with the leadership, and with Catilina himself, and had even been of financial assistance to them since the election.

The question of armaments was considered at length. To a large extent the weapons of the old street clubs were still available; they had been carefully hidden at the time. There were weapons under the floorboards gnawed by rats, and weapons had been inserted in water pipes which no longer worked. The empty grain stores weren't *completely* empty, and the ragged scraps of clothing inside didn't just cover the bottom of the vats. Pomade-head was delighted at the thought that he could now rip down the walls of the gymnasium and have the well-greased swords brought out. There were plenty of weapons; some could even be given to the Catilinarians. (Every precaution would have to be taken about that, of course.)

It was agreed that the path being taken was a dangerous one. Under certain circumstances it would mean marching against the City. Therefore great caution was necessary. Crassus, at present spending time in Sicily because of his corn deals, was not to be told the details of the conspiracy at all, so he could always say he knew nothing about it. Due to his current unpopularity, C. should only meet the top people in the street clubs and ostensibly assume a quite neutral attitude. He said he would even try to establish contact with Cicero, if possible.

C. was pacing up and down the whole time, taking long strides, but I was the only one who knew why he didn't sit down.

I found the whole thing very ominous. While his ability to learn from everything and make something out of everything is breathtaking – this clarity of mind which permits him to perceive the true meaning of even the most unpleasant incidents and to evaluate them objectively in terms of political significance (how quickly his sharp gaze had discerned behind the few malicious rioters last night the powerful figure of the Roman citizen who had become restless and remembered his own strength) – still, his sudden decisions are really dangerous.

18 November

We're heading for a catastrophe, no doubt about it. Whenever the large sums of money intended for political purposes of one sort or another cease to pour in, as is now the case, there is an acute shortage of ready cash at home. Everything's built on sand; it's as simple as that. The 20,000 sesterces from the day before yesterday disappeared immediately. While the water system had to be repaired by grooms, because the plumber would only work for cash (in the High Priest's house!), the master of the house had to pacify estate agents who were demanding half a million by midday. C. had intended to drive to the country this morning to fetch Pompeya and his mother, but then a letter came from one of the large banks, and soon afterwards several gentlemen arrived and detained him for two hours. He sent me to Mucia with a letter, and she came in the afternoon. In the meantime C. had asked Clodius to pick up Pompeya. Under no circumstances was he to return with the ladies before midnight.

So then C. dined with Mucia (I don't like her: too old), and a man from the bank sat and waited in the atrium. In vain. C. emerged with a red face and sent him away with some lame excuse. Mucia is probably tired of flogging all the jewellery her Pompey sends. It's all so immoral.

And I'd like to know where C. got the 20,000. Servilia? But her husband's supposed to check every sesterce she spends these days, since she had that affair with the boxer. Cynthia is too angry. Tertulla? Maybe Tertulla.

19 November

Clodius didn't get back from Campania with the ladies until lunchtime today. Pompeya complained that Clodius only talked nonsense with her, and she sympathized with C. a lot because he looked overworked.

C. took me with him to a pontifical banquet where Mr Cicero was present. I was therefore able to observe his attitude towards C. quite well. They've known each other since they were children, and even today Cicero seems unable to overcome completely the respect for the aristocrat which he must have felt to an overpowering extent in those days. C. treats him with the charm he shows towards those who are his social inferiors (though not towards Alexander, incidentally: C. simply treats him as an important person). Even before the oysters were finished they were arguing mildly about literary issues; C. studiously backed down, though Cicero didn't appear completely content. The great man moved on to the subject of *The War in the East*.

'Twenty-two dictators toppled!' he said with satisfaction. 'The world is civilizing itself. Just bear in mind that nobody under those twenty-two kings enjoyed any legal rights. Any person could be executed at any time, without judicial proceedings, whether he was at the top or the bottom of society. That can't happen to anyone where the Roman Eagle has been planted. That bird is dishevelled and greedy, but it does have a sense of justice. There is no other state in the world where a citizen, whether he's of high or low ranking, can only be executed with the consent of all the other citizens.'

It's common knowledge that he laid the foundation of his wealth in Ephesus, so in financial terms he's totally dependent on the regulations Pompey implements in Asia. He hardly thinks of anything other than the size of the tax contracts. Then he went on to speak very highly of Asian culture. 'We have also captured books, works of art, artistic concepts and ideas. It is said that we have subjugated Asia. Let me tell you this; the important thing now is for us to subjugate ourselves to those we have subjugated, or rather, to their culture. Our good Pompey's staff is a little incomplete, in my opinion. It contains too many soldiers and economists, too few men of letters and artists. And I'm speaking from a practical point of view, mind you, as a realistic politician. Our Catos and Catulusses have monopolized the term. According to those gentlemen you can only be a realistic politician if you are good at throwing books away. Realistic politicians don't read books, except for account books.' Then he told a witty anecdote about old Catulus, the curator of the Temple of Jupiter who, faced with two gold statues of gods which Pompey had sent, simply chose the fatter one.

I would probably have appreciated his joke more if I had been allowed to dine with them. As it was, I had a greater appetite for the artichoke he was eating than the joke he was making. That man always reminds me of a sick fish. His mannerisms were lively enough, he was immensely amusing, but there was no life in his eyes. He listened to his own jokes, as it were, and suffered if they weren't appreciated sufficiently. He appeared to be decisive, too, but as though he were by no means sure that anyone would believe it of him. It was the same with the omniscience he exhibited; it was the omniscience of a financier who constantly fears he lacks one last piece of news, one last tip which might prove crucial. As he was eating a thrush, some of the asparagus tip stuffing fell on to his sleeve; immediately he pushed the dish away and plunged into the game fricassée. He treated C. in a very similar way to that thrush. Both were somehow sinister (because of what was inside). Of course, he knows that C. still has dealings with the Catilinarians, even now.

C. deftly brought the conversation round to the topics of the day. He warmly congratulated Cicero on his anti-Catilina speech of the 8th, and for three whole courses they discussed a couple of expressions it contained which exhibited grammatical audacity. Catilina's flight from Rome was mentioned. At this point Cicero made a significant comment: 'By leaving town, Catilina has also put himself out of the game. Nobody is negotiating with him any more. And negotiating was where his prospects lay, not action. Threatening an uprising may be profitable. Actually initiating one means ruin.'

C. expressed his regret that the Consul's services to the Republic had not been sufficiently appreciated by the Senate at all. As he did so he mentioned Fulvia's name, though I can't remember why at the moment, describing her as an old acquaintance, and Cicero responded to this with a sharp, mistrustful glance. Over the fruit Cicero casually threw in something about 'a little surprise which is in store for the Catilinarians and may soon cast its shadow over those gentlemen, who aren't exactly averse to worldly goods'. Unfortunately, he didn't reveal any details about this surprise, the shadow of which was certainly what brought C. there.

Finally, over the cheese, C. also touched fleetingly on the land question. Cicero gazed at him attentively as C. eloquently portrayed the unworthy situation of the small farmers. However, he also remained evasive and vague in his comments about this subject. He has already brought about the defeat of the Democratic land reform proposals once and appears not to have changed his views. He's far too friendly with the Sicilian corn companies.

(On the way home C. said: 'That chap's about as patriotic as an Etrurian shepherd. Did you see the look on his face when I brought up the land question?')

Farewells were accompanied by pronouncements of lasting friendship and mutual trust.

20 November

Clodius and Alexander have started their underground activities in the reorganized street clubs. The mood is said to be excellent. The slogan about the 'betrayal of the bankers' has been effective. Alexander reports: 'It's as though the people have had a weight taken off their shoulders. An unemployed tanner told me: "Weapons are what we need, not elections! When there are elections I have to sell them my vote or starve, and my whole family with me. With an iron bar I can beat their heads in". And a common coachman said: "Did Pompey conquer the East by holding elections?" Entirely new forces are stirring everywhere.'

The club members bear the cost themselves, as always. They sacrifice their last assaria, sell household effects, fall behind with the rent, etc., so they can rent assembly rooms and channel their dissatisfaction.

C. really has the insight of a genius. Just think: to be able to grasp the mood of the people instinctively on the basis of a sound thrashing! Ultimately all they displayed was their deep hatred for him, yet he managed to deduce that this hatred would enable the people to take political action which they would pay for themselves. At the precise moment when he was devoid of any resources he encountered these people (in large numbers!) who were prepared to fight without being paid, and even to pay for the materials to fight with! He saw that with a single glance! That's inspiration!

Incidentally, there had already been fraternization with the Catilinarians weeks ago. Nobody waited for instructions from the leaders, even to deliver weapons to the troops.

20 November (night)

Now I know where C. got the 20,000 from. There was a nasty scene. When I entered the library I saw the Shins there with a stranger who was covered in dust – obviously a military officer. C. was standing by the fire, his face as white as chalk. The Shins was toying with a paper knife and smiled in a way that sent shivers down my spine. C. turned to me and asked falteringly whether I remembered having sent a cheque for 22,000 sesterces to a certain address last week. Of course I said I did. The Shins looked across at the officer, who merely said: 'There seems to be no confidence in our success here.' So he's one of Catilina's people! His threat naturally troubled C. far less than that smile from the Shins, who frequents the Forum.

The fact that we haven't managed to discover anything about the 'surprise' Cicero predicted is also bad news. Not even Alexander knows anything. The trade guilds, usually his main source of information, have deliberately excluded him from their meetings recently, presumably because his close ties with us have become known.

21 November

I don't know how C. came up with the unfortunate notion that he should attend a meeting of the street club leaders. Doesn't he trust Pomade-head? C. certainly knew he wouldn't be there. We got the sedan porters to drop us two streets before the basement bar, and at first our reception was not unfriendly. Some organizational questions were being dealt with. C. gave some good advice, which was also well received. But then he offered to secure funds for the purposes under discussion, and strangely enough a terrible scene developed, quite without warning. Within two minutes the badly lit, stuffy bar came to resemble a madhouse. Suddenly all the mistrust, which had been accumulating towards C. was released. 'Is he offering money again?' they shouted. 'What kind of money is it?' – 'Everything's been fine so far without big money!' – 'He's only just arrived, and he's promising to raise filthy money again!' Some of them tried to intervene, but three or four people from the crowd charged towards C., intent on smashing their wine tankards over his head. It looked as though the events of a few nights ago were about to be repeated, but then a quick-witted club leader, Clodius' deputy, threw his tankard at the lamp and led us out into the street under cover of the ensuing darkness.

This extremely hostile reaction to an offer of financial assistance struck me as quite tragic. After all, I knew perfectly well that C. hardly has a few sesterces to pay his butcher's bill at the moment; he only held out the prospect of 'funds' from innate generosity, and in order to give himself airs!

His lucky touch seems to have deserted him these days.

22 November

The Catilinarians are doing everything they can to raise morale in the squads, which had fallen as a result of the ebb in funds. They are clever at milking small incidents for every advantage. The burial of the salted fish seller, who recently met an unhappy end in the Subura, has brought them general sympathy (which is not only manifested in their flourishing street collections). When I accompanied C. to a meal given by the Chamber of Commerce in the Forum today we had to make our way through the crowd which was taking part in the funeral procession. The Catilinarians had proclaimed the slogan: 'Everyone who has to live off salted fish should attend.' The procession was huge, a lot longer than any conquering hero has ever had. The fish basket was carried behind the urn. (The fact that the police force of the Democrat Cicero hadn't even seized the basket shows a quite incredible lack of understanding of the people!) The sight of the basket caused a great uproar of a quite singular nature. Although Crassus had naturally allowed the five or six families who were to be evicted to stay in their homes, they still took part in the funeral procession; it was as if they were also to be laid to rest, or at least led under the arches of the bridges over the Tiber.

We had to wait for over an hour before we could squeeze through a gap in the procession, and then a number of highly unflattering comments were hurled after our sedan chair, not because we had been recognized but merely due to its purple Senatorial trimmings.

The speech C. made at the banquet led to an unexpected consequence. Its tenor was: 'The capital of the world consists of a few government buildings surrounded by suburbs. A sea of dilapidated tenements, crammed with miserable wretches, encircles a couple of assembly rooms, temples and banks. The war was a crime. It brought about the downfall of 22 Asian kings and the people of Rome. Apart from yourselves, gentlemen, the capital of the world only houses the unemployed these days. And one of these days the employment they find will stagger you. The leading figures among the Democrats will not be able to preach reason to the masses for much longer. And there you sit, your fists clenched tightly around your purses! Tomorrow they'll be taken from you, *with* those fists. You're facing an armed uprising, gentlemen!' That was expressed so clearly that Manius Pulcher, the head of the Asian Trade Bank, felt obliged to respond: 'Your uprising is only armed to the extent that Mr Crassus supplies the arms, my dear man.' In reply C. embarked on another long portrayal of the misery suffered by the unemployed population, but there was general laughter when some of the bankers came to his aid with exact figures to back up his touching depiction. C. turned pale and abandoned the speech. But he was lucky. At that moment some light was cast on the situation in the city from a different quarter. A muffled noise had been audible from outside since shortly after the meal had begun. The salted fish seller's funeral procession was coming back from the burial, and via the Forum at that. Nobody allowed this to disturb the meal, since everyone had become so accustomed to disturbances. But suddenly the sound of clapping could be heard from the other side of the walls, and a cobblestone came flying through one of the narrow windows. It landed in the middle of the table, in a crystal glass bowl of tuna fish. Nobody at the banquet moved a muscle. Suddenly the roar of the vast masses became audible in that luxurious hall. Apart from that, nothing happened.

Outside the procession could be heard moving on. The exact words that were being chanted could not be made out. Only the stone in the crystal glass bowl allowed certain conclusions to be drawn about their content. By the time the servants had removed it, the Forum had become quiet again. More food was served, but there was no real appetite for it. The atmosphere improved somewhat after the cheese, and then something unexpected took place. (I have this from Mummlius Spicer, who has excellent connections: sons of big bankers who are in debt, and so on. It's a disgrace that I can only ever learn something about C.'s dealings behind his back!) After the cheese Pulcher took C. discreetly by the arm, led him into another room and said, in the presence of several other gentlemen: 'You must have perceived that your threats about an uprising had little effect on us. You say your clubs, which incidentally appear to be of an illegal nature, are armed. I wonder how they are armed? There is no need for you to reply. I'm simply pursuing my train of thought. You want financial assistance for those elements which will guarantee peace and order – with weapons, of course. But peaceful and orderly people are granted neither economic control of both Asias, nor land for settlement purposes, nor state credit to buy slaves, nor contracts in connection with the resettlement of the unemployed. Weapons are simply a luxury for peaceful and orderly people. Some of our

friends here get nervous when a moneychanger's stall is stormed, a
fishwife is buried, or a speech is made against bankers; but not all
of them get nervous. Some of them would also, subject to a halfway
verifiable accounting system, supply financial support for restless
people who are opponents of the existing order; I say subject to
a halfway verifiable accounting system because the economic
situation at the moment is far from rosy. To put it bluntly, my
dear man; you really must clear up your private dealings, which
are said to be rather considerable, on your own. You should never
mix the two; that's never a good idea.' C. was apparently beside
himself with rage when he left. But he didn't totally reject the offer,
it seems.

23 November
A ray of light; up until now the Senate has stood as steadfast as
a tower in the face of the dark storm which has begun to rage
so violently through the valley of the seven hills. Now the tower
appears to be wobbling.

Information has leaked out about the proposals which the
gentleman from Asia will make when he takes office as Tribune
(on the 10 December). They'll certainly be sensational; he intends
to demand that Pompey be recalled to Italy, with his Asian legions,
to reestablish order. The big cheeses are said to have met in their
sedan chairs while visiting each other. Widespread trembling. At
least 5,000 pounds of fat was set wobbling. There was an animated
conference of the Cato clique at Catulus' country estate to discuss
the sudden change in the situation. The cry of terror from our
elders is: who will save us from the saviour?

23 November (evening)
Am thunderstruck. *Caebio has vanished.* He didn't say a word to
his mother. But she's sure he's with Catilina's troops in Etruria. I
demeaned myself to such an extent that I returned to the granary.
I just *had to* know for certain. Rufus has gone, too.

I knew it before the clerk told me.

They had both been dismissed two weeks ago. The administration of the granary has engaged slaves in their place.

It's all over.

24 November
The Senate is preparing to strike a deadly blow against Catilina! As from last night the man of the people is Mr Cato of the Senate Party! Just imagine!

There was an extremely serious row between C. and Crassus very early this morning. Old Mouldy steamed in, obviously having been up all night, and had C. brought out of his fencing lesson. 'How long have you been back in Rome?' asked C. in a hostile tone. Crassus didn't say a word in reply. Before they had even passed through the atrium he explained, gasping for breath, that a night session of the Senate had been held, and Cato had pushed through the reintroduction of *corn handouts*. 'Corn handouts, now?' said C., incredulous. 'Yes,' said Old Mouldy, looking round for a chair, 'and I'm tired; I've been standing at the corn exchange all night. The Senate didn't reach a decision until 3 in the morning. Can I have something to drink?' – 'Corn handouts! And you don't tell me until now, 8 in the morning?' C. yelled at him. Old Mouldy blinked. 'I had my hands full with the goings-on at the corn exchange, I tell you. The price of corn plunged from 20 to 2 – do you think it's easy, handling something like that?' Suddenly he got furious. 'Why do I have to tell you about it at all?' he defended himself indignantly. 'Why weren't you in the Senate yourself? If you're going to organize a coup you don't hang around brothels, you hang around the stock exchange!' – 'It's also possible to organize politics,' said C., grimly, 'not just business.' They were both very pale as they entered the library; I followed them. There was a terrible argument. Crassus admitted that he had seen the decision coming. As it turned out he had actually been speculating on a slump in corn and had therefore made a fortune from it. C. accused him of having kept the whole thing secret from him for purely commercial motives, despite it being of immense political importance. Old Mouldy denied that and argued that he had only taken the steps he did take after having visited Cato. C. gave a start. 'When did you visit Cato?' he asked. Old Mouldy fixed him with a malevolent gaze. 'Just before you did,' he replied. 'I went for the sake of the movement,' shouted C. 'So did I,' responded Old Mouldy. C.: 'So you must know that he didn't give way. Cato wouldn't budge an inch as far as concessions were concerned!' Old

Mouldy: 'Not then, before the election! After all, he knew the City would never really have Catilina elected Consul.' C.: 'So why has Cato given way now?' Old Mouldy had taken a seat. He studied C. with a judicious eye, in a not particularly friendly manner. 'You're hardly in the picture at all, my dear Gaius Julius,' he said. 'He's given way because Colonel Nepos has been elected People's Tribune, as you may have heard in the brothel, and because they're scared to death of Pompey.' C. remained silent for some time. Apparently he hadn't taken the Senate's agitation about the rumours regarding Pompey so seriously. 'So you were never really serious about Catilina, were you? Not for a minute?' he asked, his voice devoid of all expression. 'Yes I was,' said Old Mouldy, quickly, 'but it doesn't make any difference to the price of corn whether it's Catilina or the Senate who doles out the corn. It falls in any case.' C. suddenly spun round on his heel to face him. He was in a towering rage. 'But that means,' he screamed, 'that Catilina falls, too! It makes just as little difference to the people whether they get the corn from him or from Cato! And what happens to us then? And don't imagine we'll be able to extricate ourselves from the whole business just like that. Now everything is going to fall to pieces, and then there'll be an investigation.' Crassus appeared to take the point. 'Of course, it's hard on Catilina now,' he said, weakly. 'It was a good move by Cato, the old drunk.' There was a pause. When C. spoke again it was as if an old man were speaking, his voice was so hollow. 'I'm ruined,' he said. 'I've been buying land,' Old Mouldy woke up. 'What have you been buying?' he asked, as if he couldn't believe his ears. 'Land,' C. repeated. Old Mouldy seemed dumbfounded. 'By the great Styx,' he murmured. 'What did you think you were up to?' – 'But the land question *has* to be tackled,' said C., in an attempt to defend himself. Old Mouldy merely repeated: 'By the great Styx,' and his tone was not completely lacking in sympathy. 'And now there'll be an investigation. I got rid of my land, as much as I could, so I could get away if need be. The investigation will be extremely dangerous; Pompey will insist on that. You'll have to be appointed Praetor. If an investigation takes place, we have to lead it.' – 'That'll cost ten million,' said C., sullenly. 'Five,' said Old Mouldy, immediately. 'It would have cost five yesterday; today it'll cost ten,' said C., stubbornly, 'because everyone knows it's essential to us now.' – 'Catilina isn't completely out of the running yet,' his fat companion squirmed, 'things could still change dramatically. He's got an army, after all.'

Having to listen to all that made me feel sick. As far as I was concerned, the army meant Caebio.

25 November

When I got to Caebio's apartment yesterday morning his little brother told me that his mother had already gone to the halls where corn was to be handed out in the evening. He went with me to look for her.

In the enormous yards incredible noise and devastating confusion prevailed. Tens of thousands of people were looking for their issuing counters. Corn handouts had been suspended for years, so nobody could remember exactly how it was organized. Sweating officials were posting boards with district numbers.

Everyone was shoving each other, children were crying, and the police were stretching out ropes to cordon off the streams of people. What bodies! What faces! That was hunger for you. That was the whole of Rome.

It took us hours to find Caebio's mother. She was standing there, her big shopping bag under her arm, squeezed in among people who lived in the same district. But she couldn't tell me Caebio's address or anyone else who could put me in touch with him. He had simply gone to ground in Catilina's army. And every ladle full of corn that would be handed out there was a blow that would rain down on him from a sword.

As I was leaving a rumour was spreading among the crowd that the corn wouldn't be given out until the following morning, perhaps not until lunchtime. The stockpiles hadn't been filled up yet. But I didn't see anyone leave their places.

A light autumn drizzle was falling. Soaked and silent, the vast crowd stood there in the yards in front of the corn halls, waiting. I was deeply troubled as I returned to the city, which seemed empty.

25 November (evening)

A somewhat nervous mood spread throughout the City today, the fear that one of these days Catilina might not be able to keep the slaves among his troops under control. The corn handouts are sure to deplete his ranks to a certain extent. Then he'll have to fill the gaps with slaves. And a rather dangerous mood has been brewing among the slaves for some time now. The large number of cheap Asian slaves has pushed down their standard of living.

One clear warning sign has appeared; the large trade guilds are forming a united front against Catilina. They are seething with rage about the disguised assurances he has given the slaves. Cato is said to have reintroduced corn handouts for the unemployed as a concession following long negotiations with the trade guilds.

Asian stocks are falling.

25 November (late evening)
Old Mouldy has played an outrageously dirty trick on us. He pulled out of Catilina's election campaign right at the beginning, once he heard that the trade guilds weren't on board and were negotiating direct with the Senate for corn handouts. He simply changed course and embarked on rather distasteful corn specu-lation. But what he's done to us now tops the lot.

This evening C. was determined to see the bankers (the Pulcher group) and, in view of the predictable demoralizing effect of the corn handouts on the street clubs, to dictate new conditions for the continuation of preparations for a coup. The whole thing has become much too dangerous now. A week ago in the Chamber of Commerce C. was taught that it's a mistake to threaten the City with an uprising just now. Now he should threaten that the uprising will be abandoned. He went to see Manius Pulcher in the Forum this evening. I went with him, carrying the documents, most of which related to the land purchases. Pulcher seemed to be expecting us; he had other gentlemen from the City with him in his office. Everyone sat down, and then C. spoke in a business-like tone, without any preliminaries: 'You have shown a friendly interest in the success of the Democratic Street Clubs, which have reappeared. Now the leaders of these clubs fear that a section of the membership will be more or less demoralized as a result of the Senate's corn handouts. It is not uncommon for the political initi-ative of an individual, often the most valuable sort, to be hampered by severe debts. The survival of the clubs depends on whether or not, now that the remaining members are to risk *life and limb*, they can be made to feel that the victory of democracy would also be their victory. Like the businessmen you are, you have expressed the understandable wish to see detailed accounts of the sums required by the clubs, the purposes they will be employed for, etc. I have taken steps to place some figures at your disposal. Here is a list of the obligations which have to be met most urgently.'

Pulcher, who had been listening to him with an impassive face, nodded. C. took the folder of documents from me and looked through them briefly, extracted a list of his own land purchases and handed it to the banker. Pulcher took the sheet of paper and studied it in silence. Then he looked up and said, in a voice not entirely free from emotion: 'And without these slum clearance schemes, which are incidentally very extensive, you do not believe that real interest in propagating democracy can be expected from this quarter?' As he spoke he passed the sheet on to the other gentlemen. 'No,' replied C. with conviction.

Pulcher gazed at him fixedly. He is a short fat man with a face as white as chalk and a bald head. He looked at C. as if he were an arthritic bone in his toe. When he spoke again his tone was brusque. 'So you intend to cancel all the activities unless we finance your private speculation. Is that how things are?'

C. stared back at him for a minute. Then he said stiffly: 'No. I appear to have handed you the wrong piece of paper.' – 'No doubt,' said Pulcher dryly, taking the sheet from the hands of his business partners, who hadn't said a word up to then, and pushing it back to C. across the table. C. stood up. He had an admirable air of indifference. He said: 'It is my impression that this is hardly the ideal moment for a serious, business-like exchange of views. Such conversations can only be profitable if they take place in a friendly atmosphere, which might well be lacking here.'

'Perhaps,' said Pulcher, though he remained in his seat and slowly continued. 'But do spare us a little more of your apparently extraordinarily valuable time. Up to now it has been our pleasure to converse with the politician. Now we feel compelled to have a word with the private man. As it happens we are by no means uninterested in the, ah, inventory which you inadvertently showed us. A series of promissory notes, bearing your name, came into our possession yesterday. They were transferred to us by Mr Crassus and amount to a total of 9 million sesterces. With the utmost dismay we now learn that despite your extremely high financial obligations you have also entered into land speculation on an enormous scale. Perhaps you would care to offer some explanation?' C. stood there as if he had been struck by lightning. Old Mouldy had drawn his own conclusions from C.'s cry for help. He had deserted C.!

I don't think C. took in the closing moments of the conversation with any real clarity. Pulcher addressed him as if he were an employee. He curtly instructed him to continue the preparations for the bolstering of democracy that he had mentioned initially 'in whatever form you wish', and what's more, 'by the 10th of the 12th at the latest'. C. didn't dare say a word. His land speculation is catastrophic. I'm sure he has completely lost track of the land he bought, and how much of it there is. Of course, he's only paid a deposit, and he probably used Mucia's money for that. And apart from that, he must have taken out huge loans!

The 10th of the 12th is the day Metellus Nepos takes office as Tribune.

26 November

And yet now he's on great form again! Half an hour in the riding school in the morning, and in the clients' surgery he's once more the grand lord. As if there were no butchers' bills, no Mummlius Spicer, no preparations for an armed uprising and no bankers!

He's got real nerves! It's fantastic, the way he continues with preparations for armed uprising in the poorer quarters, although he himself must regard an armed uprising as hopeless, at least since Cato's corn handouts began.

Took a letter from C. to Alexander. He and Publius Macer, our confidential agent among the district leaders, are organizing the armed uprising from his meticulously clean little room. Macer, a tall character apparently made of dried leather, was sitting on a pile of books and listing the wine cellars which had been chosen as distribution centres for the individual streets. The two of them are collaborating with Clodius' street clubs to form armed cadres from those members of the trade guilds who are in favour of active opposition and those of the electorate whose names are down on the lists kept by the Democratic Election Committee. They have recently had some capital at their disposal, which has considerably strengthened discipline among the combat troops.

Alexander and Macer are able to work without arousing suspicion in Crassus' house, which is big and grand though with a rather restless atmosphere. But I could tell by the way Alexander talked about Cato's corn handouts ('That fellow's unerring instinct for mastery has led him to choose just the corn out of the Democratic demands for *land and corn*; that way he keeps the people tied to him – giving them land would make them independent'), that he no longer believes with complete confidence in the coup he's preparing.

C.'s letter must have contained instructions not to act too rashly, because Macer made the disgruntled comment: 'Every day it's something different. Today: don't be too rash, let's be on the safe side. Last week: it's going too slowly. There's never any set date. Well, a bloodbath needs just as much organization and takes just as much preparation as all the other sorts of baths the gentlemen like to wallow in.' When he caught sight of my astounded gaze he added dryly: 'I hope it's clear up at the top that something like this can involve thousands of families in all sorts of ways.'

Alexander's comment left me with no doubt that he still remembers the election. I was very worried when I left.

26 November (evening)
On C.'s request went with Paestus, Clodius' secretary, to a bar where a meeting of one of the street clubs was being held. Our papers were checked at the door. There was no drinking during the meeting, which is unheard of in Rome.

Topic under discussion: should we let slaves join the clubs? One speaker expressed the view that only isolated individuals should be allowed to join. Another, who was obviously unemployed, said angrily that slaves never stay where they belong and always ask for more. He said he was a citizen of Rome and would never fight side by side with slaves.

A tall, pale, haggard-looking man, who was hardly visible through the bar room fog, said bluntly: 'Stop all this stupid nonsense about the slaves, will you, as long as we're being bled dry by the same leeches as the slaves!'

But he was immediately shouted down. As we left we could see half a dozen people bent over him, arguing with him furiously. At the door the leader of the club assured us that the mood was good. He claimed that the Senate's corn handouts hadn't caused any disruption. The members had adopted Alexander's catchphrase, that they shouldn't let anyone throw corn in their eyes, with great enthusiasm. Work was what they wanted, not handouts.

C. had wanted to know how the clubs were bearing up to the blow of corn handouts. His reaction to my report was rather indifferent. He has become completely languid once again. He reclines in the library all day, reading Greek romances.

27 November

I had a strange conversation with an unemployed mason in the old district behind the vegetable market. Another of the seven-storey tenement blocks had collapsed. A squad of slaves was clearing the rubble away. The man was sitting on the lower half of a shabby kitchen cupboard, watching some of the surviving tenants search through the rubble for the remains of their belongings. Through the clouds of dust we saw an old woman punch one of the slaves in the face as he was shovelling, because she felt he wasn't being careful enough. Then the man beside me suddenly spoke. 'They're still fighting among themselves,' he said. 'As long as that keeps up, they'll never get any better houses than those. The poor devils are doing my job; I can't earn an assarius in this town any more. But I'm off to join Catilina, because I've heard he wants to join forces with the slaves. We'll never get the better of the scum in the Forum and the Capitol unless we join forces with the slaves. Everything, election and revolution, is just a swindle unless that happens, nothing but a swindle.' I was in a very thoughtful mood as I made my way home.

Went to see Cethegus in his home and managed to arrange for a courier to be sent to the Catilinarian camp with an inquiry about Caebio; to be on the safe side I put down Rufus' name too. Now I feel a bit calmer. At least something's being done.

I was just in the middle of a fencing lesson with Glaucos when news arrived about a big disturbance that had broken out in the halls. In the last few days the Catilinarians had been calling on everyone whose name wasn't down on the list of people entitled to handouts to go into the halls and demand some corn. The lists are old, and unemployment has grown tremendously since the Asian war. By five o'clock in the afternoon the yards were so full of people that the police who had been called to provide assistance couldn't get through. Dozens of people were trampled underfoot, including women. There were reports of two officials from the corn administration also being attacked by the enraged crowd. By night the word was that they'd been killed. Four of the enormous vats were completely emptied by the crowd.

The street clubs from two districts are working hand in glove with the Catilinarians, and once again numerous slaves were seen during the riot, behaving particularly violently.

28 November
The bloody events in the halls will further radicalize the masses. Nobody talks about 'Cato, the man of the people' any more. The total inadequacy of the state provisions has become apparent. The fact is that almost half of Rome is unemployed.

Mummlius Spicer is full of complaints about the increasing resistance he and his colleagues are faced with in the working-class districts. He feels the effects of Catilinarian agitation whichever way he turns. People no longer hand over the things he has come to collect in silence. He sat down in the atrium, exhausted, and said: 'I much prefer impounding things here, I can tell you.'

28 November (evening)
A big row in the Catilinarian camp, according to Glaucos. In a bar at the cattle market, a place where the 22nd Squad congregates, a Syrian slave was given a sound thrashing because he claimed that after the Roman legionaries conquered his home town, while they were raping the Syrian women they'd jump up and salute when an officer went past. That was four days ago. Since then nine squads have demanded that slaves be excluded. There is constant brawling, and the slaves, some of whom are better fed than the starving unemployed workmen, don't come out of it at all badly. The leaders are trying to get across the point that they don't believe

the uprising can work without the slaves, which is absolutely true. But on this point they encounter huge resistance from their free members. The slaves, on the other hand, are indignant, especially about Statilius' comment that the plebeians of Rome are not yet in such a bad way that they would be prepared to act in unison with the slaves.

I had a long talk with Glaucos about it. I may be a slave, but I regard myself as far from being in 'such a bad way' as this bankrupt aristocracy and its seedy, idle plebeians.

29 November

A warning from Alexander. He told C. today: 'I have received absolutely reliable reports that the Shins received a letter from Catilina stating that the uprising is only feasible if there is simultaneous emancipation of the slaves. We can never go along with that. It is a falsification of our concept and would brand it a crime.'

C. side-stepped the issue. He admitted that Catilina would be capable of something like that, because he had lost his grip in moral terms and was willing to do simply *anything*. However, the Roman citizens in his squads would never be a party to such a fantastic scheme.

But when Alexander had left C. did seem very flustered. He walked round the garden for over an hour, very disturbed. When Fulvia turned up for lunch he was unusually monosyllabic. I discreetly pumped her for information. Some time ago she was at a small banquet where prominent Catilinarians, whose names she would prefer not to mention, argued about the slave question – apparently after a considerable amount of wine had been consumed. The gentlemen expressed doubts about the Roman people's ability to deal with the Senate by themselves. The old misgivings; the military forces, under Senatorial officers, would receive double pay to put down every disturbance; half the population consisted of tenants, leaseholders and other people in debt to Senators, as could be seen from every election; even the slaves would defend their masters, unless an uprising held out some hope for them, and there were five slaves for every Roman citizen. So the slaves had to be won over, they had to be at least promised their freedom, later on there would be time to think again, etc. But weren't the slaves foreigners? That's true; they weren't citizens, as long as they hadn't been naturalized, and the Romans were citizens, as long as they hadn't been denaturalized, and the worst form of denaturalization was death, e.g. in an unsuccessful uprising. 'What about Lucullus' beautiful palace? He's brought so many slaves back to Rome – will his beautiful palace on the Pincian Hill belong to slaves one day?' asked Fulvia, nervously. C. reassured her, although I could see quite clearly that he was alarmed. 'If the common man can't engage in political activity without acting in unison with the slaves, then he simply won't be able to engage in any political activity,' he said, absentmindedly. When I agreed, Fulvia, who's very nice but a bit stupid, asked me: 'Aren't you in favour of slaves being freed, either?' I assured her that I was far from being in favour of it. C. looked over at me, and added: 'If our house slaves were to turn on us today, they'd do away with Rarus before they did away with Caesar, my dear.' I'm afraid I had to agree with him about that.

Fulvia soon left, a little offended by our taciturn mood, and C. went to lie down. He complained of severe diarrhoea, and we borrowed two doctors from Crassus.

29 November (late evening)
Although it's now 2 o'clock, I can still see a light in the library, where C. has decided to sleep tonight. He is having Aristotle read to him. The doctors say his stomach disorder is only a result of excitement.

He must have realized by now that the 'armed uprising' operation could be transformed into a bloody uprising of the slaves at any moment. Now that more and more slaves have been admitted into the Catilinarian ranks only the most desperate of the original volunteers remain. The street clubs have kept clear of any involvement with slaves, of course, but if it came to an uprising they would never be able to retain command. And what would be the real consequences if the slaves were to break free of all restraints of reason and morality? The citizens of Rome may be hungry now, but if the slaves stop working, the citizens will simply starve to death. How could the capital be supplied with provisions, even for a fortnight, without the large estates which are manned by slaves? Not one of the corn supply ships could sail without slaves! It's all completely insane!

Where could Caebio be? Surrounded by filthy rabble, in a barracks in Faesulae? In a tent, with the rain leaking in? It's bound to be raining in Etruria.

30 November

A merchant from Gaul came to the clients' surgery today. He had a letter of recommendation from fat Favella of Cremona, and he told us at some length about the hopes still being placed in Catilina by not only the Po valley but also the whole of Cisalpine Gaul. C. talked to him in private for half an hour.

In the morning he sent me to take a letter to – Cicero. He tore it open in my presence, skimmed through it with a peculiar expression comprised of surprise, fear and triumph, and then dashed off to his secretary's office without paying any more attention to me. What was in that letter?

The tension in town is becoming unbearable. All the indications point to an imminent explosion. At nights the Catilinarian squads drill on the Campus Martius, and the Democratic Street Clubs have been armed to the last man for some time now. Of course, Mr Cicero's police are well aware of that. Strangely enough though, Mr Cicero seems prepared to content himself with exposing the occasional plot to assassinate him. The Senate, on the other hand, is getting worked up. Apparently it's putting increasing pressure on Cicero with each day that passes; Cato would like nothing more than to see the 'whole fuss' disposed of once and for all, particularly since then the demands of Pompey, who is getting more and more imperious, could be resisted more firmly. In fact, nobody really understands why Cicero doesn't strike. Is it Nepos, the gentleman from Asia, that's holding him back? After all, the underground struggle in the Forum has started up again now, and the brand new People's Tribune, with a folder full of tax farming contracts, is playing a significant part in it. The attitude of the City is completely inscrutable. Some of the banks financed the Catilinarian coup initially, only to back out smartly, at which point another group of financiers promptly stepped in, no doubt with quite different aims. And now people say that Pompey's man, of all people, has spread his protective wing over Catilina. Why else should the Consul Antonius be dispatched to engage Catilina's army in Etruria, when everyone knows Antonius is a Catilinarian! And to top it all, despite rumours which become more menacing each day about the Catilinarians (and the Democratic Street Clubs) preparing for an uprising, on the stock market Asian shares are climbing again. I'd like to see anyone make sense of that!

1 December
No news from Caebio. Feeling desperate.

Thinking about Caebio a lot these days. Politically, too. What do I know about this person, who meant so much to me? What do we know, in these big houses, breathing the same air as the great figures of the world, about the hundreds of thousands of people in this city? Nothing. I'm just a slave. But although he's a Roman citizen, a free man, he had to depend on me for every little thing, just because I get tips. Of course, he is inferior to me in terms of education. But that wasn't what destroyed our love; it was the fact that I didn't buy him the perfume shop in time. The unemployed have no hope apart from Catilina. Yesterday I still thought only the most desperate elements could remain with Catilina, but perhaps that amounts to hundreds of thousands of people? Maybe this Catilinarian movement is a mass movement after all? Just think: Mr Cicero exposes plans for a dictatorship, the trade guilds make loud accusations, Catilina touches on the slave question, and yet despite the enormous rewards offered for information against the conspirators – 100,000 sesterces and freedom for slaves, 200,000 sesterces for free men – no witnesses have come forward. And everyone knows about the conspiracy! Does that mean they are all involved in it?

The Catilinarians are expected to strike virtually every day. The reason given for the delay is that Clodius hasn't finished his preparations. The truth of the matter is that he just can't get the go-ahead from C. to start things moving yet.

1 December (evening)
Old Mouldy was here again today, trying to persuade C. to stand for the office of Praetor (State Judicator). C. still isn't showing much enthusiasm. That tells me he still hasn't abandoned his land

speculation, amazingly enough. He doesn't want to take public office because members of the Senate are forbidden to engage in such business activities, and that does make engaging in such business activities harder. Old Mouldy appears to be more deeply involved in the affair than we are, officially. After all, everyone knows we were in no position to support Catilina financially. But Crassus was. He's said to have loaded cash on ships, but: 'He can't take half of Rome with him;' said C. coolly, 'and those miserable wooden sheds of his would inevitably collapse if he tried to move them by ship.'

Old Mouldy has withdrawn from every sort of political activity. His nerves are completely ruined. He certainly never gets a full night's sleep these days. He's afraid of the Senate's police and of Catilina's gangs. He's even afraid of the street clubs now, because he knows very well that they've taken up arms *Against the Rich*, as their slogan goes. He's afraid of Pompey, and he's afraid of his competitors in the City. But most of all – of the slaves, of the slaves! He wakes up his librarian in the middle of the night and sits there on the edge of his bed, sweating and talking until dawn about life after death.

He can't be the only one in the City who feels like that. But still, it's incredible! They're still paying up …

2 December

Apparently the Senate's furious! It seems that Cato presented them with exact details of the funds poured into the Catilinarian movement by the City, even after the election!

Disturbing news from Capua, too. There have been outbreaks of unrest in the gladiatorial training centres there. Everyone in town was talking about it today. You could even hear quite ordinary people saying: 'If it comes to civil war there'll be an uprising of the slaves, and that'll be the end of us.'

2 December (evening)

Now the City is trembling. They've been shocked to the core by the cry: 'The slaves are coming'. The Chamber of Commerce convened a meeting and decided to hold an investigation to determine which of its members had provided funds for Catilina 'and movements associated with him'. Of course Pulcher and his group, which has merged together incidentally, weren't present.

3 December

And now the blow really has been struck, but not by Catilina's side – by 'Cicero's'!

At 4 o'clock in the morning a delegation of Gallic merchants was stopped by the police on Aemilius Bridge and their luggage searched. It was found to contain letters and documents of a highly treasonable nature, signed by known Catilinarians.

An hour later Cethegus' house was searched, and a large cache of arms was discovered. The conspirators were arrested as they lay in their beds and taken to the Temple of Concord, where Cicero had called a meeting of the Senate. He presented the Senate with correspondence between the Shins and Catilina, apparently containing details about the inclusion of Capuan gladiator slaves in the uprising. The documents are being kept confidential for the moment. In any case, in view of the incriminating evidence Lentulus and Cethegus were unable to offer any denials. They were handed over to the custody of individual members of the Senate until further notice.

Which is why Statilius was brought here under armed escort around lunchtime; he had been put in C.'s charge!

C. himself arrived back home this afternoon, very pale and exhausted. He didn't eat anything or go to see Statilius.

But it seems that his name wasn't mentioned at the Senate meeting (neither was Crassus'). The feeling seems to be that they aren't so deeply involved.

Unfortunately I haven't been able to put C.'s discussion with the Gallic merchant out of my mind all day.

3 December (night)

Five districts are occupied by troops. The soldiers (one legion, made up of farmers' sons from Picenum), are bivouacked in the streets. They also cook in the streets, so their field kitchens are quickly surrounded by the rabble. The soldiers are good natured, or embarrassed, or even scared, and they readily share their bean soup. But the respectable people won't accept anything, and I've even heard that they knock the food the soldiers have given their hungry children out of the kids' hands.

4 December

Yesterday evening the most amazing rumours were buzzing around town. They were surpassed by the contents of the confiscated documents, which Cicero made public at about 8 o'clock. The huge crowd standing in front of the display cases and posters was told that *fuses and sulphur* had been found in Cethegus' house, along with precise plans for fires. Rome was to be set ablaze at twelve points!

Glaucos swears that this claim is a mere fabrication. And that the police themselves planted the stuff in Cethegus' house (no more than enough to fill a handcart, incidentally). He says the Gallic merchants had been given the documents by an agent provocateur, and that they are forgeries. Everything was faked and planted. But the letters contained a draft proclamation emancipating the slaves! Now nobody who has even a bed to call his own can support the conspirators any more. Every craftsman has his slaves.

By the evening it was also being claimed that there was a plan to block the water supply.

In the street clubs indescribable confusion reigns. Alexander called a meeting of the leaders to explain that the whole project had to be abandoned, because there was undeniable evidence that the Catilinarians had also armed the slaves in the city. Only six of the 21 leaders turned up. What's more, two of them initially expressed the opinion that they should fight it out anyway, slaves or no slaves. The others assured Alexander that their members would get rid of their weapons this evening, even without any instructions.

Apparently the Catilinarian squads have also been completely paralysed by Cicero's revelations.

Clodius has gone into hiding outside Rome.

This morning the names of C. and Crassus did appear among those involved in the conspiracy. A certain Vettino, a notorious police informer, appeared in front of the Quaestor and accused C. of being one of the financiers.

C. went to the Senate again this afternoon. It seems that Catulus called on Cicero very early this morning (at the Capitol – the

Consul slept there instead of going home), with an urgent request for C.'s arrest. But Cicero is said to have refused.

C. is convinced that there isn't any evidence against him.

And he came home in one piece this evening. He told Pompeya, who was very upset, that when someone tried to denounce Crassus in the Senate he was shouted down the moment he mentioned the name. A lot of the Senators are in debt to Crassus. And he was able to clear himself of any suspicion, too. 'I have,' he said, 'too many creditors.'

But things do look bad for those who have been arrested. The city fathers want to see blood this time. Of course, Cicero refuses to consider death penalties at all; he maintains repeatedly that they would be unlawful without the approval of the People's Assembly and would only rebound on his own head. But it seems that Cato and five associates have gone to see him now, and they must have some means of applying pressure.

They were still talking in the atrium when Manius Pulcher was announced. He entered with Afranius Cullo, perhaps the biggest financier in the City, whose name is hardly ever mentioned but whose opinion is considered crucial in financial circles. Three other known figures from tax farming companies were also with them, all very pale and nervous.

They withdrew to the library. The gentlemen came out with their request without any beating about the bush. It was really amazing. They suggested quite bluntly that C. should appear on behalf of the arrested conspirators in the decisive Senate session tomorrow, and prevent the death penalty being imposed at all costs! At first C. was very calm. He reminded them of the serious offences the people had committed, and that public opinion was not in their favour. Afranius Cullo, a grizzled little man in his fifties, let him have his say and then just repeated: 'The death penalty must be avoided at all costs. It would be the final victory for the Senate!' C. sent me out of the room.

It was an hour and a half before the gentlemen left. When I entered the library after their departure I found C. in a flood of tears. He shouted out at least three times: 'I won't do it under any circumstances. What do those racketeers take me for?'

It's obvious; if he does what the bankers demand from him everyone will realize how deeply the Democrats are involved in the attempted coup, and especially C. himself – at the very moment when the Senate Party is sharpening its axe!

Old Mouldy turned up at 11 o'clock; he's lost at least twenty pounds in weight overnight. He stayed until late in the night. Statilius kept on demanding to see C. In vain, of course.

5 December

The whole city has been up and about since early this morning. The streets are full of excited groups of people. Nobody speaks out in favour of Catilina any more. Every carpenter seems convinced that the Catilinarians wanted to set fire to their benches. In the barbers' shops people who are known in the district as Catilinarians aren't being served. It's as if the scales have fallen from the eyes of the man in the street.

There are a million or a million and a half slaves in Rome. Hannibal once stood at the gates of the city, but the slaves are inside the gates!

While C. headed off to the Capitol I took a letter to Servilia, Cato's sister. Whatever you may say about her, she really does love him. She read his letter and gave me an answer immediately.

The Forum was packed. All the banks were closed. Lots of police. People had been waiting for the Senate's decision for hours.

When I reached the Capitol the session was in full swing. I was told that C. had already spoken very boldly in favour of *forbearance towards the Catilinarians*! My heart started beating like a drum. Where I was standing I was surrounded by a load of people from the merchant classes, most of them young and all of them armed. They were members of Mr Cicero's Civil Guard, and all they could talk about was C.'s speech, which they said was a disgrace. One of them called out: 'That Caesar is the worst of them all. He's being paid – it's obvious. He wouldn't open his mouth unless he got cash down.' And another one replied: 'You can smell the stink of Catilina's money from here!' I almost burst out laughing, thinking of Afranius Cullo.

I finally managed to send Servilia's letter in to C.

It wasn't until this evening that I found out what a sensation it caused.

Just as C. had foreseen, it caused an uproar immediately. As soon as he took hold of the letter, Cato, the old jackass, who had just called for the death penalty and more or less accused C. outright of being an accomplice, demanded that C. should reveal the contents of the letter, implying that it must have been sent by someone closely associated with Catilina. C. obligingly handed him the letter his own sister had written. The old drunkard went white with rage and threw it down at C.'s feet, with the word: 'Lecher'. The episode was sufficient to make his suspicions appear ridiculous. C. is great at details like that.

Basically, nobody believed an execution could take place. All over the place people could be heard saying: 'We're not living under the rule of an Asian despot.' The law states quite clearly that Roman citizens can only be sentenced to death with the approval of the People's Assembly. When Cicero went to collect the prisoners this evening, as darkness was falling, and led them through the Via Sacra and the Forum, past the silent wall of people, everyone thought they were just being taken into custody somewhere. Although when they reached the place where the Via Sacra opens into the Forum, the Shins fainted. They had to carry him past the banks, which were closed. And the people standing right at the front, who could see Cethegus' hair dripping with sweat, might have guessed where the little procession was heading. But none of the prisoners who were being led away called out a word to the crowd, and not one of the many people who had supported the prisoners two days earlier now showed any sign of lifting a finger to help them.

They had dared to bring up the slave question!

When the Consul came back out of the Mamertine Prison, himself a changed man – sweat glistening on his forehead, hardly able to stay on his feet – to say, in a hollow voice: 'They are no longer amongst the living', there was no word of criticism from the vast crowd. And when he left the Capitol an hour later, surrounded by the best-known members of the Senate, who had just greeted him as the 'Father of the Fatherland' (all of them people who had commanded troops in great wars and brought rich prizes back to Rome, now thanking him for having saved them), the better class elements in the crowd gradually took the plunge, and isolated cheers were heard. Lamps were lit in front of the house doors, too, and women were seen waving down to him from balconies.

C. was right this morning when he said the only danger for the prisoners lay in Cicero's cowardice and his fear of showing it. This evening I heard that there had been an attempt to assassinate C. as he was leaving the Curia. The Civil Guard! Some of the Senators positioned themselves in front of him. Whatever's going to happen next?

He gave me 50,000 sesterces this evening, to pay off the most urgent bank interest. He must have got the money from Pulcher, who's bound to be scared of the Chamber of Commerce investigation.

6 December

Got up early; slept badly on account of Caebio. Headed off down towards the Tiber. Caught a scruffy fellow hunting through the rubbish bins for scraps of food. Had a chat with him. He sleeps under the bridge over the Tiber. Used to be a peasant in Campania, then he was put up for compulsory auction, ran away to Rome, couldn't find anything except temporary work in a slaughterhouse Asked him what he thought of Cicero. He said: 'Who's he?' Of course, there are thousands like him.

7 December

Days of treacherous calm.

This morning C. was gazing into the garden fish pond with its two shabby carp and said, depressed: 'Once I've got rid of these plots of land I'm going to make a serious start on my book on grammar.' How is he ever going to get rid of these plots of land? When he talked about his book like that (the one he's been going to write for the last four years) I had a vision of the carp with Mummlius Spicer's bailiff's mark on them, too.

8 December

Since the day before yesterday the whole world's been in favour of rescuing the Republic. In City banquets speeches are made celebrating the 'defeat of the dictatorship'. Cicero is the man of the hour.

Alexander on the death penalty for the Catilinarians: 'The death penalty has a huge effect in the mind of the common man. Criminals are executed; therefore anyone who's executed is a criminal. But there's even more to it than that. The people in power have shown how far they are prepared to go. They called for blood, and that means they'll be fighting to save their own skins from now on. And the worst thing of all is that the verdicts were passed by Mr Cicero – a Democrat. The Senate knows how to pick its executioner.'

Beneath the surface the police investigation continues. Reputable names are being kept out of it for the moment, because Catilina hasn't actually been defeated yet. But still, a whole series of big trials is coming up. (!) A few well-known people are being arrested. Every day there's talk of houses being searched.

The trade guilds didn't fight alongside the losers, but they've been defeated with them. It won't do them much good to expel all their members who are involved in the uprising. The Senate is taking full advantage of its victory and has announced a strict, comprehensive check of the list of citizens' civil rights.

Of course, the worst off are the members of the stormtroops and street clubs, who have now been robbed of their leaders. The police are in and out of the houses in the poor districts. They can't run away, because they haven't got the means to escape, and they'd starve wherever they went. So they just wait to be arrested. If they're lucky their little businesses will be confiscated and their furniture auctioned on the street. First they were incited to take part in the election, then to take part in the uprising.

C. is unusually troubled. The Catilinarians do seem to have a hold on him after all. Something about a letter in his handwriting. That's awful.

He went to see Crassus this afternoon. Now he's agreed to stand as Praetor. Due to the changed circumstances – when Old Mouldy gets wind of them, that is – I'm sure the post won't simply be bought for him. Now Crassus will probably only lend him the money. Up to yesterday he would have given it to him.

9 December

The police were here last night. They wanted to know where C. was around the 28th October, while he was out of town. That's the day when the Consular election took place, and Catilina's first attempt at a coup. C. was at a spa in Campania, with Mucia. We can't very well say that, though. They think he was in Etruria, with the Catilinarian troops.

When C. came home and I told him all about it, he said: 'If they ask again, I'll tell them the truth. Then they'll have to decide whether they want it repeated in open court. They'd rather abandon the investigation, if I know them.'

He could have added: and if I know Pompey. But he still tries to keep up appearances with me.

Less than half the usual number of people turned up for clients' surgery this morning. The Catilinarian affair does appear to have done us more harm than one would have supposed with the common people, the man in the street. After all, there hasn't been any official inquiry yet. But, of course, everyone knows the police sent some people round here. And a good many of our clients keep clear of any places where the police might turn up.

Very busy with preparations for the Praetor election. It really will be very expensive. Part of the profit from Crassus' brilliant corn speculation will be eaten up by it. The candidates C. will face are being financed by the Senate Party, with more or less no expense spared. Just as well that Old Mouldy knows his head is on the block this time. He's conducting the negotiations with Macer himself. We'll be appointed to the judicial position just in time. For New Year. Catilina will hardly have been completely defeated until then. And people won't be in *all that much* of a hurry to start the inquiry until he's been completely defeated.

The stock market is incredibly nervous. After the 'clarification of the situation' a rise in share prices had been expected. Instead of which they're falling. Two corn firms and a number of armament companies have gone bankrupt. One of the large banks is said to be shaky. And worse things are feared.

C. hardly ever asks about land prices any more. They've fallen sharply, as have all the rest of the prices. He listens to my reports in gloomy silence. I assume the land really was bought on Mucia's account. Which only makes C.'s position even more unbearable, especially as Pompey is bound to find out all about it when he comes back.

He is expected to return in spring.

Metellus Nepos is due to make his first proposal as People's Tribune tomorrow – that the victor in the Asian war should be recalled to Italian soil to crush Catilina.

10 December

Metellus Nepos made his proposal and was defeated. Reason; there's no longer a need for any special army to put down Catilina. *He's beaten now in any case.*

11 December

Black day on the stock market. Drastic slump of all shares. Shares in Asia fell particularly sharply. (I'm 1,000 sesterces worse off. Cicero is said to have lost a third of his fortune.) The banks closed at lunchtime.

Lots of bankruptcies. There's a vast range of theories in circulation to explain the slump. Pompey is said to have cancelled a series of tax farming contracts. Catilina is said to have conquered Praeneste. Catilina has given battle and been defeated. The Senate has recalled Pompey to help deal with Catilina after all. What's the truth?

Lots of terrible details about the slump in shares on the Forum were being related this afternoon, as Clodius told us in his mocking voice. Cittus Vulvius the banker impaled himself on his slate pencil and was seriously injured. His children are keeping share prices from him; otherwise he'd tear off the bandage. Cucca (corn imports) gathered all his clerks around when the panic started and ordered his head clerk to read the ledger out loud, to the accompaniment of sobs all round. Vitturius (land) put up a notice on the board in his office requesting any employee who was prepared to kill him to report at once. His whole staff reported to him.

A grotesque thing happened to Pirius Qualvus' family (still according to Clodius). The wife of the well-known ship owner, his son and two daughters were crossing the Forum in mourning clothes. Some of the unemployed started to mock her out loud, calling out: 'How many millions are *you* in mourning for?' Someone had to inform them that the family wasn't mourning its lost money but the head of the family, who had committed suicide upon finding himself bankrupt. Fat old Balvius Cucumbrus (tax farming) caused a commotion. Bursting out of his office, he turned to a few women gathered in front of the boards where the names of casualties from the war in Asia are posted and yelled at them furiously: 'Go home! They died for nothing!' The women protested and had to be led away.

11 December (evening)
Panic broke out when the big banks issued a clear statement saying there was now no hope of a revival in Asian trading.

This evening the Senate proclaimed a suspension of payments on all current debts until further notice. The banks are to remain closed tomorrow, too.

Cicero is said to be ill in bed.

12 December
A ray of light! The whole of the last terrible, bewildering six months is suddenly bathed in the clarity of autumn and bankruptcy.

C. came home with great news today. It was very late when he had me summoned to the library so he could dictate a letter: the rubbish carts were already out on the streets, so it must have been three in the morning. He had found out (from Mucia) that *the important big banks had been in constant negotiations with Pompey for the whole three months of the Catilinarian unrest about his seizing power as dictator; they merely couldn't reach agreement with him about the collection of taxes and duties in Asia!* Over a thousand million sesterces are at stake for the City in Asia. The banks in question supported Catilina at first because Pompey was rather dragging his feet about the tax and duty collection contracts, and they wanted to put some pressure on him. In this way they showed him that other gentlemen could also come into consideration as dictators: Mr Catilina and Mr Crassus. And, apart from his Asian legions, there were also Catilina's bands and Mr Caesar's herds of voters. So it wasn't a question of whether to side with the blackmailed Senate against Catilina (the Cicero combination) or with the blackmailed Catilina against the Senate (the Crassus combination), but simply a question of how to blackmail Pompey. That's why the required unrest in Rome was organized by arranging the flight of capital (I remembered the puzzling comment by Celer – skins and leather – which hadn't made any sense at the time), and by manipulating the price of bread. And they paid for it! Mr Catilina, Mr Caesar and Mr Cicero. And then, when Pompey the Great finally gave in (which took quite a while, due to the distance if nothing else), suddenly the cry went up to save the Republic, Cicero's great aria on democracy! In fact, what they had just consented to was Pompey as military dictator!

Catilina's election was sabotaged. But they still weren't finished. What good was a deal with Pompey if the Senate couldn't be forced to sign it? It would only be signed if it were presented by Pompey, skewered on his Asian sabre. And Crassus wasn't finished, either. The big banks took the precaution of not letting him into the secret of their negotiations with Pompey, since the two of them are enemies. But he still didn't have the corn handouts he wanted to blackmail out of the Senate after having given up hope of getting them from Catilina. He carried on paying until around the 13th of November, when he did finally get the corn handouts from the Senate, not because they were afraid of Catilina, but because they were afraid of Pompey, who would have liked to defeat them in person. Because by that time the big banks were trying to enable Pompey to march into Italy. That meant that Catilina had to present a 'danger'! So the floodgates opened again and money poured out for Catilina and the clubs.

So it's no wonder we were all groping around in the dark. The whole Catilina business never had the slightest chance, from start to finish. And there we were, buying land! It's worthless now. If Catilina had won, and put through his settlement programme, C. would be one of the richest men in Rome today. If Catilina had held on at least until Pompey and his army had arrived on Italian soil to put him down, the settlement programme would still have been put through, this time by Pompey, and we would still have made money. The City lost the game by not keeping the unrest going for long enough. They got cold feet themselves! Now their Asian contracts with Pompey aren't even worth the paper they're written on. The Senate will never ratify them. And the unemployed masses in Rome got cold feet too, and lost their game. They had fear instilled into them by the Senate and the City, so they got scared of the slaves! This collapse is going to shake the whole Empire to its very foundations.

Then C. said something which really surprised me: 'But still, we were on the right track when we saw the whole thing as simply an opportunity to make money. We were looking at things in exactly the same way as the banks. That says a lot for our instinct.'

13 December
Can hardly keep on hoping for news of Caebio. Cethegus is dead and buried, and every connection with Catilina's headquarters has been completely severed. Don't have any strength left.

15 December
The stock market collapse is still having repercussions. A lot of small firms are caught up in the bankruptcies, and thousands more craftsmen have been put out on the streets. There's no hope now of contracts deriving from an extensive settlement policy. All the projects were cancelled in today's Senate meeting.

People in the barbers' shops are more upset about this than they were when the Cimbri and the Teutons attacked. One man I know, the owner of a small bronze works, said out loud: 'I might just as well have let Catilina burn down my business!'

Catilina – apart from that there isn't much talk of him. There he is, somewhere in Etruria, his hordes of soldiers dispersing gradually, waiting for the government troops to arrive. Now the big banks' last attempt to save him, by sending Antonius against him (who was ready to defect to him at any time) has also failed. Antonius let himself be bribed a second time. Cicero had to hand him his own province, Macedonia, and in return he transferred command to a lower-ranking general who is loyal to the government.

My poor Caebio!

17 December
These last six months have proved one thing at least; C. isn't a politician of major importance and never will be. For all his brilliant abilities! What Rome needs more than ever – a strong man, who goes his own way without flinching, and imposes his will on the world, putting a vast plan into practice – that just isn't him. He hasn't got either the character or the ideas for that. He's

in politics because there's nothing else left for him. But he's not a natural leader. Our future looks bleak to me.

20 December
Now the Praetor election is over. If C., the State Judicator, heads the inquiry into the Catilinarian affair he may well succeed in allowing Gaius Julius, the politician, to get out of the whole business free from all suspicion. We owe Old Mouldy another tidy sum, 9 million sesterces.

The Catilinarian coup wasn't good business.

691. End of the year
I've made an inventory of our official income. Hopeless. For example, we haven't made more than a miserable 320,000 sesterces in the whole year from the post of High Priest (and that's including a cheque from the Egyptian linen mills for the new augurs' cloaks and compensation for the postponement of the Ceres festivities). It cost us 840,000 to get the position. And we pay eight per cent interest! Of course, we could have done better if C. had really worked at it, instead of just organizing a haul every now and then in the most careless way imaginable. He takes 20,000 sesterces for proclaiming an augury that prevents the election of a Quaestor and then holds a pontifical banquet that costs 22,000. The worst thing of all is that the City quite shamelessly accepts everything as a 'favour', and we have to swallow it because we have promissory notes outstanding. An eternal cycle!

Book Three
Classic Administration of a Province

Clambering up the rocky path to Mummlius Spicer's villa in the bright, fresh early morning, I heard singing from the olive groves over to one side. The sound rose to a crescendo, ebbed and then rose again quite evenly. I could not make out the words; presumably the song was in a foreign language.

I was deep in thought. The cool sea breeze, the view of the pleasant landscape around me, and the song were soothing after the night's reading. The capital of the world, swathed in dust and bloody chaos, receded to the back of my mind. It was as though the wind were dispersing the ominous clamour. I suddenly exhaled, struck by the realization that it was, after all, three decades since the events of which I had been reading had taken place.

The singing increased in volume, filling the air in an odd manner. Spicer was standing at the gate to his property, talking to a slave.

He greeted me, and we gazed across the fields for a moment.

'What are they singing?' I asked.

'It's Celtish,' he replied. 'I use Celts for olive cultivation. Celts and Dalmatians, but I keep the nationalities together. You wouldn't have been able to do that twenty years ago. You had to mix them up, to keep the antagonism going. Troubled times. These days I'm getting quite good results with teams from one region. The teams even compete against each other, from national pride.'

We set off up the path. While he was talking he didn't look at me, but I had the feeling that he was curious to hear my impressions of Rarus' diary. So, in a few words, I told him that I had yet to collect my thoughts, since the roll he had given me finished at the end of the year, when the events in question still hadn't reached their conclusion.

'You can have the next roll straight away,' he said, calmly. 'Although the notes about the next year, 92, are not so detailed. I glanced through them myself this morning. The writer is subdued by his personal misfortunes and only notes down his experiences sporadically. You know: Caebio.'

We waited in the library for a servant to bring the second roll, which was in Spicer's bedroom. The gentle odour of all that leather blended pleasantly with the bouquet of the white wine the old man pressed upon me.

He said: 'There are a few more things you should perhaps be told. In the summer of 92 I managed to get hold of the smaller promissory notes outstanding against C. I was working with a bank. I had a great many other cases, but he made more and more demands on my time. In the end I was concentrating entirely on him, you might say. His financial embarrassment became the greatest chance of my life. At the end of 92 I was made one of the directors of the bank with which I had been handling C.'s case. I was a sort of specialist in C.'s financial affairs, as far as they were concerned. His total obligations at the end of 93 amounted to about 30 million sesterces.'

Then the roll was brought, a very thin one this time, and I set off home.

The singing of the Celtish slaves followed me the whole way down to the lake.

The Diaries Of Rarus II

1 January 692
Great commotion in the house. C.'s investiture.

Arrival of the eagerly awaited envelope from Nepos, at last. The gentleman from Asia took his time about it. But now it's here. Of course, the Praetor's robes weren't ready. There was a terrible scene with the tailor. In the end the embroidered bits were held in place with pins. C. arrived at the Forum an hour late. Odd state of affairs in the 'capital of the world' when the tailor refuses to hand over the robes for the highest justice official in the empire until his bill is paid in cash!

But then the ceremony itself was very dignified. Relatively large number of people there. There are still a lot of scared people throughout the whole city, because the investigation into the coup is a threat to almost every household. The street clubs are placing their entire hopes in C. Touching scenes. An old woman broke through the line of people, tugged C.'s sleeve and cried out: 'Don't forget about Taesius!' She must think he knows everyone in the clubs by sight! C. said some friendly words to stop his lictors, who were about to drag the old woman away. As he moved on he said quite loudly: 'I am less interested in the offences of the people at the bottom than in those of the people at the top.' This was relayed everywhere in a very short time.

There was also applause when he didn't go to the Capitol first, as 'is fitting', to pay his respects to the new Consuls of the year, but started working immediately. As it quickly became apparent, he preferred to have the city fathers come to him in the Forum.

He had hardly settled himself in his ivory chair on the platform, and his six lictors had only just taken their places around him, when he ordered in a business-like voice that the curator of the Temple of Jupiter should be brought before him to answer to the people for his handling of the accounts. The sensation was enormous.

The curator was Catulus, the grand old man of the Senate.

The ceremonies in the Curia hadn't finished when C.'s lictors appeared and summoned the oldest and most respected man of the illustrious assembly to the Forum, to make a statement about the expenditure of funds during the reconstruction of the Temple of Capitoline Jupiter. The entire Senate, in a state of considerable agitation, followed the old man, who left the lofty building in a complete daze.

C. was still in the middle of his speech when they came running up. He launched into an unmistakable reference to the gilded bronze sheets which form the roof of the temple, reminded everyone that the cost had been raised by voluntary donations throughout Italy, and then his exact words were: 'The farmers of Italia did not, instead of buying ploughs, donate this money, just so that the Roman constructors could, instead of building a temple for the people, build villas for themselves.' But the first thing the city fathers heard when they came dashing up was Pompey's name.

For C. was now demanding that instead of Catulus, Pompey the Great should be charged with the completion of the temple. This name, the name of Pompey, should be inscribed in the very stones of the temple, for this name, Pompey, was a name to inspire confidence, and so on … But the present curator should present his books to be examined.

He was interrupted by a cry of rage from the Senators. Catulus wanted to get up on to the speaker's platform; C. refused to permit it and ordered him to remain standing below. An awful argument about matters of protocol ensued. C. cut short the dispute and announced a lunch break.

C. withdrew to his official chambers, the Senators marched off together to Cato's house, to discuss the matter, and the people lay about in the Forum in happy anticipation, not wanting to lose their places.

C. was lying there over breakfast, surrounded by several gentlemen who were congratulating him on his technique, which had allowed the name of *Pompey* to be mentioned no less than eleven times in five sentences, when Cicero was announced. He approached C. with a smile, apparently very amused, and even cracked a few jokes, but he soon proved to be a mediator sent by the Senate. He expressed his 'conviction' that C. would be content with the success of his little campaign; he had actually managed to ensure that virtually the most malicious suspicions possible would be attached to the name of old Catulus, even if the man were to present the most perfectly kept accounts. After all, if he did so people would just say he had a perfect accountant. The worst thing for Catulus was that never in a million years could he consent to present his accounts, because doing so could be interpreted as giving some credence to the disreputable suspicion.

'How would it look,' he said forcefully, 'if someone stood up and proved in a long speech that he *hadn't* stolen two silver spoons from his mother!' Catulus' honour really did prevent him from uttering one word in response to such an accusation. The old man had gone home straight away, incidentally, and taken to his bed, ill with all the excitement.

He was still talking when a messenger arrived with a letter for C. from Catulus.

C. read it, put it away and said to Cicero gravely: 'Catulus has written to me saying that his books are in order.'

The crowd was disappointed after the lunch break when C. ordered that the case should be dealt with in the usual manner and turned to some other, trivial cases.

Fulvia came this evening, with her friend Curius. I hadn't seen him since that remarkable day, 4 December, when C. made his speech in the Senate defending the imprisoned Catilinarians. He was the one who had saved C.'s life when Mr Cicero's young men attacked him as he was leaving the Curia. At the time I was amazed by his love for C., but a week later it turned out that he had proof of C.'s links with Catilina and, observing all the rules of the game, wanted to blackmail him – or pocket the 200,000 sesterces reward. During the meal C. said to him: 'My dear Curius, as Praetor I have opened an inquiry into all the people who are involved in the Catilina conspiracy. I've heard that I am one of them. A certain Vettius is said to be in possession of a letter to Catilina which bears my signature. I shall have this accusation looked into tomorrow, without delay, and woe betide me if I discover that I really am guilty of any misconduct. You see, if you want your reward, you'll have to hurry up.' Curius laughed, but I know he went to see Novius Niger, an enemy of C.'s who is heading the investigation, later that evening.

2 January

Since C. had agreed to give his full support to Nepos, the People's Tribune, when he makes an appeal tomorrow for the recall of Pompey and his Asian legions to deal with the Catilinarian unrest, he found himself in considerable difficulties today. He had to clear himself once and for all of the accusations being made all over town that he had been behind Catilina himself, and that's why he made no objection to the judge in charge of the inquiry, Niger, who is really his subordinate, extending its scope to include him. Of course, the inquiry would have to arrive at a negative conclusion, but only as regards himself, since the conspiracy as a whole has to appear to be very powerful and dangerous; otherwise Pompey couldn't be asked to help deal with it. C. solved the problem brilliantly. In the first hours of the morning session he allowed Novius Niger, a morose young man who already suffers from a liver complaint, to conduct the inquiry by himself, though only in a series of minor cases involving some gladiator slaves, owners of small businesses and members of street clubs; that way there could be no talk of bias. C. himself went to the Senate and challenged Curius to speak up if he had anything to say against him. So Curius said he had heard from Catilina himself that he was in constant contact with C. C. didn't make any attempt to deny this contact, but he asked Cicero to produce the letter C. had sent him just a few days before the Catilinarians had been arrested, which contained various disclosures and warnings. Cicero confirmed the existence of this letter in a few surly sentences, and the Senate, which didn't want to press matters any further anyway, curtly refused Curius the reward for information concerning a conspirator. Then C. went over to the Forum, where Niger was conducting his inquiry. He took his seat on the ivory throne and told the young man in a sharp tone that he had heard reports that the authorities conducting the inquiry had collected material against him, the Praetor, in person. He was not aware that any blame could be attached to his person but was quite prepared to relinquish his Curial throne and go straight to jail, without a word of protest, if conclusive evidence were presented against him. On the other hand, however, if no such material were forthcoming he would have him, Novius Niger, taken to jail, because in that case he would have instigated proceedings against his superior without justification. Niger began to look even yellower than usual and sent a court official to fetch Vettius, the man who had claimed in the preliminary hearing to have C.'s letter to Catilina. He had refused to hand it over to the authorities before the case was to be tried. Everyone waited in silence. C. sat there, warming his thin, powerful hands over a basin of glowing charcoal. It was cold.

Then the lictors returned and reported that they had not found Vettius at home. It turned out that he had already been served with a summons the previous evening. C. gave Niger a strange look, and demanded that he should be arrested immediately for contempt of court. Niger, with a certain dignity that was quite becoming, demanded the usual seizure of property. The lictors retired again (and it was said later that the unfortunate man's entire furniture really was sold by auction on the spot, at ridiculously low prices), and Vettius appeared. His clothes were torn, he had a head injury, and he stammered something about having been attacked on the way to the Forum. The letter was gone. C. stood up so abruptly that his chair tipped over. He had the man thrown in jail, and then he left. This evening he also had Niger thrown in jail, as he had warned he would. This clearly demonstrated to the man in the street that C. disapproved of the sentences Niger had secured for the members of the street clubs, yet C. had achieved what he needed: proof of a widespread and dangerous conspiracy against the state! A masterpiece! This evening, when Glaucos brought the letter he had taken from Vettius, C. said dryly: 'If they want law and order, instead of people being attacked in broad daylight, they'll just have to call for Pompey.'

A long conference with Nepos tonight.

3 January

Crassus' dilapidated houses were shrouded by the bitterly cold January storm as we made our way to the Forum. The lictors were chattering away, and C. was wrapped up to his chin in his big coat of Gallic cloth. The Forum was packed with gladiator slaves; Nepos had them brought here on carts from Campania during the night. They were miserable and frozen to the bone. I also saw some war-cripples among them, veterans of Pompey's campaigns. The moneychangers' stalls had been closed. Trouble was expected. Nepos was already sitting on the bench in front of the Temple of Castor (incidentally, his hips really are as slender as Fulvia said), and I expected him to start reading out his motion for the recall of Pompey as soon as C. sat down next to him. But he made no move to do so. A tarpaulin screen had been set up next to the bench to afford some protection against the strong wind. The screen was blown down twice by the gale, and each time the Colonel got to his feet to supervise its re-erection. C. sat there motionless, waiting, like a huge, coated vulture.

Then Cato appeared, made his way through the gladiator slaves, forced a path up the steps to the temple, and took his seat between C. and Nepos – as Tribune he has the right to sit there. He seemed amazed that nobody tried to block his way. But the armed men were not there to attack him; they were there to defend C. and Nepos.

Of course, they both knew the motion would be rejected, just as the first one had been on 10 December. The whole point was simply to provoke an infringement of the constitution, to provide Pompey with a reason for drawing the appropriate conclusions from the use of force against his People's Tribune.

The comedy quickly got under way. Nepos got to his feet and started to read out his speech. Cato constantly interrupted him and even held his hand over his mouth. (Thus Nepos' greatest fear came to pass; last night he said grimly: 'Cato doesn't wash his hands'.) Then Nepos also became furious and signalled to some gladiators standing nearby. Cato, whose bright red face showed evidence of early drinking again, tore Nepos' manuscript out of his hands. Then the gladiators grabbed him and dragged him away. A war-cripple gave him a kick with his good foot. Stones which had been brought along specially were thrown from down below. Cato pulled himself free and ran off into the temple, a funny little figure. C. had been watching the whole performance with an air of boredom. Now he called upon the Tribune Nepos to read out his motion. Nepos declared that he was unable to, as his manuscript had been taken from him. He went on about this high-handed act for a long time, until Cato returned, now himself at the head of his band of armed men. And those fellows really started lashing out. They had big sticks and aimed for the heads. C. slowly stood up and went into the temple, still conveying the impression that he had simply lost interest in the proceedings.

Actually, getting away wasn't so easy. In fact, he had to take off his coat, and even his Praetor's robes, and put on the skirt of a gladiator slave before he dared escape through a back door.

When he got home he had a hot bath straight away. We heard that the Senate had decreed he and Nepos should be relieved of their positions. Well, that'll be straightened out all right. Nepos is already on his way to the ship. Pompey will be pleased with a breach of the constitution like this. Preventing a People's Tribune from speaking out is an infringement of the people's basic rights!

23 January

During the third day of the journey in a covered wagon on the military road to Arretium I heard from merchants who were making their way down from Florentia that the battle between Antonius' troops and Catilina's was in full swing. They said it was at a place called Pistoria. Since that's at least two days' journey from here, the battle might already be over. They were in a great hurry to get to Rome before the outcome was known there, for business reasons. And the icy wind that rattled the canvas roof against the wooden frame made it hard to hear them, so I couldn't understand everything they said. Fearful that I would arrive too late, I didn't have a moment's peace for the whole of that day and the whole of the next night.

I was taking a full set of legal papers for Caebio. Even if he had been put in prison, at least that would enable me to take him back to Rome.

We got to Arretium in the afternoon, and everyone we spoke to said there was still no news of the battle being decided. But over the previous few weeks large numbers of deserters from Catilina's forces, bands of them in their hundreds, had passed through the town with news of his army being disbanded. We didn't meet any of them ourselves. We made our way through Florentia in the grey light of dawn, and it looked like a ghost town. But that was only because it was so early. Just beyond Florentia we met peasants coming from the battlefield, people who hadn't been involved in the fighting but had seen the battle, and whose faces were so haggard and pale, it was horrifying. According to them the battle still wasn't over. But Catilina didn't have the faintest chance, because Quintus Metellus' fresh troops were on the northern slopes of the mountain behind him, ready to confront him if he should manage to escape the clutches of Antonius' army. *The only thing facing him and those with him now was death.* My stomach turned over and I had to vomit.

A peasant had climbed up on the wagon in Florentia. He had some news for us too. The Catilinarians' provisions had run out; that's what stopped them marching over the mountain pass to Gallia and forced them to give battle. So their last battle was fought under the same banner which had characterized the entire uprising: the banner of hunger.

The peasant was looking at me curiously, and the coachman, a Roman boy called Pistus whose heart is in the right place, made him be quiet. I sank into a restless, exhausted sleep.

When I woke up I found that our wagon had come to a halt, hemmed in by others. A large convoy carrying the wounded was coming in the opposite direction. The escort squad was running all over the place, cursing, and the wounded were lying in an apathetic daze on the wagons, most of which were open, with no more than basic dressings for their wounds. Our papers were checked over and over again; it felt to me as though the Roman soldiers were enemy troops. Everyone said the battle had been over for hours, Catilina was defeated and dead, and everybody with him was dead. From that moment on I started to hope again. Strangely enough, I kept on repeating to myself that it was a good job I hadn't come too late after all.

We drove on through the squads of troops marching towards us, past campfires. The soldiers were marching grimly, not singing the way the victors usually do. I didn't see any prisoners, not one, but I refused to admit to myself what that meant.

At a crossroads we encountered a company which was taking the captured banner the Catilinarians had fought under, the Eagle of Marius, to Faesulae. Roman soldiers had once defended the nation against the Cimbri under that banner.

Dusk was descending as we reached the battlefield proper, just before Pistoria.

My first impression was that there wasn't very much to see. The area was slightly hilly, so you could only see one part of it at a time. Small squads of soldiers were digging up the frozen ground, as hard as stone, by the light of flaming torches. Other squads were searching the piles of bodies, which couldn't be clearly made out and looked like bundles of rags. Snow had apparently fallen a few days before and still lay among the bushes.

I got out of the wagon, weak at the knees, and headed along the road without any definite plan. To right and left lay the bundles of rags, and the torches swept this way and that. The wind had dropped, or at least I had the impression that I wasn't freezing any longer. The coachman walked beside me, glancing at me from time to time. When another squad examined our papers I heard some more information about the course of the battle. But I can't remember what they said. I do remember one detail quite clearly, though; one officer said Catilina had preferred to confront Antonius' troops, because that meant he would be facing soldiers who had been recruited from the capital's unemployed. Metellus' army was composed of sturdy peasants' sons, freshly conscripted from the Picentes. But the slaughter couldn't have been more terrible if it weren't have-nots fighting other have-nots.

My coachman (Pistus) tried to find out how the identity of individual soldiers could be established. One of the legionaries shrugged his shoulders and said: 'There are at least 7,000 of them.'

We walked on, this time across the battlefield. Once I stopped and watched a squad some distance away throwing dead bodies into a shallow hole in the ground. It was a large squad, and the hole was some considerable size. It was cordoned off by ropes. Just like the way the Campus Martius is divided up for the elections.

When we continued we found ourselves in an open field. The dark piles were thick on the ground here, too, but there were no mopping-up squads in sight.

I didn't once bend down to take a closer look at a face. But still I felt as though I were searching. To keep it in mind, I thought.

There was no way of distinguishing between friend and foe here, anyway; they were all Romans, all wearing Roman uniform. And they all came from the same station in life. When they advanced to fight each other they had obeyed the same words of command. In fact, Catilina's army was no more made up of people with the same interests than Antonius' was. Shoulder to shoulder with Etrurian peasants who had seen their land confiscated stood the former military colonists of Sulla who had been given that land. The big landowners had taken it away from them in turn. Unable to resist the prospect of a bearable existence that Catilina held out to them, they fought in desperation against the veterans recruited in Rome by Mr Cicero; they had ended up back in the city because they were in debt with their land and could no more resist the prospect of an allowance of 50 sesterces a day than the indebted peasants of Campania. Neither the victors nor the vanquished managed to reach out for the splendours of the two Asias, which is what the battle was about. The soldiers of the Asian kings hadn't been able to defend them, and the soldiers of the Roman generals hadn't been able to capture them.

Incidentally, not one slave was found among the Catilinarians who fell. Catilina had been forced to expel the slaves from his ranks after the change of mood on the 3 December. So it had simply been Romans fighting other Romans.

After several hours the coachman led me back to the wagon. As we were walking back a soldier who was talking to an officer indicated a spot in the dark, snow-covered field with a vague gesture of his hand and said: 'He's lying over there, in the middle of a pile of our men.' That must have been Catilina.

7 April
Moved into the High Priest's official residence. As we left it, the old house in the Subura was inundated with creditors, you might say. I do believe they were squabbling over every column in the atrium. Here in the Via Sacra the renovation work isn't finished, of course, because there's no money to pay for it. Pompeya is being put up in a hall.

The last hope for C. (and his creditors), now lies in Pompey's return. But he must bring his legions with him, which is easier said than done now the Senate's so united again.

If it weren't for Pomade-head we often wouldn't know how to keep the household running. He helps us out with little amounts.

As for me, I try to numb my senses as best I can. I go to a different dog race almost every night.

19 June
We've been given the province of Spain for next year.

From time to time, to the right of the rocky road, we noticed a wooden construction on one of the rocky ledges projecting over the pine groves of the lower slopes, surrounded by dwarf trees; it proved on closer inspection to be half a warship. My Sempronius had made some enquiries about it in the tavern and told me it was the front part of a small warship which Vastius Alder, the poet, had had brought to the grounds of his house here. A few decades ago he conquered the city of Acme with this ship. I met the poet at Spicer's house in the evening. They had been dining together. He bore somewhat of a resemblance to a mummy, and you could just picture his servant bandaging him up for the night in those strips of white material that hold mummies together. He lived entirely for his reputation, which he strove to maintain as much from his verses as his campaigns. His personal bravery was beyond any doubt. He had battled in the turmoil of hand-to-hand fighting, at the head of his legions, with his sword in his hand. However, his sword may well have been picked up in an antique shop in Campania Street rather than in the state armoury. And he certainly chose the settings for his military campaigns with a view to the opportunities they provided for the use of choice phrases in later descriptions. He had enriched the Latin language with more new words than anyone before.

In conversation he was chivalrous and completely natural, exquisitely modest. Our host had apparently informed him of the purpose of my visit, and with great courtesy he turned the conversation to the object of my interest.

'A great man,' he said, moulding pieces of bread on the table into little figures with his delicately proportioned hands, 'just the sort of figure historians need. The man of the people and the man of the Senate. People like that are depicted and copied from one book to the next over thousands of years. A few strokes in watercolour are enough. Forgive me, Spicer, but I doubt whether a poet who wanted to write about him would need to put more than two lines down on paper. It isn't every surface that produces patina, and art is patina, don't you think? Take an Etrurian peasant's stool for example, a practical object: after four generations it attains artistic value – what wood, you say. As far as poetry is concerned the man we're talking about is something Brutus stuck his sword into. You can say a thousand times: the founder of an empire, commercial practice on a global scale! Commercial practices don't take on patina. After all, what's art for? I fear I'm hardly impartial.'

It was so quiet in the beautiful, low chamber that one could hear the dogs barking around the slaves' huts outside. The banker and former bailiff sat leaning backwards in silence, a grey, bulky, bony figure. The light fell sharply on the poet's head, which seemed to have been formed from yellow wax but was possessed of two lively, black eyes.

The poet didn't speak again for quite a while. He spoke rather haltingly, incidentally, as if he were experiencing difficulty finding the appropriate expression for every case; there was nothing commonplace about his mode of expression, if you listened to him.

'Of course, you can even find something adventurous in the life of the founder of an empire. The great dealer did forget himself once. It caused a row in the moneychangers' stalls that still hasn't completely died down. You know which episode I'm talking about, because living dangerously did produce an episode for our dealers on a worldwide scale; forgive the use of the plural, gentlemen. Catilina! The disgrace. The conspiracy. Letters, and locked doors! Daggers and oaths. Manifestos in every pocket and signals to be given in the Senate. If I touch my Adam's apple with my index finger, that means ... Hell, open up your jaws! Lists of outlaws. The power. The police. The finger that doesn't touch the Adam's apple. Traitor! Fresh whispering. Cicero has convened a night session of the Senate. A horseman galloping through the night. The banks close. The blood bath. Ending up with a police investigation, but one survives, of course, one denies everything, one wasn't around, one was in bed, with a slave – yes, one had a witness.'

The poet laughed scornfully. By now he was playing catch with the lumps and little figures of bread.

'Our dealer, mixed up in the infamous Catilina conspiracy! Implicated by a letter, most probably written in that famous terse style of his! What, it can be used for that, too? To poke a hole with the tip of a toe in the oh-so-thin brocade tablecloth around which the sibyls and corn dealers sit, and see what crawls out to the top of the seven hills from the depths of the seven marshes? The discharge from Crassus' bug-ridden tenements, mixed in with the creatures that no longer resemble man nor beast, staggering in from their mouldy scraps of land to be present for the reckoning up. It wasn't an eagle that they carried before them – some other sort of bird, more likely. Jupiter in the Capitol scratches himself for decades when he thinks of those weeks. Yes, that's where the great Democrat found his electors. For those defeated at Zama and those defeated in the two Asias were living quite close by: just down in the cellar. That would turn out to be quite a different triumphal procession; please take your place at the very front, red bearded Emperor, please stay in place quietly on your warhorse, in that case! They would have carried a captured field from Campania with them in that procession, and every loaf of bread in Italy, those "masters of the world who are not masters of their own four walls". But what are we talking about, after all, it wasn't our dealer; Sallust proved it, he's as mild as a lamb, he'd eat out of your hand, and he wasn't there anyway. Do forgive me.'

He was again silent for a while, as if listening to the gentle murmurings of the lake. Then, as neither of us said a word, he continued:

'But that was really enough to accomplish everything. At the appropriate time, when an investigation into embezzled funds was threatening, the threat of foul air rising from the depths was deployed yet again; something about revolution was muttered, a vague gesture in the direction of the suburbs was made. Then the police understood and became more tactful. A casual mention of the hungry masses (in terse, military prose), and one was greeted in the Senate once more. Of course, one had no sympathy with this stinking tide oneself; the toga that one was handed had to be wiped clean of disgusting stains. One was well aware that they would use their "liberation" to place their stunted bastard brats in the laps of the Vestal Virgins, to grow radishes instead of chrysanthemums in the greenhouses, to seal up the holes in the walls of their hovels with priceless Grecian canvases, and to shit on grammar – for which their inadequate education always excused them in the eyes of a few intellectuals. One was well aware of this, one had studied one's Greek culture. One was aware, but one had to engage in politics. And one continued to engage in politics until one finally did let the flood enter the Curia – or, at least, the spray from its tidal wave; not the starving peasants, of course, just their enslavers, the profiteers. Not the bankrupt craftsmen, of course, just the people who had lent them money. No, the gentleman didn't forget "the misery": the great Democrat remembered "the despair of the pauperized". What else could he have blackmailed the pauperizers with? The Senate was too small. It had to be enlarged. There were too few privileged robbers; their numbers had to be increased by including the unprivileged robbers. Under the threatening eye of the dictator those whose police had brought in the stolen loot shook hands with those who had gone out to fetch it themselves. And what of the plague that one had promised to keep down, to banish, to decimate, in return for so many sealed envelopes! Well, hadn't it been decimated by the time it streamed into the Curia? Wasn't that just a small part of the whole plague? In fact, it was really only the part of the plague that had some coins to jingle together. A very small part. But a powerful one. And loud. You have to be able to shout if you want to haggle. Look at his Senate: a market hall. Would you care for a contemporary theme for a painter? *Roman Senators in Search of Lice.* Yes, Spicer, he really was a great man, your clerk!'

Vastius Alder got up to leave quite early, saying that his health left much to be desired, and Spicer and I walked to the door of the villa with him.

'The only reason he's leaving so early,' the old man said to me in a low voice, 'is so he can note down that nonsense of his right away. During the last few minutes he was wriggling as if his pants were on fire. Didn't you notice him desperately trying to learn by heart the words he was saying to such a small audience?'

The difference between the banker and his guest was extraordinary, almost beyond description. They were both of humble origins; Spicer was the son of a freed slave, and Vastius was actually a freed slave himself. Both of them had played in the gutters of the capital as children, and both sat in Caesar's Senate as grown men. But the banker still licked his lips while he was eating, and the poet and soldier had come so far that he had almost started licking his lips again.

We watched the poet's lamp for a while as it descended. The poet's palazzo was on a hill separated from ours by a steep-sided valley, thick with undergrowth. It could be seen shimmering through a sparse olive grove in the light of the moon, which was almost full. From this point the rock with the wooden bow section of the ship was not visible.

When I mentioned it, prompted by curiosity, Spicer responded reluctantly:

'If posterity does gain anything from that, it'll be admiration for our engineers' skill. How much trouble do you think it was to get that relic up on top of that hill? He even issued orders for them not to damage a single tree while they were winching it up. It took a great deal more wits to get those planks of timber up here than it did to get them to Acme all those years ago.'

'Our famous friend's tendency to plant relics on the top of hills does have its disadvantages,' said Spicer when we had taken our seats again. 'On the other hand, what's missing from little Rarus' diary is some sign of greatness. He has the little man's optimism about little things and his pessimism about big things. His description of the events of 91 gives an impression which is overall too pessimistic.'

He balanced the thin roll I had returned to him in his gnarled hands and then put it back on the table.

'Following the Catilinarian affair, which had admittedly turned out badly, C.'s position certainly wasn't the same as it had been; it was stronger, understandably enough. It's the same in politics as in real commercial life. Small debts are no credentials, but large debts place things in a different light. A man who owes a really considerable amount enjoys respect. He is no longer the only one who worries about the money he owes; his creditors do, too. Substantial business opportunities have to be pushed his way, so he can repay the money. He has to be kept in good spirits; otherwise he'll lose hope and let events take their course. And it's impossible to avoid him, because he has to be pressed for payment constantly. In short, he's a force to be reckoned with. And it's the same with a politician who has suffered enough defeats. His name is on every tongue. The people who supported him have ended up in a bad way, so they need him even more. That's because they have become accustomed to him and think he's the only one who can bring about any improvement in the situation. The people who have given him commissions to perform can't completely desert him, either; he knows too much. The biggest difficulty is to get into big business; once you're in there, it would be hard for the others to throw you out. It isn't so important that a man's actions should have good results; the important thing is that they do have results. The bigger the results – even if negative ones, I'd say – the bigger the man. The Catilinarian affair took C. to the top. It's true that it brought the Democratic "party" to its knees, but still, it took him to the top of the party. It was a tremendous defeat, but if anyone wanted something from the people who had been defeated, they had to approach him. He even put up with the kicks.

The Democratic cause was in a really bad way. The Senate had accepted that it would have to pay to have the City defeated. The corn handouts for the unemployed swallowed up an eighth of the state's annual revenue: 25 million sesterces. But the money wasn't wasted, not to mention the fact that it wasn't the Senate's anyway. State revenue had increased by far more than twice that amount due to the conquests in Asia. The City's share of that revenue had been quite considerably reduced. And Pompey "the Great" now had to decide whether he could really demand more than a triumphal procession from the Senate. The Democratic organizations, which he could still have banked on for support in the autumn, were in ruins. In their betrayal of the little man the City had adhered to all the rules of the game, except the one that says the victim shouldn't notice anything. Following the final, brutal extermination of the Catilinarians the broad masses underwent a change of mood. The troops who had been victorious at Pistoria told of the bravery of the desperate rebels, who didn't even have crusts of bread left in their packs. These tales were told in run-down tenement blocks, with walls covered in mould, to people who, if they had any possessions at all, were in the clutches of the banks. And it was Cicero, the Democrat, who had put down this uprising, and "Pompey the Great" had squabbled with him for the honour of doing so. Pompey had become unpopular. But the Senate had the power. The numbers of police in the capital had been doubled, and their files were spiced with compromising material. The street clubs had been totally disbanded; even the fencing teams had been dissolved. The Senate would be able to recruit fresh, reliable legions from peasants throughout Italy, should it prove necessary. The peasants weren't at all interested in a solution to the land question that consisted of burdening them with competition in the form of the city's unemployed. As if that Pompey with his insane importation of slaves hadn't been enough!

And the City was as bankrupt as it could possibly be.

The City was longing for Pompey more than ever. It was in urgent need of *a strong man*. It expected real energy from him. His fame resounded around the Forum. There's no doubt about his genius, said the bankers; he proved it in Asia. If he dealt with Mithridates so effectively, why shouldn't he deal with our Cato? The man has a reputation to hang on to.

C. was waiting for Pompey too, of course. If Pompey came, with his legions, there would be no police inquiry into the events of January, which would otherwise have to be set up as soon as he resigned his office with the police, in the autumn. The moment he ceased to be the judge, he would be the criminal. So he was keeping a watchful eye out for Pompey the dictator.

But Pompey the Great was shrouding himself in silence. He was winding up his business affairs in Asia, and didn't seem to be thinking about politics at all. He was still making contracts with the City for the collection of taxes and duties. They would have to be ratified by the Senate, it's true. But he was bound to be bringing his legions with him, and there couldn't be much wrong with contracts which were the heart's desire of victorious legions. The City presented a cheerful, confident countenance. But Asian shares were being quoted at remarkably low prices. If you want to know the City's real opinion on reports from the front, you have to read its stock market reports.'

The old man gazed at me thoughtfully for a while. It looked as though he were deciding how much to tell me. But perhaps he was just wondering how to make me understand what he did want to tell me. It's possible that he might have noticed traces of boredom in my expression. He was well aware that I didn't share his innate interest in convoluted business deals, or in business deals of any sort. At that time I didn't realize that a purely economic analysis of a great political event – an occurrence of significance to the history of the world – could offer genuine insights. My attitude was quite consciously one of patient forbearing.

He suddenly spoke again.

'I'll tell you how we dealt with the consequences of the Catilinarian rumpus. I say we because I had a part to play, too. As you know, Pompey didn't come with his legions; he came without them. At the beginning of 92 nobody thought the great conqueror of both Asias would possibly do anything like that. In the summer Crassus had fled from Pompey to Macedonia; they had been deadly enemies since their joint Consulship. Even the Senate was expecting all sorts of fun and games from Pompey, who had landed in Brundisium with an enormous fleet, until Crassus reappeared in the Forum. When C. saw him, he knew Pompey wouldn't bring his troops with him. Crassus had his contacts.

C. asked me to call on him that afternoon. He was standing by a statue of Minerva, supervising a dozen slaves, who were packing. He said: "Pompey's coming back as a private individual. Crassus is back again. I'm thinking of setting off for my province. Can you arrange that?" I said: "Do you have to go?" – "Yes," he replied, giving me a sharp look, "if you let me go."

I had gathered together most of his financial obligations and taken charge of them. Under certain circumstances it would be a fatal blow to the bank which, with my collaboration, had sorted out the confusion of his financial affairs (more or less the bank's only activity). "Do you have anyone who could stand surety for you?" I asked. "No," he said, as he continued to supervise the packing. "In that case, there's no chance of your being allowed to leave for your province," I said, firmly. "Your debts amount to 30 million." In fact he owed a lot more than that. At the time I didn't know anything about his insane land speculation. He didn't mention it, of course, but he did say: "They amount to even more. My creditors are in a desperate situation, my dear fellow. I do hope you haven't given up your old job completely?"

I replied emphatically that I certainly had done so, and I had absolutely no intention of giving up the fight. I walked out, furious, while he continued to direct the packing with his usual serenity.

The entire household was being broken up. The only reason he could continue living there was that it belonged to the state, not to him. He had been obliged to send away his wife, Pompeya. The terrible scandal with Clodius had just come to light.

The Ceres Festival had been held in C.'s house that year, since he was Praetor, officiated over by the Vestal Virgins and the wives of the nobility. It was absolutely forbidden for men to go anywhere near the festivities, but Clodius had smuggled himself into the house in women's clothes in order to sleep with Pompeya. He had been discovered and was awaiting trial for blasphemy. C. was fond of his wife. Clodius, "Pomade-head" as Rarus calls him, had made a vain attempt to calm him down by insisting that he hadn't sneaked into the house for Pompeya's sake, but because of his own sister, Clodia – the whole town knew about his affair with her. And he said he only became jealous of Pompeya because of Clodia. C. had thrown him out and petitioned for divorce from Pompeya.

When I returned in the evening I unfortunately had to address this distasteful matter, too. I had my men with me, and a court order with which I could prevent C. from leaving the city. I stationed about 50 men around the building before I went in. I knew he was very fast when he was in danger.

First of all I asked him to show me the documents which contained figures about the state's annual revenue from the province of Spain. In all (duties, taxes and tributes), it came to about 25 million. The outlook was hopeless.

"That's very high, for Spain," I said. "How do you intend to extract anything sizeable for yourself on top of it?" – He said: "I'll manage, because I have to." – "You'll squeeze 10 million out of the place," I said, "and then you'll be saddled with court cases." – "I'll get 20 out of it," he said, "and the cases will never come to court. I'll stand for Consul while I'm in Spain."

The instant he said that, I remember quite clearly, something inside me snapped. For a second I considered bursting into tears; I had a family after all. Then I decided to stick by him until the end. It was madness, but he inspired me with confidence. I couldn't help myself; he inspired me with confidence.

We started going into the details, and that's when his row with Clodius came up. It turned out that the only person who could help him by that stage was Crassus. And there was only one way to get him to supply that help. The Catilinarian affair had to be dredged up yet again, and milked for a few more drops; for the moment, C. was still Praetor. He could have Crassus brought before the court. When the question of providing evidence came up, Clodius occurred to us.

Somewhere in one of the clubs evidence was still being stored which indicated that Crassus had provided financial support for the Catilinarian movement. The evidence was in Clodius' hands. He had arranged for it to be kept in order to protect himself. Now he would have to cough it up. C. agreed that I should go and fetch Clodius.

C.'s removal wagon was in front of the house. I told my men to confiscate it, just to be on the safe side; I didn't know whether Clodius would come or not.

But he came along with me straight away. The two gentlemen exchanged cool greetings but then quickly got down to business. Clodius needed a witness statement from C. for his trial and was prepared to pay for it with evidence against Crassus. We had just settled that point when C.'s mother came in. A little old lady, very elegant, but a bit of a battle-axe. The moment she saw the man who had disgraced the family honour in the company of the dishonoured husband, she really let herself go. She said exactly what she thought, not just about Clodius but about her son, too. She said she was expecting him to throw the fellow out. The expressions she used were a great deal more forceful. I was amazed to hear what kind of expressions the aristocracy would use to defend their honour.

C. was in an unenviable position, because he needed Clodius. He rose to the occasion. When his mother asked him whether he intended to put his "fancy business" before his own honour, he replied with dignity and assurance: "Certainly." He said he completely refused to let private feelings influence political questions. His brief comments gave me the impression that at that moment he was determined to place the destiny of the Roman Empire before his own. His mother was speechless and apparently formed a different impression, but she left the room. We completed the deal, I set off with Clodius to fetch the evidence, and C. sent for Crassus.

I'll never forget that conversation with Crassus.

At first the fat man just laughed when we suggested that he should stand surety for C.'s debts, amounting to 30 million. "Why are you making a run for it anyway?" he asked. – "In certain quarters the fact that I spoke in favour of Pompey's recall is held against me." – "Oh, is it really?" said Crassus, drawling slightly. "In that case you should ask your friend Pompey to stand surety for you, shouldn't you?" – "I can't offer him anything in return," said C. shamelessly. "And you have something to offer me?" asked Crassus, amused. "I may have," replied C. "As you know, I'm Praetor." – "Yes, I do know that; it cost me 10 million." – "It's been worthwhile," said C. nonchalantly. "I've been able to keep my hands clean in the Catilinarian affair." – "That was the point of the Praetor deal, not the recall of the legions from Asia," said Crassus, somewhat annoyed. C. looked at him sharply, but not without a certain amount of sympathy. Then he said: "I only hope you'll be able to keep your hands clean too."

Crassus jumped up as if he had been stung. "What's that supposed to mean?" C. continued calmly: "In my capacity as Praetor some evidence against you has come into my possession which I had set aside at the time in my capacity as leader of the clubs, my dear friend." – "What sort of evidence?" asked Crassus, hoarsely. "A few moneybags with the name of a company on them. It's clearly a case of financial support for an illegal organization."

Crassus was breathing heavily. "This is blackmail," he said. "Yes," said C., coolly. – "You mean to say you're trying to sell me a few leather bags for 30 million sesterces?" – "No," said C., and his tone wasn't hostile, "they're hardly worth that much. All you have to do is stand surety. I'll pay you back the 30 million as soon as I get back from Spain. I just want to put your trust in me to the test." – "I don't have any trust in you," said Old Mouldy through clenched teeth. – "In that case, you're in for some sleepless nights," said C. – "Where are the bags? I want to see them before I talk about things that are of no interest to me."

I could see his point. I placed five leather bags on the table. The fat man gazed at them for a moment in silence, thinking of all the denarii he had poured into that campaign at the beginning, and then he started thinking about all the denarii it cost to get himself out of it again.

Then he and I started to bring some order to his lieutenant's affairs. The Pulcher group, which had invested in the Asian market in a big way, had suffered very heavy losses during the stock market crash in December, and it had to see some of the money it was owed, especially as the great Cullo was behind it. I was repre- senting about 11 million myself. Crassus supplied me with surety for 6 million of it. He promised to "have a serious talk" with some of the other creditors. We succeeded in striking a bargain.

C. sat in the corner, reading a Greek romance.

Some historians have claimed that Crassus stood surety for him because he had a high opinion of C.'s daring, enterprising spirit. I can assure you that his opinion was not a high one.'

Voices were raised in the night outside. The old man interrupted his account and listened. The voices seemed far away and faded again. He got to his feet and bent forward to fill my carafe from the earthenware amphora. As he was pouring he paused once again, listening. There was dead silence outside. Then he sat down and continued his story.

'I haven't made any secret of the fact that I was impressed by the way he dealt with his creditors. His unquestionable superiority over them derived from his concept of money. It wasn't that he was greedy and intent on transforming "yours" into "mine". He simply didn't recognize the difference between "mine" and "yours". He took the view that he had to be supported at all costs. It often surprised me that creditors came to share his open indifference to his debts rather than being warned by it. I have described the conversation with Crassus in some detail because it shows you his "wonderful serenity, which never deserted him".

What's more, he wasn't just taking Crassus for a ride at that point but me as well. He didn't say a word about his land specu-lation. I don't intend to explain at this point how he managed to maintain those operations through the period of his collapse and the whole year of his Proconsulship in Spain. Rarus gives an account of that matter in his diary for the year 94. In the year 92 only Pulcher and a few other banks connected with his knew anything about C.'s purchases of land. It was no accident that he had us deal with Pulcher as the first priority. In Spain he operated mainly in collaboration with the Pulcher group.'

He suddenly stopped speaking and leant backwards, listening. The voices outside had been raised again. They came from the direction of the slaves' huts and were now mingled with the barking of watchdogs.

We heard rapid footsteps, and the little Gallic foreman appeared in the window. He informed us that one of the slaves had broken out.

'Take the dogs,' said Spicer. 'But keep them on their leashes; otherwise we'll lose another one.'

He struck the brass gong and had a coat brought. We went outside. Past the huts, where the cracking of leather whips and the screams of pain from the interrogated slaves could be heard, following the slaves who were leading the pack of dogs. There was no need for torches; the night was bright enough for the search.

The old man strode on in silence. His movements conveyed solidity and power, each one carefully considered. He looked ominous.

At a bend in the path we came across the veteran from the Gallic war. He had a little dog with him, and it was only with difficulty that he restrained the animal, which wanted to follow the pack.

Spicer asked him curtly whether he had seen anything of the escaped slave. The stocky little man looked him straight in the face and slowly shook his head. As we walked on he gazed after us without moving a muscle.

Spicer said with suppressed annoyance: 'He knows something, of course. Rabble stick together.'

We did not go very far, as there was nothing we could do to help. But as we stepped back inside the library we heard the wild yelping of the huge hounds heading down to the shores of the lake.

The old man poured himself a glass of red wine. His hands were not trembling, but his voice indicated the effort it had cost him to keep his temper. His face, which was always grey, was now ash-grey.

'No,' he replied, when I asked what would happen to the runaway slave, 'I refuse to have anyone killed. I paid money for them. I'm not one of those fools who have people's bones broken and then expect them to work in the olive groves. Incidentally, the death penalty doesn't deter them. They aren't as fond of life as we are.'

He gradually calmed down as he spoke of Caesar's administration of Spain, which is widely regarded as a classic example. But he continued to listen for sounds from the night outside as he talked, and his account was more caustic than usual. It wasn't until much later that I understood why he not only failed to employ the euphemisms which were readily available for the procedures but deliberately stressed the violence and brutality involved.

'C.,' he said, 'left Rome in such a hurry that he didn't even pick up his instructions from the Senate about the size, equipment and wages of his army. It's my belief that the story of his famous "magically rapid journey" was spread by all his creditors.

But he didn't leave Rome without picking up his instructions from the Pulcher group. It was in charge of closing deals to provide military supplies for Pompey's army from the Etrurian iron mines. The mines, the largest in Italy, were more or less depleted. C.'s administration of Spain really was the first to proceed in accordance with sensible – that is, businesslike – criteria.

That is something you can't appreciate from the historians' accounts alone. For certain reasons, mainly so that C. could celebrate a triumph, he had to present the whole thing as a war. There was talk of a war against mountain tribes who were carrying out raids in the valleys to plunder the settlements. There were accounts of the population leaving the towns and taking refuge in the mountains, so they had to be brought back. Governor's reports are generally written in that sort of style. C.'s operations were far more interesting.

The main point, the really new aspect, was his treatment of Spanish businessmen: not only as Spaniards, but as businessmen, too. He gave them support when he could, even against their own fellow countrymen. The primary objective at first was to implement the pacification of Spain. No methods were to be rejected in attaining this end, not even the most violent ones.

His most famous measure to promote civilization was the resettlement of the Lusitanian mountain population in the river valleys. The Lusitanian entrepreneurs were complaining bitterly about a dire shortage of workers for their silver, copper and iron mines. The inhabitants of the mountain regions preferred a tranquil, pastoral existence on the highland plateaus to working in the mines. The industrialists pointed out, quite rightly, that on those inaccessible plateaus they were evading the clutches of the tax officials with great success.

For decades Roman governors had ignored the complaints of domestic industry and refused to take sides in the struggle between the Lusitanian bourgeoisie and the stubborn pastoral population. The mountain people were at a very low level of civilization. There were hardly any slaves. They were unable to exploit the significant mineral deposits without outside assistance, due partly to their primitive machinery and partly to the lack of a suitable workforce.

However, his Roman troops only marched into those regions when it became known, after C.'s arrival, that even human sacrifice was practised there. The elimination of such a barbarous state of affairs called for prompt and relentless intervention. It might lead to loss of life, but it will be worthwhile in the end. The Roman cohorts who marched into a coastal inlet, because there were no roads and they thought it was a dried up river bed, didn't lose their lives in vain when the rising tide washed them and all their equipment and supplies out to sea. On those same slopes the villas of both native and Roman businessmen can be seen today. And the mountain valleys, once filled with the roar of battle and the moans of the wounded, now resound with peaceful hammering from the quarries and the merry cries of the slaves.

The short war didn't end without bloodshed, and not all C.'s operations were successful. But he was not unpopular with the soldiers. The bonuses he handed out were decent. And he was able to demand a triumph in Rome with a good conscience, without having to do what certain other generals did in order to reach the requisite number of 5,000 enemy soldiers killed and also include all the civilians who had lost their lives.

In this campaign Roman cohorts fought shoulder to shoulder with native cohorts; Lusitanians comprised a third of the army. The Roman tax contractors, and therefore the City, also enjoyed the most cordial relations conceivable with the local bourgeoisie. With the help of the Pulcher group C. managed to secure tax concessions for the province by proving that the country had suffered during his military operations. Before the contracts for tax collection were put up for auction he secured an arrangement between the various bidders and the Pulcher group which prevented the usual attempts to outbid the competition. He left the mines in the hands of the local industrialists and obtained a moratorium on debts for the Lusitanians. He developed an acceptable mode of operation which enabled local industry to continue functioning and work off its debts by exploiting the country's labour force to the full. Two-thirds of the proceeds from the mines went to the City on an ongoing basis.

The campaign in the mountains had yielded a rich harvest of slaves. But of course that didn't settle the matter. The former shepherds, used to a lazy life up on the plateaus, kept on running away from the towns and had to be brought back by force. C. did what he could.

His success was epoch-making and did more than anything else to make the new system popular. Despite the reduced tax levels the Empire's revenue was constantly increasing, and the City had every reason to be content. It got as much ore as it wanted. Today it employs over 40,000 slaves in the mines and extracts an annual income of 45 million sesterces from the silver mines alone!

But C.'s reward for the pacification of the province was also suitably gratifying. The historians disagree as to the actual source of his earnings. Brandus is of the opinion that he only accepted money at all because he was anxious to have tangible proof of the Spaniards' great gratitude for his unselfishness. He emphasizes that C. refused all but voluntary donations. Nepos believes that a man at the head of an army is too proud to beg and assumes that he ordered the donations to be made. Some say he took the money from his enemies: others, from his allies. Some say it consisted of tributes: others, of shares in the silver mines. Some say he was paid in Spain: others, in Rome. They are all right. As everyone knows, C. could do several things at once. He made about 35 million sesterces in a single year. When he returned he was a changed man. He had shown what he was capable of. He had also shown what a province was capable of. And his historic remark – that he would rather be the first in Spain than the second in Rome – had been justified.

My confidence in him had proved well founded. Our small bank was not a small bank any more.'

The little Gaul appeared in the room once again. He was pale and dishevelled, physically exhausted.

'Couldn't get anything out of them,' he said.

The old man stared at him without any expression in his face, and the Gaul seemed to turn a shade paler. He quickly turned round and left.

The old man turned his blunt face to the darkened window, remained silent for a few minutes, and then continued in a measured tone:

'The changed man returned to a changed Rome. Democracy was rising again after the terrible defeat of 92. The question of how the half of the world which Pompey had conquered could be digested had only been removed from the agenda by the Senate's brutal victory under Cato; it hadn't been decided. Conditions had become unsustainable again. The City's activities couldn't be dispensed with, but it was equally impossible for them to continue. Immense numbers of slaves were flooding into Rome and the whole of Italy. But the larger the available workforce, the less work there was. The industries, which had served the war, were wasting away. And the price of corn was fading away drastically as a result of the free corn handouts. The owners of the large latifundia therefore had an incentive to change from corn farming to grape and olive cultivation. They needed tenant farmers. You won't be able to understand the struggles of the next few years, including the civil war, if you overlook these fundamental facts. The common man was in demand again. Democracy had another chance.' And as he stood up and reached for the little box that contained the rolls of parchment, he added:

'You will see from the diaries that Democracy was implemented in full.'

I headed back to my villa, lost in thought, with the roll comprising Rarus' diaries for the years 94 and 95 in the folds of my tunic.

The night was warm, the sky overcast. The escaped slave was in luck.

I had to pass the slaves' huts on my way, and now not a sound could be heard from inside.

Book Four
The Three-Headed Monster

The Diaries Of Rarus III

(*The period 12 February 694 to 27 July 694. Abridged by the editor*)
Authoritative historical opinion, as represented by all the more
penetrating historians, regards these events as an attempt by the
Senate to prevent Caesar from celebrating a triumph over Spain.
In Rome the Democratic forces are making every effort to have a
general from their own ranks elected Consul. Caesar, faced with a
choice between honour and power, (a triumph and the position of
Consul), chooses power without any hesitation.

12 February 694
The triumph is absolutely essential. If for no other reason, to put
a stop to the insolent jokes Cicero is circulating about C.'s Spanish
campaign. He's telling everyone that C.'s triumph will be staged
by Pulcher from the Asian Commerce Bank. And that the names
of the battles will have to be checked carefully, to make sure they
aren't the trade names of banks. He says the major battles were
actually between debtors and creditors, the only casualties were
shares, and it was contracts that were broken, not the power of
the enemy. He claims that C. took so many financial experts and
profiteers with him that the troops had to be billeted outside the
camps, and that the most the soldiers had to do was to guard the
safes now and then. Stupid jokes, but they do influence people who
don't know what's what.

It's expensive, of course. But we *must* get the Consulship
for next year. And that's precisely why Macer is demanding a

triumph so vigorously. He says the heads of the districts have been sounding out opinion (in the most discreet way) and have come up against mistrust among the voters. The fact that the money wasn't paid out at the last minute during the Catilina elections hasn't been forgotten. If the triumph takes place, everyone will see that the candidate has got some cash behind him. The town will have to be entertained, of course, and coins will have to be tossed about, even if they are just half-assaria pieces. A triumphal procession gives craftsmen a chance to earn something. How does Spanish silver benefit the ordinary people, if it goes straight into the banks? The only thing the bakers, butchers, potters and weavers get from war is the triumph. Anyway, it shouldn't be imagined that it's only a question of money. The man in the street certainly has to take the money – he needs it – but he'd rather take it from someone he trusts. The administration of the city can either be run meanly or generously. As far as the craftsman is concerned, everything depends on that. Over half of all businesses are still out of action, because they are geared to supplying the war and no war is being waged. Of course people would rather vote for a general. Spicer is also in favour of a triumph, in private. 'People don't understand a triumph,' he says dryly, 'if they think it's just a circus. It's simply a way of raising credit. We've got to cough up, precisely because our financial position isn't all that healthy. The whole city has to reek of our money. As far as finances are concerned, it's better to ride through town on a triumphal cart with empty pockets than to walk into one of the banks in the Forum with full pockets. I wrote and told him: it isn't good in the City for you to be branded a businessman. You're a statesman, a general. That's your business; get it into your head. Don't be cynical about tradition, for God's sake. I've been told you said: What's the point of all the glitter? A remark like that could cost you a fortune. Listen to what Messrs. Cincula, Skins and Leather, have to say. Show people you take your profession seriously, and they'll trust you with their money. You need the triumph.' And Fulvia says: 'The triumph, definitely! The Senate will have a fit. It's like when I order new clothes for myself from Aristopulos. Then they have a fit. Whenever I'm unhappy, and my bank account is in a mess, I simply order myself ten new outfits. I've had some regrets in my time, but never about being well dressed. It isn't just that silk excites them more than the most beautiful skin could; it's that their mouths start watering when they see how expensive you are. Definitely the triumph.'

The question, if it was a question at all for C., was decided by Pulcher. He said: 'We have to eliminate the stench of the gutter from the toga. Let me just mention one word: "Catilina".'

Then strictly confidential investigations by Spicer also indicated that the forces behind the Asian Commerce Bank are demanding a triumph before they make election finance available. Gaius Matius has petitioned for a triumph for C. in the Senate, and submitted the documents.

Incidentally, I don't understand Spicer's comment about our financial position not being 'all that healthy'. C. must surely have made a pile of cash in Spain!

20 February
Of course, the Senate commission is creating all sorts of difficulties about the triumph. It's being claimed that the number of dead foes we've stipulated includes Spanish people who died of disease, as well as allies. When we contend that C. also had occasional military skirmishes with allies, they threaten an investigation into the circumstances. In short, they're messing us about. If they knew we wanted to stand for Consul on top of all this, it would be the end of us. That plan really has to be kept secret for as long as possible.

Asked Spicer straight out about our financial situation. 'I can't show my face to the creditors,' was his answer. 'Everyone's trying to press cash into our hands. We're completely sound.' I'm reassured.

27 February
Matius says the Senate found out yesterday that C. wants to stand for Consul. Now he thinks there's absolutely no chance of approval being granted for the triumph.

29 February
The triumph has been approved! None of us understands why.

7 March

C. sent instructions to Spicer weeks ago from Spain to start preparations for the triumphal procession as soon as it was approved.
We're working out a plan. Everything has to proceed as quickly as
possible, because C. has to announce that he's standing for Consul
by the 12 July at the very latest. The triumphal procession will
practically be a substitute for our electoral campaign. So it has to
be ready to go by the end of May, and it has to look good. The bad
thing is that C. is still sitting tight in Spain. He doesn't seem to have
wound up his business with Pulcher yet.

8 March

I must make an effort to remember Pompey's triumphal procession,
because ours is bound to be compared with it. It didn't take place
until last autumn. Pompey had to wait for over a year for all the
valuables to arrive from Asia.

I was watching the festivities from the eighth floor of a house in
the Upper Subura with Pistus, the coachman. (He's the young man
who took me to Pistoria that time.)

The procession was gigantic. After all, it was a triumph over
the whole of the East, as far as it is known to the civilized world.
Anything that could possibly have been transported by ship had
been transported here. Early in the morning I saw half temples in
the cattle market, being pulled on huge wagons by elephants. They
wouldn't go through the narrow lanes and had to be left where they
were. There wasn't nearly enough time to show all the stuff in two
days. A whole pile of the loot had to be left unused.

Two huge boards were carried at the front of the procession with
the campaigns listed on them in very condensed versions. The boards
were so high that they got caught up in the washing lines stretched
across the lanes. They were lowered, with the writing facing upwards,
so they could be read by the people looking down from the windows.

The sentence that concluded the account claimed that the
campaign had doubled the annual income from Asia.

An absolutely endless procession of wagons followed the
boards, laden with armour, war engines, and ships' prows; and
behind them there were donkeys laden with silver worth 500
million sesterces bound for the Treasury.

There was a small wagon with a collection of precious stones that had once belonged to King Mithridates, arranged by jewellers. There was a card table carved out of two vast yellow stones, three beds of state – one made of pure gold – and 35 crowns made of pearls. Three colossal gold statues of gods. A small temple to the muses, ornamented with pearls and crowned with a sundial. The throne and sceptre of Mithridates. A statue of him in silver, and a huge bust in gold. Weird tropical plants, an ebony tree. In this way the wealth and gold of half the world were dragged through the narrow, stinking streets of Rome.

At one point a piece of washing – a patched shirt – fell down on to the procession from a washing line stretched between the houses, and it landed right on top of a captured golden god. One of the soldiers who was marching alongside grabbed hold of it, put it on and walked off with it, waving up to the cursing owner of the shirt.

'That's *his* spoils of war,' muttered Pistus angrily from beside me.

On the second day the triumphant Pompey presented the loot he had taken alive.

The defeated kings stumbled over the uneven cobblestones. Princes and hostages, the son of the Armenian King Tigranes with his wife and daughter. Mithridates' seven sons. His sister. A Jewish King. Some women from the Scythian royal house. Two notorious pirates.

Then came some more enormous boards, this time covered with paintings. The flight of Tigranes and the death of Mithridates. Among them grinning barbarian idols. The portrait of a famous Bithynian priest who was also a banker.

And then Pompey the Great came along. On a wagon decorated with pearls, wearing a tunic said to have belonged to Alexander, surrounded by legates and tribunes on horseback and on foot.

'They should be showing me off to the crowds, too,' said Pistus the coachman. 'He triumphed over me as well.' He had lost his job, forced to give it to one of the slaves Pompey hauled back to Rome.

The people yelled out when they saw gold, whether it was being carried on a wagon or worn by one of the captured kings.

I saw an entire family perched on a ledge of one of the columns of the Temple of Peace, just under the roof – they must have climbed up a rope to get there – for eight whole hours. They had hauled some bread and a few dried fish up there with them. The woman was holding a baby wrapped in rags to her breast. The three little boys yelled themselves hoarse when the two kings were led past in chains.

But the applause that rang out was definitely less enthusiastic in the poorer districts than in the wealthier ones.

10 March

We're going to have a large part of the good quality Spanish spoils of war manufactured in Rome, using only top firms. Firstly, because the real Spanish stuff doesn't look Spanish, and secondly, because we haven't got enough of it. C. didn't capture ivory bedside tables in Spain; he captured concessions for lead mines. Instead of removing golden idols from temples he left them there – and now gets a share of the takings. So we have to make up for a lack of massive, savage objects by using our wits. What we've got in mind is 2,000 tuba players with instruments made of silver from the Spanish mines. C. has sent us a list of Spanish place names, and a load of chieftains from the mountain tribes are on their way, too. About 200 selected beautiful women. And the high point of the whole thing will be 500 little ploughs, with parts made of Spanish iron, which will be raffled among the peasants of Campania afterwards. Furthermore, C. distributed part of the loot to his soldiers in the form of silver shin guards, which they had to promise to wear for the triumph. That'll give our procession a social touch, which was utterly absent from Pompey's.

Managed to hold out the prospect of a large order for the triumphal procession to the haulage company Pistus used to work for. The firm agreed to take on Pistus as a supervisor as soon as the deal is finalized. Pistus jumped up and down in delight.

I've been living like a widow for the last two years. I've accepted the kindness Pistus has offered me, good fellow that he is, the way you accept well-meant comfort from a lively, attractive young person. My relationship with him doesn't mean any more than that. I've paid just as much attention to his friend, the blond legionary Faevula. I must admit that the rivalry between them has amused me now and then. But I really have felt just like a widow, gazing at her youthful suitors with more than a touch of resignation, her experience a thing of the past, her heart full of mourning.

It's fun to take the two of them out. Pistus cracks more jokes than a donkey cracks farts. His only subject of conversation is dog racing. He isn't interested in anything else. Betting on the dogs has become the common man's main sport. You can place bets in every barber's shop. Some of the dogs are more famous than any politician. Fortunes change hands at the races. Pistus reckons this is the common man's only chance to become modestly wealthy. And everyone who can put a few assaria aside for a rainy day certainly does gamble. Pistus says: 'They say it's a passion, but that's just nonsense. It's simply business. You just tell me how else a plebeian can hope to lay his hands on a bit of cash!' Every time he goes on about how wonderful yet another new dog is, Faevula just smiles at him patiently, and says, slowly: 'Why does he need to be so wonderful? He just needs to get the other dogs drunk on his piss.' He thinks the whole thing's a racket. But of course he bets too. Racket or no racket, if you're lucky you can win. And then you can start something really worthwhile. He wants a vineyard of his own.

11 March

Faevula is the son of a peasant from Campania. He was only in the last six months of the Asian campaign; he's quite young. I often go with him to the soldiers' bars around the cattle market, as part of my sociology studies.

The soldiers discharged from Pompey's army sit round there, cursing.

He discharged them as soon as they set foot on Italian soil again, as stipulated by law. He gave them their pay, promised them some land, and asked them to come to Rome for his triumphal procession. The pay was quite a decent sum (5,000 sesterces); you'd be able to start a business with it if you had some land. You could buy a few slaves, some vines, vine stocks and a winepress. Pompey the Great had kept his promise and asked the Senate to give them some land, but the thing had dragged on a bit; actually, it was still dragging on. The gentlemen take their time about everything, and in the meanwhile you use up all your capital in bars and on rent. Some of them have already lost all their money, their comrades support them for a while and then avoid them. They're learning that it's easier to occupy Asia than a dry corner of a bar. They defeated King Mithridates, but it isn't so easy to defeat a Roman landlord. You can't get into a bar by waving a sword around, you have to flourish some cash, and the men who are still inside get scared when they think of the men outside, so they use up the money they've got left.

Pompey can't show his face in the Forum any more without being jostled by his former legionaries. A pile of them crowd around him and accuse him of not doing enough for them. He's said to have stayed in one of the baths for five hours recently, because the entrance was besieged by legionaries. The election organizers assure everyone that as a result he's very keen to grease the palms of the People's Assembly, which will make a decision on his applications. But since he's an old skinflint he reduces the payments whenever he can, according to Macer.

In one of his letters C., who still hasn't set sail for Italy, enquired with great interest about an incident in Pompey's struggle with the land regulations. On Pompey's orders one of the People's Tribunes had the Consul Metellus thrown in jail when he refused to debate the land laws in the Senate. When the Senate wanted to visit the Consul, the Tribune placed his Tribune's bench in the doorway and sat down on it. Of course the law decrees the death penalty for anyone who lays a finger on a People's Tribune. Metellus shouted that they should fetch a mason and break a hole in the wall next to the door, so the Senate could get in to see him. So that's what happened in the end, and Rome laughed about it for a whole week. C. apparently attaches great significance to this new method of achieving what one wants while still abiding by the law. We sent him a detailed report.

20 March

It was C.'s idea to make silver the theme of the triumphal procession. 'So they refer to it as the silver one,' he wrote. He must have assumed it would meet with Pulcher's approval, because it is important to introduce the Spanish silver mines to the Forum. But Pulcher turned up today in a rage about it. 'Damned vulgarity!' he yelled at Spicer. 'How often do I have to remind you lot that we waged war in Spain; we didn't do business. Now he wants to march back into town like a commercial traveller in silver goods! No taste, no seriousness, no discretion! Don't you know what war is? War is corpses, smouldering ruins, fatigue, legions marching forwards with dignity – by Jupiter, is it really so hard to hit that note?' We had to admit that he had a point. It's so easy for things like that to slip your mind.

21 March

Enormous scandal. The whole town's talking about how Pompey had tables set up in his garden yesterday afternoon and quite openly paid out cash to people who have a vote. What a crude fellow! Not long ago I saw him face to face for the first time, in the Forum.

A well-built man with fine, pale skin and very black eyes. His broad forehead has furrows across it, and his eyebrows are raised, as if he wants to be taken for a thinker. His black hair is artificially curled and all messed up, but by a hairdresser; his manner is very calm, and they say he loves it when people talk about how composed he is in every situation. The freed slave Pompey's said to be living with these days, Demetrius, was walking next to him, wearing lots of make-up.

25 March

C. intends to be in Italy by mid-April.

27 March

Pompey's application for land to be distributed to his veterans has been rejected. He was too stingy with his money. Now it's obvious why he gave out the bribes so openly; so the soldiers would think he was doing something for them. The grotesque thing about it is that now the poor fellows have to suffer because anything even slightly connected with war is extremely unpopular. These days the war in Asia is cursed on all sides. It destroyed commerce, the insane imports of slaves ruined agriculture, and it has had Rome simmering on the brink of civil war for months.

The tenant farmers and smallholders, who are working themselves to death at the moment to switch to vine and olive cultivation, are afraid of a new war more than anything, with its military service, taxes and subsequent civil war. War is detested so much that the Senate is doing everything it can to suppress certain disturbing reports which are arriving from Gaul and has adopted a very conciliatory policy there.

12 April
C. isn't coming until the end of April. If the triumph is to take place at the end of May, he will only just be in time.

27 April
C. is still engaged in business negotiations in Spain. We have to postpone the triumph until the end of June. That will be expensive.

5 May
Gaius Matius has returned from Spain. C. simply can't reach an agreement with Pulcher and the Spanish businessmen. Matius says: 'It's easier to defeat the Spaniards than the Romans.'

22 May
Spicer got a letter from C. where he wrote: 'What good is the finest triumph over Spain to us, if Mr Pulcher triumphs over us?' That's true enough, but how are we supposed to keep on starting this enormous machinery and then stopping it again, and extending those expensive contracts? And apart from that, people in the city are already beginning to say that C. is afraid of being prosecuted in Rome for his conduct during the Catilina trial. That's absolute nonsense; it's just the financial transactions that are necessary after every campaign.

8 June
If C. isn't here by the middle of June, the triumph will have to be held during the election period, and a special dispensation will be required. And he still hasn't set off.

12 June
Spicer is getting terribly nervous. We were crossing the Forum together when he said to me in a very depressed tone: 'My whole triumph is dying before my very eyes. The only way I can under-stand C.'s obstinacy about the Spanish affair is that it's his first

genuine commercial transaction. He can see real money within his grasp for the first time. So he's behaving like one of those starving seagulls which bites into a fish that's too big for it and then gets dragged down into the depths.'

If Spicer's getting poetic he really must be absolutely desperate.

21 June
C. has apparently set off at last. Is there any chance that the triumph can still be held?

23 June
It's a catastrophe; when Spicer went to the Asian Commerce Bank today to pick up certain funds which had already been assured for the triumph, he was coolly informed that Mr Pulcher's negotiations with C. had not yet been concluded. What is to be done? Now every day is precious. Even with things the way they are now, there's no chance of our being ready by the 10th, and that's the last possible date for the triumph. Spicer doesn't think we could make it by then, even if the money were made available tomorrow morning. What's Pulcher up to? C. seems to have set off from Spain without having settled things with Pulcher.

30 June
C. has finally arrived. And it's high time; the triumphal procession is swallowing up an incredible amount of money; Spicer has already stretched our new credit to its absolute limit, the Asian Commerce Bank suspended all our credit a week ago, and we've had to halt all our operations. Now we really need the Spanish money urgently.

He's taken up residence in a new palace in the Alban Hills which he had built specially for the period before the triumph, when he isn't allowed to enter Rome. I haven't seen him for two years now, and I'm curious to see if he's changed.

1 July
He's just the same. When Spicer and I saw him again today he strode towards us with his rapid, nervous walk, extending both hands, and the first thing he said was: 'Do you have any money? I'm completely broke.'

He was coughing as he spoke, surrounded by a cloud of dust; one wing of the huge new palace is already being pulled down again because he didn't like it.

Spicer went as white as a sheet. He was absolutely speechless. C. gazes at him for a moment, amused, and immediately started to tell us about his new construction plans. He forced poor Spicer, who was in a state of shock, to clamber over the blocks of marble and listen to a half-hour description of the passages that were to be chiselled out of the stone floor.

To put it in a nutshell, it's the same old C.

This afternoon Spicer gave me some clues as to the state of affairs. When the commercial affairs were being wound up in Spain C. fought like a lion for his package of shares in the silver mines, right up to the last minute. He wasn't just fighting because of their value but also so he could be more certain that Pulcher would keep to his agreement and support him in the City as candidate for the post of Consul. Pulcher's counter move was to make it clear to the City that it had to insist on a triumph. He was hoping that C. would then need him to finance the triumph. But C. simply raised a loan with the shares as collateral, so at the moment he still has the shares. However, as a result he's delayed things so much that there's absolutely no way the triumph can take place before 20 July, and he has to register as a candidate on the 12th! So now he needs a special dispensation from the Senate. Spicer's very much in favour of handing the package to Pulcher, because otherwise he's quite capable of arranging for the Senate to refuse the dispensation. Of course, that would mean a considerable loss, as the value of the shares will rise dramatically as a result of the triumph. And then C. really will have been cheated out of his share of the Spanish deal. But Spicer thinks everything depends on the Consulship, and doesn't want to mortgage C.'s land for even higher sums under any circumstances. He believes the land has far greater commercial potential.

2 July

Today Gaius Matius, our inside man in the Senate, arrived with Macer. We immediately got down to the details of the election campaign.

Cornelius Balbus took part in the discussions; he's a Spanish banker who represents the Spanish companies which are exploiting the mines in southern Spain as a joint venture with the Pulcher group. He's a bald, greasy man with bulging eyes and nervous twitches, and he's generally considered a financial wizard. His prime interest is in the establishment of a system whereby the City can exercise control over Senatorial administration in the provinces, and he claims there's even a substantial group in the Senate which is dissatisfied with the present predatory administrative policy. It is composed of people who either have considerable property in Asia Minor or are secret shareholders in the tax collection firms. There has been a general tendency recently for more and more Senatorial families to conduct their financial affairs through the City. The drastic fall in the price of corn has meant that considerable numbers of landowners are short of ready cash, and the only place they can obtain it is from the banks. All these people would welcome the cautious implementation of a moderate Democratic programme at this very moment, whatever Mr Cato says. Balbus suggested allocating shares in City ventures to members of the Senate in return for services of any sort rendered to the City. This would be the best way to bind them to Democratic interests.

He made no mention at all of Lucceius, the Democratic candidate for Consul, but a lot of what he said was relevant to Lucceius, so I began to realize why he had been nominated in the first place. When he was one of Pompey's legates he advanced large sums of money to Asian towns, so they would be able to pay their tributes, and now he's completely in the hands of the banks. Every three days Oppius reports to him on the size of the losses he (Lucceius) has suffered due to the drastic measures taken by the Senatorial administration.

In the course of these comments he made veiled allusions to Pompey himself having a sore point, which he would not like to become public knowledge under any circumstances.

It seems that Pompey is wondering exactly what use he should make of his popularity with the soldiers, and therefore with the people in general. When he returned from Asia last autumn it seemed natural to go over to the Senatorial party, which is direly in need of a popular man. He did make the attempt, requesting the hand of Cato's sister even before he arrived in Rome. Alluding to C.'s well-known affair with Mucia, Cicero said: 'I know why Pompey wants to get married again; Caesar is tired of Mucia and wants to get his hands on Cato's sister.' Cato refused his permission for the marriage, and Pompey grew accustomed to the thought that he should place his popularity at the service of democracy. The City made some inquiries and established that he was up for sale. And then the gossip died away completely; the City had bought him. It happened like this: even during the military campaign some of the tax contractors and their bankers had come up with a scheme to prove to the general how unfairly they were being treated by the state. He was persuaded to get involved in a typical City deal himself. With the assistance of the Oppius Bank he lent Nicomedes, the King of Syria, a sizeable sum of money so he would be able to pay reparations to Rome. Pompey the businessman lent funds to the Syrian court which Pompey the statesman demanded from it as tributes. He charged up to 50 per cent interest but soon felt 'in his very bowels' the sort of blows between the legs dealt out to our businessmen by the Senatorial administration of Rome. The constant looting and plundering, the pillaging of the cities by the governor, the removal of harvests and slaves, etc., etc., made it quite impossible for the king to pay Pompey the interest. But Oppius was demanding his interest from Pompey! His financial difficulties were compounded by fear of the scandal which would result if it ever came out into the open. So, in short, the City has good reason to regard the general as one of their own.

C. was lounging in his chair, listening with amusement to the stream of daring speculation, cautious allusions and amazingly expert knowledge issuing from the Spaniard's lips. The people he always manages to come up with!

Matius, who is rather a snob, didn't appear to share C.'s liking for the Spaniard at all, and Macer's battered countenance didn't react at all to any of his numerous jokes. However, this changed when the battle plan for the election was discussed in greater detail and it turned out that Balbus has excellent connections with the Oppius Bank. As early as last autumn he had entered into discreet negotiations with Lucceius, via Oppius, about the possibility of a joint candidature with C.! And his suggestion that *two* Democratic candidates could be pushed through hasn't been rejected at all. Pompey wants to have his Asian agreements ratified at all costs; Asian shares are in a very bad way. Up to 10 million is to be made available for this election by the City. The only condition Oppius/ Lucceius have laid down for supporting C. is that everything should proceed strictly in accordance with the law, with no Catilinarian excesses involving the rabble, no democratic 'experiments' and, above all, no reference to the land question. (Oppius' position is that coming to grips with the land question would jeopardize the import of Asian slaves.) Macer breathed a visible sigh of relief. He's going to make a direct approach to Lucceius in the next few days.

Matius is to apply to the Senate for a special dispensation which would allow C. to enter the city before the triumph takes place in order to register as a candidate.

Our hopes were high as we left the Alban Hills.

5 July

The application for a special dispensation submitted by the tireless Matius has been rejected! Spicer went off to see C. immediately. He'll hand Pulcher the package they've been arguing about tomorrow. Matius is going to see Cicero. The dispensation will have to be fought for.

7 July

This morning, as I was braving the oppressive heat to supervise the hanging of the new Gobelins in the library, Spicer comes in and peers round. 'Has he been here?' – 'Who?' – 'C., of course.' – 'In Rome?' – 'That's right.' – 'Nonsense. He isn't allowed to enter Rome before the triumph.' – 'Isn't allowed! He wasn't in Alba last night. We're going out there right now.' He gave me a few clues on the way. Camilla, Matius' wife, has suddenly returned to Rome. And her husband has gone to see Cicero's estate, on C.'s orders! The worst thing about it is that not long ago Camilla arrived in Alba late one evening 'to collect her husband', who had of course left long before, and then it was 'too late to make the journey back to Rome'. We went to Spicer's apartment first of all, so he could pick up a pile of bills. When we got to Alba he forced C. to look through them, but as evening was approaching C. threw him out, and me as well. Spicer muttered something about 'carrying on in the morning', and C. laughed. Then Spicer displayed surprising strength of character. He stared at C., his face immobile, and said without any preliminaries: 'The triumph has cost 4 million up to now, and a scandal would cost more than that: everything, in fact.' – 'True enough,' said C., cool as a cucumber, 'and now I'm getting rather tired.' Spicer turned on his heel and got into the coach. When we reached the slaughterhouses in the Second District he got out. As this is some way from his own apartment, I got out at the next corner as well and followed him, convinced he was on his way to Matius' house. But he went down one of the narrow alleys behind the slaughterhouses and spent some time in one of the rundown houses there. He has acquaintances everywhere from his days as a bailiff, and the fellow who emerged from the doorway with Spicer must have been a bankrupt down-and-out. The man set off at a fairly rapid pace, and Spicer went home.

It would be insane of C. to take a risk like that and come to Rome, now, just for the sake of a pair of pretty breasts!

8 July

Wonderful development. C. is in Alba with his head bandaged. He was attacked last night on a country road not far from Alba as he was going for an evening ride. The attacker escaped.

I went out there with Spicer when we heard the news. He wouldn't see us. Spicer seemed very worried.

The doctors say it was just a blow with a sandbag, and everything will be fine again in two or three days.

I went back to the alley behind the slaughterhouses this evening. The man is a former weaver in very bad circumstances: known as a ruffian, incidentally. He went out last night and didn't get back until this morning.

10 July

Went to the dog races with Pistus and Faevula. Thanks to some tips from the expert Pistus we made ourselves a tidy sum from a few bets.

I've promised to let Faevula have 8,000 sesterces if he does get any land allotted to him. He came back home with me and was in very high spirits.

I'll borrow the money from Spicer.

C. is in good health again.

11 July

Matius is fighting for the dispensation like a man possessed. He's back from Cicero's country estate. Cicero had already been well prepared by Oppius and was quite amenable; he said he was willing to vote for the dispensation but doubted that his support would have much effect. There was a trace of compassion for him in Matius' report.

Cicero doesn't count any more, and he knows it. The Senate has used him and dropped him. His hands are stained with the blood of craftsmen. He accepted money from the 'fathers', so he's corrupt; he betrayed their enemies, so he's a traitor. These days only the City has got any time for him. It has a weakness for people with bad consciences.

The diabolical thing is that a majority in the Senate in favour of the dispensation has already been organized, but Cato has actually managed to postpone the vote until the last day. It's to take place tomorrow, and if C. doesn't announce he's standing for election tomorrow, it's too late for him to be a candidate.

12 July

Today the situation has changed completely.

From early in the morning C. was waiting in Alba for the dispensation to be granted, so he could register as a candidate.

The Senate session began at 11 o'clock, and Cato rose to speak about an application for construction work which had become necessary because of a burst water main in the centre of town. His face was rather red, probably because he had drunk two jugs of Falernian wine instead of his usual morning ration of one jug, but at first he stuck more or less to the point. Nobody was listening to him; everyone was waiting for the vote on the dispensation. When Cato had spoken for about an hour on the necessity of ensuring adequate water supplies for the city centre, he launched into a general account of the water system throughout the city. That lasted until 1 o'clock, as every subsidiary pipeline was described in detail. The Senators were just returning from the passageways when, after staring at the ceiling for a few minutes, the speaker employed an elegant turn of phrase and embarked on a history of the water supply system since the foundation of the city. By about 3 o'clock in the afternoon he had got as far as the Gracchi. Matius told us that the atmosphere in the hall was incredible. Jokes were followed by shouts of indignation. At times the speaker's voice couldn't be heard at all, but he carried on relentlessly, and his words, incidentally, were devastatingly innocuous.

At about 4 o'clock I entered the building myself. There were a lot of Senators in the passageways, most of them apathetic by this time. I saw some fat old boys sitting in the corners, leaning on columns, fast asleep. Only a few Senators were sitting in the hall itself, in complete disarray, and there was Cato, plump, with chubby cheeks, his lively gaze fixed on the beams of the roof, talking about Sulla's decrees against placing contracts for civil construction work through the clubs. At one point he lowered his voice, as if he had run out of material, and the audience was galvanized into action. One of the Senators rose awkwardly to his feet, and hurried out. The hall filled up, but only for a few minutes. The speaker's voice had been raised once again.

We had set up a line of communication between Rome and Alba. Three times Matius thought C. would soon be able to set off, and three times C. took a cold bath, so he wouldn't arrive with his toga drenched in sweat. At about 2 o'clock he got impatient, and in the afternoon he rode right up to the city boundary, where all sorts of people had turned up to greet him. At 5 o'clock in the afternoon C. rode across the city boundary – without a dispensation. At half past five he registered on the Capitol as a candidate for Consul.

Immediately afterwards, surrounded by a large crowd which had recognized him, he made his way to the session of the Senate, where Cato was still speaking. He strode slowly through the passageways, and the Senators who supported him gathered eagerly behind him, chattering away. He still had a black eye from the attack he had suffered the previous week, and he was wearing a candidate's white toga, which traditionally has no pockets, so the candidate can't bring money with him to give out as bribes. When Cato saw him enter the hall at the head of a crowd of Senators he wound up his speech with three words.

So the triumph has gone up in smoke. It has cost us 4 million sesterces up to now; the entire profit from the Spanish Propraetorship. You can't make money from politics these days.

13 July

Poor Pistus is in despair. Nothing has come of the job with the haulage company. 'Pompey put me out of a job and held a triumph,' he said, 'and Caesar didn't hold a triumph but still put me out of a job.' Faevula was touching. He suggested I should give the 8,000 Spicer owes me, which I was going to give to Faevula so he can start a small olive farm, to Pistus so he can start a haulage business. But Pistus wouldn't hear of it. 'It would just be money thrown away,' he said. 'People like us can't run a haulage business these days, unless you can buy a hundred slaves.' He's going to carry on gambling on the dog races.

Finished the opinion survey today. Presented the results to C.:

Cruppulus (wool): Whatever happens in politics, weapons decide things, short term and long term. The politicians won't have the last word, the generals will. So we don't need Caesar, we need Pompey.

Celer (skins and leather): If it's up to the Senate, it'll be Cato. If it's the army, Pompey. If it's us, Cicero. If it's the streets, Clodius. – And Caesar? I asked. – Well, C.'s got his creditors after him.

A Senator: The best way to dispose of Pompey is not to block his way – down to the rabble. If he starts playing the part of a Democrat, there'll be no part for him to play in a Democracy. Caesar can tell you all about that.

Second Senator: The City has got the war in Asia on its conscience. The value of our estates has dropped by half. Now they want to snatch away from us any income we could derive from the new governorships, too. If they succeed, it will be impossible for us to maintain our estates in Italy any longer. That's where the real danger lies.

Third Senator: Caesar is a Catilina who is attempting to use legal means.

Fourth Senator: We don't need slaves, we need tenant farmers. As far as that goes, I'm with the better Democrats. Cicero is a spent force.

Tax contractor: What good is Asia to us if we don't exploit it? What we don't need now are more adventures, or more adventurers. Nothing scares me more than that Caesar.

Banker: A strong man is what's required. Unfortunately, Caesar is just crafty. We're crafty enough ourselves.

Another banker: Democracy won't have a chance like this again. The old families are bankrupt, unable to change over to wine and olive production on their estates without us. The Senate without an army. Asia in chaos. The Roman citizen is the only one who can solve the land question. If C. could put a stop to his womanizing, he'd be in power.

A poultry dealer: Caesar? Isn't he in Africa?

A shirtmaker: It's that C.'s fault that the clubs have folded up.

A dockworker: He's still the only one of those big shots who's on the people's side. But they got rid of him.

A ropemaker (unemployed): His games weren't bad.

Peasant farmer: Anything, as long as there's no more war. If my boy Reus has to join up, I won't even be able to keep the vineyard going for one more year.

Another peasant farmer: The city folk can't buy anything these days. It's Pompey's fault, him and his slaves. And that Lucceius, the one they want to make Consul now, he's an officer, too.

Blacksmith: I used to make swords. I can't change over to making ploughs now. The farmers get them patched up by the slaves on the big estates!

Butcher: I was for Catilina, I'm not hiding it. They've bought up Caesar.

Mason: I've got some work again. Pompey is building a theatre. I'm going to vote for his man, Lucceius.

Head of the potters' guild: Caesar's the one, of course. The only popular man in the whole of Rome.

Former member of a street club: We get our instructions, and we stick to them.

Storekeeper in the market halls: Bibulus.

A cabinet maker (unemployed): Catilina was the best of the lot.

A shoemaker: I've got other things to worry about. Three children, and nowhere to live.

A legionary: I don't give a shit about land and property. One or two campaigns and I'll buy some myself.

A mule driver: Caesar, he's the one with the debts, isn't he?

14 July

Pulcher has given Pompey the impression that C. abandoned the idea of a triumph because he realized he would be utterly incapable of matching Pompey's Asian triumph. And that C. knows the business in Spain couldn't be called a campaign, and that he isn't a general at all, just a politician. And that he's completely serious about his peace programme. So Pompey, great pompous ass that he is, pretended not to believe any of it, but then said that the man (C.) was a chameleon, and that it was quite possible, if the Roman rabble wanted peace, that he would immediately be filled with disgust at the mere sight of a regimental standard.

15 July

The Democratic election committee had posters put up today saying the Senate is planning a war against the Parthians.

17 July

A big speech by C. to the district heads of the election committee.

'Romans, there are some Romans for whom there are too many Romans in Rome. For me, Rome is Italy, with its blossoming groves and its fields lying fallow. You, Romans, live in miserable tenement blocks, four people to a tiny room; it could perhaps be said that there are too few rooms, but some Romans say there are too many Romans. These people are of the opinion that a few Romans are enough for Rome, and that there's really only enough of Rome for a few Romans. The rest will just have to emigrate. Go and wage war, they say; conquer foreign lands and then live there! You are that rest. There are only 200 Romans, as far as those 200 think, and then there are the rest of the Romans, and the rest should get out of Rome and stop being Roman. Become Syrians, they say, become Gauls! Romans, people are assuring you that war will help you get everything you need. Well, we've just been through a big war: the war in Asia. And business really did pick up at the beginning. There were some orders. Then imported slaves from Asia started to arrive. There were still orders, but now the slaves were doing the work. There were some Romans who made a profit. The war was enough to secure them a profit. And they made enough profit to carry on delivering the military supplies. You, the rest, went hungry. And while all the battles and victories didn't increase the number of homes for you, the rest of the Romans, you, the rest, did decrease in number. Romans, the land question must be solved – not in the East or in the West – but here on this peninsula, here in Rome. The fact is that there are some robbers living in palaces and mansions, and the rest of the people live squeezed together in tenement blocks. The fact is that some Romans cram all the delicacies of Asia into their bellies, and the rest stand in line for corn handouts. Bibulus and his friends in the Senate – they are for war, they are for promises. My Democratic friends and I – we are for peace, we are for land. Romans, let some Romans vote for Bibulus, but you, the rest of the Romans; vote for Caesar!'

Balbus is the one who has drawn C.'s attention to the immense significance of unemployment in Rome. Half of Rome is out of work. On street corners the wood sellers, who haven't got any more wood to sell, stand around with the poultry merchants, who can't sell any poultry, and talk about the fishmongers, who can't make a living from selling fish these days. The bakers queue up outside the bread depots for bread, and the shirtmakers explain to the barbers that they can't get their hair cut anymore because the unemployed potters aren't buying shirts these days. And the city fathers in the Senate still go on about the lower orders being work-shy!

18 July

The Democratic posters, alluding to the intention of some powerful gentlemen in the Senate to unleash a new war (against the Parthians), are causing an incredible commotion throughout the whole city. The Senate has announced that the accusation is completely unfounded. But nobody believes that. 'They can't milk the cow,' is what people in the barber's shop are saying. 'All they can do is slaughter it. No wonder they always want to steal new cows! And we're supposed to finance the robbery!'

It was an excellent move by Macer, revealing that the 200 families are warmongers (whether they happen to be planning a war just now or not). Advocating war is going to be out of favour in Rome for a long time.

19 July

Caesar to a delegation from the clubs: 'Why didn't I hold my triumph? Because I didn't want to become Consul as a soldier. A triumph should be awarded for a year of peace, not a year of war.'

It was quite apparent that this comment made an excellent impression.

20 July

Now quite a lot of Senatorial cash is also being poured into the election campaign. This time the city fathers have dug deep into their pockets. Up to now, the so-called natural influence they possess was enough for them. Tenant farmers obviously have to vote for the owners of the land, and all the debtors from the craftsmen class have to vote for their creditors in the Senate. Entire districts of the city have been informed that the owners of the tenement blocks will put the tenants out on the street immediately if Bibulus isn't elected.

This has led to considerable confusion in the Democratic election committee. It is becoming uncomfortably clear that getting both candidates through won't be possible. Since Lucceius is providing the money, there can hardly be any doubt who will have to be dropped. On the other hand, in political terms Lucceius is nothing.

And C. is out of circulation again. Yesterday, without any warning, he set off for Alba. Matius wanted to go out there after him, and it took a lot of effort to persuade him not to; he would almost certainly have found his wife there. It's really scandalous the way C. leaves everything to his supporters, when the situation is so difficult and decisions are so crucial, for entirely frivolous motives.

23 July

A big meal. Lucceius, Matius, Pulcher and a few Senators. Lucceius is a tall, skinny man with a washed-out face and restless eyes. He suffers from frequent attacks of fever, which he picked up in Asia. He was effusive in his praise for the absent Macer for the excellent slogans but made no mention at all of the threatening situation which has arisen because of Bibulus' certain victory, assured by the immense sums of money spent by the 200 families. The atmosphere during the meal was tense below the surface, but not because of the relationship between Lucceius and C.; last night C. and Matius had a terrible argument. Matius has finally found out that C. and his wife are having an affair. Of course he can't make a scandal about it now, so soon before the election. He's most bitter about the fact that C., shameless as ever, is taking advantage of the situation Matius has been forced into. C. actually made several comments of the most tactless variety during the meal, such as remarking that nothing disgusted him about his public activities more than the public's interference in the private life of everyone who held office. Matius, who is basically colourless and insignificant, won my complete sympathy with his dignified conduct.

24 July
Oppius is said to have remarked quite openly in the City that Bibulus and Lucceius together would mean Bibulus as Consul, and Bibulus and Caesar together would mean Caesar as Consul.

26 July
Mutius Ger has just left. He is one of Lucceius' business associates in the Senate and had come to sound out C.'s position on the withdrawal of one of the Democratic candidates, which has now become necessary.

He didn't mention politics, of course, and kept to the subject of business. He was quite well informed about certain financial problems C. is experiencing, and seemed frankly eager to learn what wishes C. might have as regards financial compensation. He kept on stressing Lucceius' generosity.

C. listened to him like someone who had no idea about business matters, especially his own, but would welcome the opportunity to learn from a competent authority, and it was quite a while before he casually mentioned that he disliked mixing politics and business. I always admire the ability of people like C. (and Ger as well), to say things which everyone knows are completely untrue.

But what is really going to become of our candidature?

27 July

Lucceius has suddenly withdrawn from the election, which has occasioned general surprise. And the only thing I've heard is that Balbus and Oppius went to see Lucceius. Those two apparently informed the horrified candidate that due to an indiscretion, certain material concerning Pompey's commercial dealings during the Asian war is either already in Cato's hands or has at least reached people who would not hesitate to place it at Cato's disposal for the election campaign. Today not many people in Rome know that for a few hours a huge scandal about the Democrats was brewing. The revelation that Pompey (and, not far behind him, Lucceius and some others) had exploited the last war for financial gain would have introduced a shrill note of discord to the Democrats' slogans about peace! Well, now there won't be any scandal of that sort – and the day after tomorrow C. will stand in the Consular election as the only Democratic candidate.

The Democratic slogans look very effective. Wounds caused by the war are to be healed. There is to be assistance for the business community, and craftsmen, to convert their war production programmes to the provision of supplies for peaceful reconstruction, settlements, etc. Legionaries, who are to be thanked for the victory, will be rewarded. And peace is to be maintained for at least one generation.

Today all the walls are covered with the simple slogan: *Democracy is Peace.*

Proposed Contents of the Rest of the Novel

The unfinished novel as it stands here consists of the first three books and the first part of a fourth.

The remainder of the novel – the second part of the fourth book and two further books – was intended to depict the irresistible rise of the 'great dealer' Julius Caesar as his attempts to evade the bailiffs sent him on the path to dictatorship. In the rest of the fourth book the Democratic programme is implemented in generous fashion with a brilliant 'solution' to the land question by means of the famous Lex Julia (Caesar's land law), which is revealed as a gigantic land speculation on the part of the historical triumvirate consisting of the banker Crassus, the general Pompey and the demagogue Caesar. Alongside commercial interests there are also plentiful 'purely human' factors at play. Pompey discovers that his wife had embarked upon an affair with Caesar while he was waging war in Asia, and that she invested a sizeable fortune in Caesar's land speculations. This naturally motivates him far more than the promises he made to his war veterans about putting the Democratic land distribution plans into practice.

Sexual relationships play a significant role in this book overall. Caesar succeeds in arranging for his daughter Julia to marry the cuckolded Pompey, thus placing the relationship between the two of them on an even more intimate footing.

In the meantime, despite skilful abuse of his public office, Caesar's debts mount steadily. It is no longer necessary for him to engage in politics solely due to his financial needs, but he is obliged to make money from all his political enterprises. At the same time, his political activities now display on a general, long-term basis a need to safeguard the interests of the ruling classes. And since he performs his acts of violence almost always within the legal framework, the value of this legality is revealed with surprising clarity. The Republic gives birth to the dictatorship virtually without any labour pains.

The Roman citizenry, which has been transformed into a huge mass of the unemployed due to the prevalence of slavery resulting from the conquest of the East, descends still further into abject poverty. The land settlement programme is good business for the City but little more than a drop in the ocean for the army of the unemployed. More and more measures are required to appease the masses in their misery. Only a new war can bring in the money necessary for the enormous handouts and public works programme.

Caesar prompts panic in the capital by cleverly engineering reports that Gallic tribes are about to attack Italy, and (by means of huge bribes and an assassination using poison) obtains the consulship for the two parts of Gaul. It proved to be impossible for the ruling classes (represented by the City and the Senate) to reach agreement on dividing the spoils from the Asias: now the Gallic Trading Company is founded. Since Caesar has good reason to fear that the moment he is no longer Consul he will be swamped by court cases and financial demands, he makes an early departure for his new province in order to wage war there.

The fourth book contains more long passages from the diaries of Rarus, once more depicting his private life. After the death of Caebio he has found himself two new male friends, the coachman

Pistus and young Faevula, one of Pompey's legionaries. Pistus lost his job due to the enormous numbers of imported slaves from Asia and now spends his time at the dog races; he claims this is the only chance for a Roman citizen. Faevula, a farmer's son, wants to become a settler, but 'forces of circumstance' lead to him becoming a legionary once again, this time for Caesar. The fate of these two young men reflects the fate of the Roman people in this period when the Republic is collapsing.

Conversations with the general Lucullus, the librarian Alexander and the fatally ill poet Lucretius form an obituary for the freedom of the general population.

The fifth book deals with the Gallic War. Side by side with his banker, Mummlius Spicer, Caesar makes his way to the rich, blossoming pastures of Gaul. The banker informs the general that his main profit will flow not from the pockets of the Gauls but from those of the Romans. He will earn money from every war supply contract and every soldier. Naturally the lower classes of the victorious nation share the burdens of war with the lower classes of the defeated one, and similarly the ruling classes of the victorious nation also share the profits with the ruling classes of the defeated country.

The war begins with the Roman campaign against the Germanic tribes, but since the tribes have already crossed the Rhine; this takes place in the middle of Gaul. The Gauls practise a policy of non-intervention. A national uprising, of the sort which later takes place in Gaul under Vercingetorix, is betrayed by the Gallic princes. They then become involved in the commercial activities of the Roman City.

Since Caesar conducts his campaigns in accordance with the advice of his banker Spicer, he makes a considerable amount of money. He dispatches the tributes from the subjugated tribes to Rome on time, but he profits from variations in the price of gold, and the high interest loans granted to the defeated princes by the Gallic Trading Company in Rome, which they require in order to pay the tributes, are handled by his banker. He is also in a position to establish huge slave schools in Capua. But his expenses are enormous. It is only by launching massive construction projects in Rome that he manages to maintain his position and prolong the war.

Of the six books which comprise the novel, the fifth is the most idyllic. In the field the city dweller comes to embrace the beauties of the countryside. The over-sophisticated aesthete develops an interest in the machinery of war. He is amused by the negotiations with the Gallic aristocracy. Caesar adores negotiations more than anything else.

The book consists of a long narrative from the banker and former bailiff Spicer and a small collection of letters from the legionary Faevula to Caesar's secretary, Rarus, in Rome. Faevula falls in the Battle of Aduatuca, where two Roman legions are eliminated to the last man because Caesar had stationed the troops in remote, enemy territory: he wanted them to secure their own rations so he could save money on the cost of the provisions. Faevula never did succeed in achieving his aim of owning a piece of land. However, the fate of another of Caesar's veterans, a man we encountered in the first book, illustrates the destiny of many who did achieve this goal: his smallholding is devoured by bank debts.

The first three books of the novel show how Pompey's conquest of the East ruined half of Rome and half of Italy; the last three books illustrate the point that the conquest of the West by Caesar completed the ruin of the Roman people, the peasants and the craftsmen. While the second book depicts the effect of Pompey's wars on Rome, in the sixth book the effect of Rome on Caesar's war becomes apparent.

The war in Gaul is not yet over and could, in the opinion of Mr Spicer, continue for several decades when the situation in Rome forces Caesar to return. Pompey has shifted his allegiance to the Senate party. The bankrupt members of the City, threatened by counter-revolution from Pompey's Senate, gather in Caesar's camp at the Rubicon and plead with him to march on Rome with his victorious eagles in order to protect their moneychangers' stalls. At the same time, the Senate sends him his papers of dismissal. But the man, deeply in debt and accused of every possible crime, hesitates to march on Rome. For several weeks the bankers negotiate the new constitution with him. After a complete nervous breakdown he is finally carried across the Rubicon in a state of semi-consciousness.

However, Caesar is not the only one to foresee trouble ahead: the City is also pessimistic. In order to ensure that Caesar safeguards their mastery of the slaves, the City has to secure Caesar's rule by enslaving themselves. The maintenance of slavery as the foundation of the economy will lead to general slavery of all sections of society.

[This is Brecht's own description of the contents. It is preserved amongst several other outlines and sketches for the novel. See *BFA* 17, pp. 349ff.]

Historical Events and Personages

The dates in the novel are according to the Roman calendar, AUC (ab urbe condita = from the founding of the city); here we give the BC equivalents.

Year BC	
264–241	First Punic War
218–201	Second Punic War
149–146	Third Punic War
133	Tiberius Sempronius Gracchus becomes People's Tribune
123	Gaius Sempronius Gracchus becomes People's Tribune
106	Birth of Gnaeus Pompeius (Magnus)
	Birth of Marcus Tullius Cicero
104–101	Second Sicilian Servile War
102	Victory of Romans over the Teutons
101	Victory of Romans over the Cimbrians
100	Birth of Gaius Julius Caesar
90–88	Social War between Rome and Italy
	Roman citizenship extended to Italy
	Rome and Italy form the Italian State
89–84	First Mithridatic War
88	Lucius Cornelius Sulla and Lucius Cornelius Cinna become Consuls
83–82	Second Mithridatic War, launched by the Roman Governor of Asia, Murena
83	In spring Sulla marches to southern Italy with 40,000 troops (from Asia and Greece), supported by Pompey and Marcus Licinius Crassus
82–79	Dictatorship of Sulla (died 78)
78–75	Expedition against the pirates of Cilicia
76	Pompey is given command of Roman forces in Spain
74–64	Third Mithridatic War; Lucullus commands the Roman forces
74–71	Servile War, slaves led by Spartacus

70	Pompey and Crassus become Consuls
	All rights of the People's Tribune are reinstated
	The Censors Gnaeus Cornelius Clodianus Lentulus and Lucius Policola Gellius exclude 64 Senators from the Senate for corruption
68	Caesar becomes Quaestor
67	Following an application by the Tribune Aulus Gabinius, Pompey is given a naval task force to combat piracy, along with wide-ranging powers
66	Pompey is given command of Roman forces in the Third Mithridatic War
65	Caesar becomes Aedile; he stages lavish fencing games
63	Marcus Tullius Cicero becomes Consul
	Caesar is elected High Priest (Pontifex Maximus) after paying huge bribes
	Defeat of Lucius Sergius Catilina in the election for Consul in 62 BC
	Catilina conspiracy: on 5 December Caesar makes a speech in the Senate opposing the death penalty for Catilina, but he is defeated by Marcus Portius Cato (the Younger)
62	Caesar is elected Praetor.
	The Catilinarians are defeated in a battle near Pistoria
	In December Pompey lands in Brundisium and dismisses his army (end of the Third Mithridatic War)
61	Caesar journeys to his province, Spain, as Propraetor
	Pompey holds his triumph
	Pompey is unable to get acceptance for his proposals to grant land to his former legionaries and to recognize the order he imposed upon the East
60	Alliance of Caesar, Crassus and Pompey (First Triumvirate)
59	Caesar becomes Consul
	Pompey marries Julia, Caesar's daughter
58–51	Gallic War
56	Renewal of First Triumvirate
49	Caesar crosses the Rubicon
	Beginning of Civil War
49–46	Civil War: Caesar against Pompey and the Senate
46	In December Caesar is named Dictator
	Caesar passes a law restructuring debts
46–44	Dictatorship of Caesar
44	Caesar is murdered

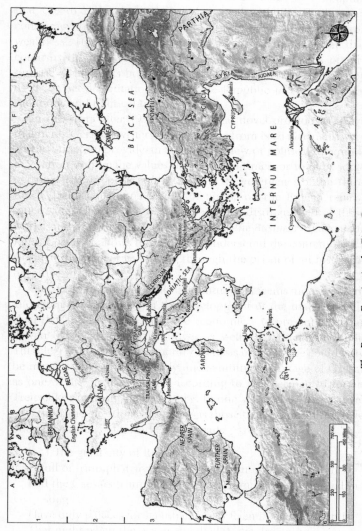

The Roman Empire in the First Century BC

Temporal Structure of the Novel (264 BC–44 BC)

Sections within Novel	1st Book	2nd Book	3rd Book	4th Book
Narrated Time (first time level)	679–691 AUC [75–63 BC]	11 August 691–end of year [63 BC]	1 January–19 June 692 and 691–694 AUC [62 BC and 63–60 BC]	12 February–27 July 694 AUC [60 BC]
Narrated History (Caesar)	Early history of Rome: Punic Wars, the Gracchi, Sulla. Caesar's background as a lawyer, the story of the pirates, public offices held.	The Catilinarian affair, Caesar as liaison between the City and Catilina. Holding the office of High Priest (Pontifex Maximus).	The end of Catilina. Spain. Caesar, as Praetor, investigates the Catilinarian affair. Caesar goes to Spain as governor (Propraetor).	Triumph and Consulship. Preparations for the triumph. Election campaign.
Narrated History (Rarus)		Relationship with Caebio. Caebio is unable to find work, joins the Catilinarians.	Rarus searches for Caebio, goes to the battlefield near Pistoria where Catilinarians were defeated.	Rarus describes Pompey's triumph. Rarus has a new relationship with Faevula.

	1st Book	2nd Book	3rd Book	4th Book
1st Transmission Level (Diaries of Rarus)		Documentation: first section of diaries.	Documentation: second section of diaries.	Documentation: third section of diaries.
2nd Transmission Level (Spicer as eye witness and commentator, oral)	Spicer provides annotations to Rarus's diaries, an overview of early history.		Spicer's account.	
3rd Transmission Level (Eyewitness reports, oral)	Legionary describes serving in Gaul, Carbo on Caesar.		Alder on Caesar.	
4th Transmission Level (Historian, first person narrative)	Historian meets Spicer, visits Caesar's legionary, meets Carbo in Spicer's house.	Historian reads first section of diaries.	Historian meets Spicer, reads second section of diaries, meets Alder in Spicer's house, listens to Spicer's account.	Historian reads third section of diaries.

	1st Book	2nd Book	3rd Book	4th Book
Narrated Time (Second time level)	24 BC, first and second day: historian arrives at Spicer's house and sees his estate, 20 years after Caesar's death.	24 BC, night	24 BC¹, third day: information about keeping slaves; a slave escapes.	24 BC, night
5th Transmission Level (Third time level: the narrator/historian 'writing' this account looks back on his visit to Spicer; we sense that his biography of Caesar has not been written.)	Unspecified later date; 'At the time ... Later, when I knew Spicer better ...' (p. 20)	Unspecified later date	Unspecified later date: 'At that time I didn't realize ...' (p. 155), 'It wasn't until much later that I understood ...' (p. 162).	Unspecified later date

¹ In Book 3 the narrator comments (p. 137) that the events he has been reading about in Rarus's diary took place 'three decades' ago, and since those events were in 63 BC that would mean the date when he reads the diary is 33 BC. However, this is likely to have been a mistake on Brecht's part, since the narrator's visit to Spicer clearly takes place over three days, and we are told at the outset that the date is twenty years after Caesar's death, i.e. 24 BC.

The Business Affairs of Mr Julius Caesar